Fingerprints of You

Fingerprints of You

KRISTEN-PAIGE MADONIA

SIMON & SCHUSTER BFYR

New York London Toronto Sydney New Delhi

Grateful acknowledgment is made to the following
publications where portions of this book first appeared:
*American Fiction, Volume 11: The Best Previously
Unpublished Stories by Emerging Authors* and
Sycamore Review.

SIMON & SCHUSTER BFYR

An imprint of Simon & Schuster Children's Publishing Division
1230 Avenue of the Americas, New York, New York 10020

Text copyright © 2012 by Kristen-Paige Madonia
Illustrations copyright © 2012 by Terry Ribera

For information about special discounts for bulk purchases, please contact
Simon & Schuster Special Sales at 1-866-506-1949 or
business@simonandschuster.com.
The Simon & Schuster Speakers Bureau can bring authors to your live event.
For more information or to book an event, contact the Simon & Schuster Speakers
Bureau at 1-866-248-3049 or visit our website at www.simonspeakers.com.
Book design by Krista Vossen
The text for this book is set in New Caledonia.
Manufactured in the United States of America
2 4 6 8 10 9 7 5 3
Library of Congress Cataloging-in-Publication Data
Madonia, Kristen-Paige.
Fingerprints of you / Kristen-Paige Madonia.
p. cm.
Summary: After spending her life moving from place to place with her single mother,
pregnant seventeen-year-old Lemon takes a bus to San Francisco to seek the father she
never knew, as well as truths about her mother and herself.
ISBN 978-1-4424-2920-8 (hardcover)
ISBN 978-1-4424-2922-2 (eBook)
[1. Coming of age—Fiction. 2. Mothers and daughters—Fiction. 3. Single-parent
families—Fiction. 4. Moving, Household—Fiction. 5. Pregnancy—Fiction. 6. Fathers
and daughters—Fiction. 7. San Francisco (Calif.)—Fiction.] I. Title.
PZ7.M26572Fin 2012
[Fic]—dc23
2011018447

For my mother and father.
Everything that is good in me is there because of you.

Fingerprints of You

BOOK ONE
Sandstorms

In this way, in increments both measurable and
not, our childhood is stolen from us—
not always in one momentous event but often
in a series of small robberies, which add up
to the same loss.
—John Irving, *Until I Find You*

CHAPTER ONE

MY MOTHER GOT HER THIRD TATTOO on my seventeenth birthday, a small navy hummingbird she had inked above her left shoulder blade, and though she said she picked it to mark my flight from childhood, it mostly had to do with her wanting to sleep with Johnny Drinko, the tattoo artist who worked in the shop outside town.

"Stella-Stella," he said when we entered. He sat in a black plastic chair in the waiting area, flipping through a motorcycle magazine, and he looked up and smiled. Big teeth, freckles, alarmingly cool. "Good to see you."

He put the magazine down as the bell above our heads dinged when the door closed behind us. He was tan and toned and a little bit sweaty, and he wore a dirty-blond ponytail that hung to his shoulders. His sharp eyes were so blue, I thought of swimming pools and icicles the first time I saw him. My mother told me about Johnny Drinko after he gave her the orange and blue fish on her hip, but I'd expected him to be as unlikable as the other burnouts Stella hung around with back then. I had not expected *him*.

"And you brought your kid sister this time." He winked at her, and I popped a bubble with my piece of pink Trident, listened to the hot hiss of the tattoo needle inking skin somewhere inside the shop.

The hummingbird was Stella's third tattoo, but it was the first time she let me come along, so she was nervous, her hips shifting from left to right inside her tiny white shorts. It took a lot to make her shaky, and I could tell she wanted a beer or maybe a highball of vodka, but I knew she'd go through with it since I was there watching. Once she made her mind up, there was no going back. It was one of the things I liked and disliked about my mother.

"Lemon's my kid," she said to Johnny, and she tucked a panel of frizzy bleached hair behind her ear.

She'd gotten a perm a few weeks earlier and was still adjusting to the weight of the nest hovering above her shoulders. It was the first and last perm she ever got, but I'll never forget the vast size of her head with her hair frazzled and sprung out around her face like that.

"I figured it'd be good to bring her along, let her see how much it hurts," she said, and I thought of our argument the week before when I announced I wanted a tattoo of my own.

"Like hell," she had said when I told her about the sketch of the oak tree I found in an art book at school. We were in the apartment, and she was making baked chicken for dinner. Again.

"You have two," I reminded her.

"I also have nineteen years on you and my own job." She peeled back the skin of the bird's breast and shoved a pat of butter underneath.

I rolled my eyes. "I've got my own money," I said, which was true. I'd been saving my allowance and slipping five-dollar bills from her purse when she wasn't paying attention.

"You're not even seventeen yet, and I'm your mother. No. Chance. In. Hell," she said, and she put her hand up like a stop sign as if directing traffic, signaling that the conversation was indisputably over.

Johnny Drinko wiped his palms on his jeans and ran his eyes over the curves of my body. "Lemon, huh? How'd you get a name like that?"

And then my mother used the laugh she saved for men she wanted to screw when she wasn't sure they wanted to screw her back. "Look at her." She nudged me forward toward him. "Sharp and sour since the day she popped out."

It never ceased to amaze me that she insisted on using this line for explaining my name, when really we both knew she picked Lemon on account of her obsession with the color the September I was born. She was a recreational painter, and each month she randomly selected one shade to use as the base for all her work. September of the year I was born was the month of Lemon, a muted yellow paint she found in an art store when we lived in Harrisburg.

Johnny Drinko sat down behind the cash register and lit a Marlboro Red while my mother leafed through binders of tattoo sketches. The shop smelled like plastic wrap and cigarettes and sweat, and I could feel Johnny watching me from behind the counter, so I cocked my hip and put my hands on my waist, reciprocating.

I'd lost my virginity that spring to a senior at school, and even though we only did it four times before he got suspended for selling weed at a soccer game, I considered myself to be experienced. The first time the pothead and I tried it regular, the second time he did it from behind, and the last two times he used his tongue first, so even though I was just getting started, I thought I knew what felt good and what didn't. I'd learned enough, at least, to recognize that a guy like Johnny Drinko could teach me all the things I still wanted to learn.

I moved next to his chair and looked at the photos taped on the wall behind his head: Polaroids of bandanna-wearing bikers and big-haired blondes with crooked teeth showing off sharply inked dragons and crosses on forearms and ankles. "Roughnecks" we called them, the townies who never left town, never went to college or got a real job, the grown-ups who never grew up. There were also photos of sports-team emblems tattooed on fine-tuned athletes and pictures of girls in low-slung jeans sporting new tramp stamps: fresh flowers and vines inked at the base of their spines. Aerosmith played from a set of cheap speakers mounted on the wall, and a fan blew warm air inside from a corner by the window while Johnny leaned over a leather notebook sketching a tree with long-reaching roots and thin, naked branches.

"You going to the race next month?" he asked me.

I shook my head, and behind us my mother said, "Oh, I think I like this one" to no one in particular.

Stella and I lived in a small city in southern Virginia that had a NASCAR racetrack built on the outskirts of town. We'd been living there for over a year and a half, and race weekend happened twice a year, but the closest I'd come to going was parking with the pothead in a cul-de-sac near enough to the track that we could listen to the buzz of cars between beers and awkward conversation.

"I must have inked a hundred NASCAR fans last spring. This one guy had me do a foot-long car driving up his back. It was pretty cool, really." Johnny nodded to the photos on the wall. "I did a good job."

I shrugged and popped another pink bubble, my trademark gesture that fall. My mother called the habit white-trash, but my friend Molly-Warner read an article in one of her magazines about the importance of drawing attention to your lips when flirting with boys, and she insisted we follow the rule.

"His old man had been a racer, got killed back in '81 in a crash," Johnny said between drags off his smoke. "That tat was really important to him."

I could see the black ink of a design inching up the back of his neck, and I suddenly wished my mom wasn't there so I could reach over and take a drag off his Marlboro. I needed my mouth around the tight white tube where his lips had just been. I was looking at him, and he was looking back, but then a woman with bright red hair pushed aside the white sheet that separated the waiting area from the tattooing room, spoiling the moment. She had wet, glassy eyes and a square of Saran Wrap taped below her collarbone.

"All good, Suzie Q?" Johnny asked, and they moved to the register.

"It's a keeper." She smiled at him and then at me.

I nodded like I knew exactly how it felt to walk into a room without a tattoo and to walk out of the same room permanently adorned. She shifted her attention back to Johnny, who was eyeing her with a slick smile slapped across his face, and I had a quick but detailed vision of them screwing in the truck bed of a white pickup. She was on top, bucking back and forth with her palms pressing into his chest, and his eyes were closed while his body pulsated beneath all that pumping. He might have liked it, or maybe not. I couldn't decide.

My mother called my name then, and I looked up and winked at Johnny before I turned away from him, checking to see if I could get his attention the same way Stella and the redhead had.

It took about twenty minutes for Stella to settle on the hummingbird, then she handed Johnny the sketch and leaned over the counter where he sat. "You mind?" she said, and she took a smoke from his pack. I thought of her mood swings back when she quit and the nervous way she used to chew her fingernails. She caught me watching her when she brought the Marlboro to her lips. "See something you like, kiddo?" she asked, and then she followed Johnny Drinko to the customers' chair behind the white sheet.

The other tattoo artist, a man with a thin black braid, finished cleaning his gear while Johnny completed the stencil and poured ink into tiny white paper cups sitting on the stand next to his chair.

"I'm taking lunch," the other guy said, and he pulled off a pair of pale blue surgical gloves and tossed them into the trash.

And then it was just me, my mom, and Johnny Drinko squished inside the heat of the tattoo room.

That was the third town we had lived in since we'd left Denny, and I liked it best, because of the low mountains and the sticky summers and the way our apartment smelled like fresh bread all the time, since we lived next to the sub shop by the mall. It was a rough ride to get there after the six months at the Jersey Shore with Rocco from the pool hall, and I was glad to be in Virginia, where my mom seemed calmer and the men she dated were quieted by the innate laziness of a small town. My best friend, Molly-Warner, had a car and a fake ID, and we had spent the summer making out with boys from school and smoking cigarettes at the public pool in town. I'd finally found my lady curves, as Stella called them once while watching me under raised eyebrows, and when school started that month, Molly-Warner and I would head to the neighborhood park after class and spend our afternoons in our bikini tops, lying out, reading books, and gossiping about our teachers, our classmates, the latest school scandal. Stella liked to take her notebooks up to the Blue Ridge Parkway on the weekends to sketch split-rail fences and ragged farmhouses she'd paint back at home. It was the first time I felt like we were ready to put Denny and Rocco and those last years behind us, and I hoped we stayed in town until I finished high school. It was my senior year, and I was sick of moving boxes and cheap motels and having to make friends every time my mom picked a new place for us to live. I needed to finish driver's ed. I needed to stay in one place long enough so I could recognize the faces in the crowd when graduation finally happened. I'd finally found a group of friends, mellow kids like me and Molly-Warner who partied a little but also knew how to keep out of trouble, and the librarian at school liked me enough to drop the late fees I'd accrued over the summer. Plus, Stella had a good job working in the jewelry department at J.C. Penney, and I could tell she liked the cheap rent and the apartment that smelled like bread too.

Johnny Drinko was pressing the hummingbird stencil against my mom's skin when she licked her lips and said, "Get me a mint from my purse, Lemon. I need something to suck on."

It was not the first time I'd watched my mother throw herself at a man. She'd been throwing herself at men in each town we passed through ever since we left Denny after the black eye. She was pretty and thin and wore cute clothes, and after all the drama when she and Denny split up, I was just glad to see her back on her feet. I knew she liked the game—the chase and the satisfaction of getting what she wanted—but there was something about Johnny Drinko that made me nervous, something I sensed right away that day at the shop. He was mysterious like he had a secret, and controlled like he knew what he wanted, and that had me worried. If Stella wanted him and he didn't want her back, if the game lasted too long, she'd walk away. While we'd been living in Virginia, things had finally evened out, but I was constantly afraid she'd get bored or, worse, vulnerable, and I knew it would be someone like Johnny Drinko who would send us moving again.

I used to tell my friends my mother was made of metal and glass. She was smooth and sturdy on the surface, but there was always that part in danger of shattering, a childlike aspect that never disappeared. I resented that unpredictability and tiptoed around the threat of her cracking apart, of her dragging us out of one city and into the next.

"Let's motor," she said as she took the breath mint from me, sucked it between her lips with a smile, and settled into the chair. Then I watched Johnny Drinko ink a perfect permanent hummingbird above her shoulder blade.

CHAPTER TWO

THE NEXT TIME I SAW JOHNNY DRINKO, he was sitting in my living room on a Tuesday afternoon in early October. Molly-Warner and I had ditched our last class and headed to my house because I knew my mom would be at work. Molly-Warner wanted wine coolers and I wanted something to eat, and Johnny Drinko was on the couch watching *The Crocodile Hunter* when we opened the front door.

"What are you doing here?" I said, and Molly-Warner mumbled "he-llo" behind me.

He looked good and cool, his golden arms stretching out from the sleeves of a tight black T-shirt with the Rolling Stones tongue printed on front. His hair was loose that time, thick waves drifting above his shoulders, making me think of surfers in California or Hawaii. He smiled and checked us out from the couch as I combed my hand through my hair and sucked in my stomach.

"Stella gave me the key." He leaned for the remote and turned down the volume.

I tossed my backpack onto the floor by the door and tried to decide if I liked or didn't like seeing Johnny Drinko in our apartment. My afternoon had gotten a lot more interesting with him sitting there looking at me that way, but I didn't like that he'd seen my mom, that they were together earlier, and that she'd invited him over.

"Business was slow at the shop, so I closed early." He leaned back in the chair and put his feet up on the coffee table like he owned it, and I decided that, overall, I did in fact like his presence taking over our apartment like that. "Your mom said I could hang here."

We moved into the room, and I hitched my weight on one hip, hooked my thumb through the belt loop of my jeans, and arched my back a little. I'd topped out at five feet five inches that summer, and I'd been experimenting with bangs, so with the layers growing out my brown hair finally had some shape, some curl. I didn't bother much with makeup, but my skin was still a creamy summertime brown from all those hours at the pool. I knew I wasn't model-hot like the popular girls in school, but it could have been worse, so I didn't mind Johnny looking at me like that. Even if I was nervous, having him there made me feel important, him looking at me and me looking back at him. I was glad Molly-Warner was there to see it.

"Who's your friend, Lemon?"

Johnny Drinko taught me and Molly-Warner how to make tequila sunrises, and we drank them in the living room while we finished watching the episode "Journey to the Red Centre." The two of us sat on the floor in front of the TV, and Johnny stayed on the couch, but I could smell him from where I was, the distinct mix of sweat and tequila with the chemical scent of ink from the shop.

When the credits started rolling, Johnny Drinko rose to his feet and announced, "Jesus, I need a cig," but I told him Stella didn't let me smoke in the house, which I guessed was true since I always hid my Camel Lights from her. He shrugged, and Molly-Warner and I followed him out when he left the apartment.

The three of us stood in front of the sub shop and took turns using Johnny's Zippo to light one of his Marlboro Reds. I'd recently discovered the Beats, and something about the way he propped himself against the wall of the building and clamped his smoke between his thumb and pointer finger reminded me of the cover of *Desolation Angels*, a photo of Kerouac I'd studied a hundred times when I'd read the novel that summer.

"You girls old enough to smoke?" He inhaled deep.

"What do you think?" Molly-Warner said, and rolled her eyes.

Molly-Warner and I met in chemistry class the year before. She was still a virgin, but there were rumors at school that she gave good blow jobs, which made me feel a little better when I first told her about sleeping with the pothead. He wasn't the most admirable character, a lanky kid who'd probably never make it to graduation, but she believed me when I said he'd been nice about the whole thing and that he had a quirky sense of humor.

"I'm a sucker for anyone who can make me laugh," I told

her, which was true even though it didn't have much to do with me sleeping with the stoner. We'd never talked all that much, when it really came down to it.

Molly-Warner was my most confident friend even though she was a little bit fat, and she had short, spiky hair that made her look tough and unpredictable. She wasn't weirded out when I told her about all the different places my mom and I had lived, and she'd been nice to me from the start even back when I was the new kid in school, the daughter of a single mom who lived in the junky apartment complex near the mall. She never was one to judge. Both her parents worked at the furniture factory in town, and they bought her a used Toyota when she turned sixteen so they wouldn't have to worry about driving her to school. She was my only friend with a car, and I was her only friend who didn't mind talking about what it felt like to have sex.

"Did it make you feel important?" she asked one afternoon as she wove her way through town with one hand on the steering wheel and the other hanging out the window.

I had my nose buried in a not-very-good collection of Jim Morrison poems, and I shook my head and kept my face turned down toward the book. "Not really."

"But it was exciting, right? To be with him like that?"

She hit the brakes, and I looked up, eyeing the red light that put the car on pause. She was staring at me like I was supposed to say something significant as she raised her dark eyebrows high, punctuating her face with them like two big quote marks. I didn't want to disappoint her, but I also didn't like to lie.

"I guess it . . ." I tried to find an easy way to describe the weight in my stomach the first time we did it, the distinct and lonely feeling that comes when you realize something important has happened and that, if you had blinked just a second longer, you almost would have missed it. "I guess it felt good to do something memorable," I said.

She returned her eyes to the road with a "humph," trying to translate my statement into something satisfying, a recommendation maybe, or a promise.

We lied and told Johnny Drinko we were nineteen, and when he said he was twenty-seven, I decided he was too young for my mom anyway, that he probably didn't know she'd be thirty-six in November. She had a convenient habit of letting the fact slip through the cracks.

"You girls like living here?" he asked as a woman and her son nudged past us and headed into the sub shop.

I looked at him and tried to decide if *he* liked living there, but it was too hard to tell, since he was wearing sunglasses and watching Church Street in front of us as the cars moved down the road.

"It's okay, I guess." I shrugged.

"It's a shit hole is what it is," Molly-Warner said, and I wished I could sound as assertive as she did when I talked. It was something she was always telling me I needed to work on.

"Oh, yeah?" Johnny eyed her up and down, and I tried to telepathically tell her to suck in her gut. I wanted him to think I was the kind of girl who had interesting thin friends with strong opinions.

"There's nothing to do here—it's the same shit all the time." She flicked her cigarette onto the pavement.

"That's kind of what I like about this town," Johnny said. "It's mellow, no surprises. I dig that."

I wanted to tell him that's exactly how I felt, that that was what made the town my favorite place Stella and I had lived, but I kept my mouth shut and finished my smoke instead.

We were pretty drunk by the time my mom got home, so my voice was slow and slurred when I tried to explain why Molly-Warner and I were sitting around in our underwear taking tequila shots and playing strip poker with Johnny Drinko. She said something about us acting like prostitutes, and then she told me to get some clothes on and go to my room. Now. Johnny was on his feet pretty fast considering how many cocktails he'd had, grabbing his T-shirt off the floor and pulling his tennis shoes on as he headed toward the door.

"It's cool, Stella," he said as he dug in his pocket for his keys. "We're just hanging out."

Molly-Warner and I stood in the doorway that connected the kitchen to the living room, and we held hands and smiled as we watched my mom throw her cell phone at Johnny's head.

"Are you insane?" she yelled right before the phone hit the wall.

We stopped smiling then, and I started to feel a little queasy when Molly-Warner began to cry, the tequila sneaking up on me and uncoiling in my stomach, stretching out. But I squeezed my friend's hand and whispered, "Shh, it's gonna be fine," and then Johnny called my mom a crazy bitch, and he opened the door and headed down the hallway.

She followed him out and stood at the top of the stairs, yelling, "They're only seventeen, you sick shithead" until he was gone. I hoped the neighbors weren't home from work yet.

My mom kicked Molly-Warner out, and I sat on the couch as I watched her slam the door and call my friend a dumb slut. Then she turned her eyes to me.

"Are you crazy? Have you lost your mind?" she asked.

Which made me think of her at the Motel 6 the week after we left Denny, of the way I dragged her out of bed on the sixth day and dumped her in the shower. It was fast and furious, the misery and depression clinging to her like Velcro she couldn't get unstuck. I was only fourteen at the time, but I watched as my mother lost herself over Denny, a drunk who treated us like crap, a loser who took all her money.

"Jesus, Lemon. He's twice your age," she said, which wasn't even close to being true, but I let it slide.

I looked at her in the tight black miniskirt and the chunky wedge heels she'd worn to work. I looked at our tiny apartment, the stacks of dirty dishes taking over the coffee table and the trash spilling out of the bin in the kitchen. And for the first time I realized how embarrassing it was to have a mother who acted like a child, to live in an apartment where two people in the building couldn't take a hot shower at the same time. I decided I'd outgrown Stella's choices: I wanted a permanent address, a home with enough space for us to unpack all the boxes, a family that made more sense than we did.

"Look at you," she said. "He works at a tattoo parlor, for Christ's sake."

"You're the one who gave him the key," I said, even though I knew it had nothing to do with me and Molly-Warner getting drunk with the man I figured my mother wanted as her boyfriend.

"What does *that* mean?" She came toward me. She ran her eyes over the empty shot glasses that had left sticky rings along the edge of our coffee table, at the tequila that had spilled and ruined her stack of *Vogue* magazines piled on the floor. At my jeans on the carpet next to the couch.

"It just means he was here when I got home. He was here because of you." I stared at her. "They always are."

Her face changed right before she slapped me—it was hot and tight and far away, her face like sculpted metal and her eyes like broken glass.

I brought my hand to my cheek, my skin throbbing and my eyes watering over. And when she turned away, headed to her bedroom, and slammed the door behind her, I knew we'd be moving within the month.

The last time I saw Johnny Drinko was that weekend, back at the tattoo shop. He was ringing up a man with a buzz cut and a square of Saran Wrap taped to his forearm, and I stood outside the window, looking in as Johnny handed the guy a credit-card receipt. The customer left, and then Johnny came out, lit a cigarette, and squatted down next to me. I didn't say anything for a long time, but then he reached over and hooked his finger under the edge of my silver anklet.

"I hope I didn't get you and your friend in too much trouble," he said.

I remembered the way his skin looked when he took off his shirt at our apartment, the way the black tattoo on his back reminded me of the Egyptian hieroglyphics I'd learned about in social studies the year before.

"Nah, it's no big deal."

He dropped the silver chain but kept his grip on my foot as he rubbed his thumb along the curve of my heel, making me hot and anxious in a way none of the boys from school ever had.

"You seem like a good kid. It's too bad." He stopped.

I fidgeted with the button on my corduroy miniskirt and

imagined how his breath might taste. Like sweat and cigarettes, tequila and ink, maybe. "It's too bad what?" I asked.

I thought of the pothead and the way I kept my shirt on the first time we did it in his car down at the cul-de-sac. We were rushed and awkward, childish, and it embarrassed me as I stood outside the shop with Johnny Drinko. I imagined it would be better with Johnny, that he would be smarter and less clumsy. He would make me feel grown up, and I would finally understand why Stella wanted to be with men like him.

He ran his hand up my calf and squeezed my leg. "It's too bad about you being so young." He rubbed his thumb along the slope behind my knee. "And me being so old, I guess."

When I followed Johnny Drinko into the shop and behind the white curtain, I was thinking of my mom across town behind the jewelry counter at J.C. Penney, how she was probably planning the move, deciding what we would need to leave behind this time and what we would have space to take with us.

And then Johnny sat down in the same chair my mother had sat in a week earlier and pulled me toward him. Behind him I saw myself in the glass mirror above his work counter, me looking down at him as he tugged me to his lap. He tasted different than I expected. I'd been right about the cigarettes, but there was also something cinnamon and hot, like the thick red After Shock liquor Molly-Warner and I drank sometimes at her house. At first his tongue was slower than the pothead's, but it sped up as he shoved his hands under my shirt, his fingers darting back and forth across my skin, pinching.

"Should we lock the door or something?" I asked when I pulled my face away from his and tried to catch my breath.

"I already did," he said.

My mom and I bailed on the month-to-month rental by the sub shop and moved to Morgantown, West Virginia, the following week.

"I'm doing this for you," Stella said after we loaded up the car and turned in the key to the landlord. But I just rolled my eyes and looked out the window as she pulled out onto the road.

I didn't get a chance to see Johnny Drinko again, but I copied down the address of the tattoo shop from the phone book and promised myself eventually I would find words good enough to write down and send to him from the road. I lost the address on I-77 somewhere between Beckley and Bridgeport.

The day we left, I ran into the pothead when we stopped at the gas station near the mall. At first he pretended he didn't know me, but when Stella went inside to pay, he came over to the car and leaned down at my window.

"I heard about what you did, Lemon," he said. He reached inside to graze his fingers across my cheek, but I shook his hand away. "You screwed that guy down at Atlas Tattoo."

I squinted and looked behind him at my mother, who was handing her credit card to the man at the register.

"When you turn out like your mom, just remember who taught you first," he said before he laughed and walked away.

And in that instant I realized I had become a girl worth talking about, a person worth remembering once I moved away.

CHAPTER THREE

A FEW WEEKS LATER WE WERE SETTLED in a squat two-bedroom house in West Virginia with the same water-stained ceilings and sluggish showerhead dribble as all the other places we had rented, but this time around was different because by the time I enrolled at my new school the first week of November, I was almost six weeks pregnant.

I spent my first days dodging teachers in the hallways and categorizing students into the distinct groups I'd seen in every school I'd gone to. There were Preps and Hipsters and Weekend-Warrior Partiers with trust funds stitched into their back pockets, the kids who threw ragers at their houses when their parents flew to Vail or Vegas or Key West for vacations. There were the Jocks and the Geeks and the Film Kids, who kept video cameras in their backpacks. The Adrenaline Junkies were the guys who went skydiving or rock climbing on the weekends, and the Low Riders were the country boys who stuck small wheels on big trucks and cranked rap music from their dashboard speakers. I usually slipped in somewhere between the Art Kids and the English Nerds, never committed enough to join the lit magazine staff, knowing we could move again at any time, but too much of a bookworm to be considered an angst-ridden Art Punk or Emo. It always took a while to make friends, but this was the large kind of public school that made it easy to disappear.

Then, a week after I told Stella about the pregnancy, my new friend Emmy Preston found out her dad was being sent to Afghanistan.

"You're shitting me," I said.

"I wish," she said back, and then neither of us said anything as I tried to wrap my brain around it slowly, the shock of it moving over us like fog. It was bigger than all the arguments with Stella, bigger, even, than my frustrations at having moved again before I finished driver's ed.

Like a lot of the dads in Morgantown, West Virginia, Emmy's father enlisted as a reservist for drill pay. That November, when their infantry unit was activated, over a hundred and fifty of the town's men would have to board a group of old, beat-up school buses and leave for a place that, until then, had existed for us only on television and in newspapers. Now the war infected their families, and Emmy handled the news like the rest of the reservists' kids: with silent acceptance and a vacant shrug of the shoulders.

Emmy and I had met in Contemporary Lit on my first day at school, and out of twenty-six other kids in the room, she picked me to lean over and ask with a big wide grin, "WantToGetStonedAfterClass?" She had flawless tan skin and quirky rectangle-shaped glasses she had to wear for reading, and later she said she picked me because of my nose ring, a small silver hoop I wore after I'd secretly gotten my nose pierced when we first moved to West Virginia. I carried the nose ring in my pocket and removed or replaced it depending on the proximity of my mother.

"You were new and I was bored with my scene. Everyone likes new, right?" she once said. "Plus, facial piercings score major points in terms of hipness. Even if you can't drive." She nudged me then and smiled.

After class that first day, when I told her my name was Lemon, Emmy said, "Sure it is," which I was used to, and I followed her out of the building and figured there were worse things I could do than smoke a joint with this long-haired blonde in skinny jeans and a red hooded zip-up. I was almost a head shorter than she, so I had a perfect view of her gold necklace as I walked beside her, the small four-leaf clover resting inside the V of her collarbones. We walked through the back of campus, down by the gym and up a small hill to an empty field, and all the while people watched her. I could feel their eyes on Emmy like the glare of summertime sun streaming through a car window.

"I lost my virginity here last summer. It was the football field a million years ago," she said as we crossed over the turf, "but now they never mow it, and the only thing it's really good for is smoking between classes and hiding when they take us outside for gym," and I knew immediately Emmy and I would be very good friends. She would be the person who taught me never to apologize for who I really was.

And in the same way, it took my mother less than thirty seconds to decide she did not like her when they met. Emmy came for dinner, and while we waited for the pizza guy to arrive, Emmy tried to convince Stella to get a better job that paid salary, a better haircut with highlights, and a better house on the north side of town near West Virginia University.

So while Emmy prepped for her dad's deployment over at her house, my house became angry and loud as Stella processed the reality of my pregnancy. Once she knew about the baby, it seemed like happy hour happened more frequently. "Get me a beer, Lemon," she'd say when she got home from work, shifting her eyes away from my stomach with a dramatic "ugh" or "hmph."

I was a neon sign in a storefront. I was the intercom voice in the public library announcing someone had left their car lights on. When she looked at me, my body was a stack of catalogues that kept showing up in our mailbox. Unwanted and unnecessary, a waste of natural resources.

Stella also started sleeping with her boss, Simon, a freelance photographer who'd hired her to help him stay organized after he landed an ad campaign with The North Face for a shoot in Dolly Sods Wilderness Area. Simon had grown up in Fort Collins, Colorado, a place that seemed as foreign and far away as Kabul, Afghanistan, where Emmy's dad was deployed. He'd spent a few years working on a farm in Costa Rica, and even went to college for a little while to study photography, but ended up on the East Coast because he fell in love with a woman who didn't love him back enough to stick around. That's what he told me, at least, one night when we stayed up to watch *Saturday Night Live* together. And then he said he decided to stay in West Virginia once he'd arrived, because he liked how slow it was. He liked the heat in the summer and the green in the spring, and mostly he liked the way

Morgantown encouraged people to take their time. The way he said it made me homesick for the apartment that smelled like bread, and my friend Molly-Warner, and it even made me miss the smell of skin and ink a little bit, since Johnny Drinko said something similar the day we made tequila sunrises.

Stella claimed his upbringing out west made him more cultured and interesting than the other men she'd met in town. I think she liked the way he paid attention to her paintings and the way he'd show up with new brushes or art books, little gifts none of her other boyfriends would have thought to buy. He liked all the same late-night television I did, and he was good at explaining how Spanish conjugations worked, one of the subjects I'd fallen behind in since the distraction of the pregnancy, so I liked him okay. Better, at least, than Denny in Philadelphia or Rocco in New Jersey.

November turned the town a dark rusty color as orange and red leaves began dropping to the ground, and Emmy and I wasted time hanging out down by the lake every day after school. Sometimes we'd do our homework, and sometimes we'd just listen to music or play cards. She was good at gin rummy, and I was a blackjack badass. By then Emmy was kissing a boy from our physics class, a long-haired guitarist named Dylan who worked after school as the poetry editor for the Morgantown High literary magazine. Dylan liked to listen to the Shins and he liked to smoke pot, but mostly he liked to drive us around three wide in the cab of Emmy's old blue truck, since his parents hadn't bought him a car and he usually rode to school on his dirt bike. He was the kind of guy who would never outgrow his long hair, who would never hold a nine-to-five.

"Do you think he's too quiet or too artsy?" Emmy would

ask me before he'd show up at the lake. "Do you think he's too nice? Or too boring, maybe?" she'd ask as she sucked on a cigarette and stared out at the water.

I'd nod or shrug, thinking of how similar Dylan and Emmy were, how brave and fearless, carefree. Emmy was one of the popular kids who hung out in the parking lot between classes smoking cigarettes but also landed her name on the honor roll, while I was the kind of kid who just aimed to blend in. I was the new girl, an increasingly curvy loner who'd had to walk home from school before I met Emmy and Dylan, and it constantly surprised me she'd chosen me to be her partner in crime. I asked her about it once when we were parked down at the lake and she was venting about a girl in our class, Jenny Myers, who'd just gotten a new Mini Cooper. I knew she and Jenny had been friends, but we never hung around with her, and I wondered why she'd bailed on her old friends and replaced them with me.

"Aside from the obvious fact that I'm ridiculously intelligent and adorable, why'd you pick me and walk out on them?" We were good enough friends by then, and I was feeling honest—honest and maybe a little worried she might walk out on me, too. Plus, I'd heard some of the girls had been giving her a hard time, the girls with the right clothes and the right boyfriends. I'd seen the notes scrawled on the bathroom doors. They called her a fake and a traitor, and I wanted to give her a chance to talk about it.

"I spent three years with the Preps and the Partiers, you know?" she said, and I nodded.

Before I came along, Emmy was part of a close-knit crew of Partiers, and she'd told me she and Jenny Myers and Allyson Carter and Maggie Rothbright had founded their

clique freshman year in French class; the group of boys followed shortly after.

"And I knew who I was supposed to be when I was with
them. But it was never really me. Those kids come from families with money, and I always felt like I was playing catch-up."
We were standing in front of her truck, and she dug the toe
of her red Vans into the mud. "This summer I just got sick of
it. It's like I knew they were just friends of convenience, party
friends. I knew we wouldn't keep in touch after graduation,"
she said, and shrugged.

And I understood exactly what she meant. I'd felt the same
way about most of my friends in high school too. All the kids I'd
spent the last years with never felt important, except for Molly-
Warner and Emmy, maybe because I always figured we'd move
before anyone had the chance to really get to know me.

"And then you showed up," Emmy said. "You rescued me,
really," and I loved the way she said it like that. "Plus, you
were cool. And not cool in a knowing-about-the-best-parties
or having-the-best-clothes kind of way."

I shook my head. "I am definitely not that kind of cool."

"No, you're authentically cool, though," she said. "Cool in
the way that you can be totally happy sitting in my truck bed
reading a book while me and Dylan make out in the front
seat, *and* you'll actually have something smart to say afterward." She pulled out her pack from her back pocket and lit a
smoke with her lucky yellow lighter. "You actually care about
what you read and don't just pretend to be reading because
you think it will make you seem smart."

"That would be totally lame," I said, and she nodded
because she knew by then how important books were to me
even if she didn't share the interest.

"And it's cool that you don't care if you have a lot of friends, if you're popular," she said.

"I have no skills at being popular."

"And I love that," she said.

"Rumor has it, popularity is overrated," I said back.

"Exactly. You rescued me, really," she repeated, and then she elbowed me and smiled before she took a long drag.

The afternoon Simon found out I was pregnant, Dylan showed up at the spillway on his bike around five, and I sat on the grass and read the pregnancy book Emmy stole from the library, while they got stoned and made out in the front seat of the truck. I'd Googled some details already and had learned about dating the pregnancy by the first day of my last period and warding off the nausea by eating small meals and sipping, not chugging, my liquids, but the book broke it down week by week and had more information about nutrition and development and childbirth than I ever could have needed. Eventually Dylan drove me home, one hand on the steering wheel and one hand on Emmy's knee as she sat between us on the bench seat and mumbled the words to a Rolling Stones song on the radio. It was the middle of November, and Dylan liked to drive with the windows rolled all the way down and the stereo turned all the way up, which was one of the things Emmy and I liked best about him. I watched Dylan instinctively rub his thumb over the plane of her knee, the gap of tan skin between skirt hem and boot shaft, and I wondered how long you had to be with someone before that kind of thing became second nature. Except for the pothead, the boys I'd made out with back in Virginia were inconsistent interactions, guys I'd had classes with. And none of them would've taken the time to ask your last name, let alone hold your hand at school.

"Looks like your mom's man-friend got a new ride," Emmy said when Dylan parked the truck behind a glossy blue, four-door Tacoma in my driveway. "That thing is gorgeous."

Mom and Simon were sitting on the front porch with Simon's dog, Pace, lying at their feet next to a half-empty bottle of liquor. She was laughing, and from the driveway she looked young. Young and maybe a little drunk, but mostly she just looked happy as Simon reached over and pushed a strand of hair from her face.

I took my nose ring out, slid it into my pocket, and opened the door as Emmy turned down the radio.

"Am I allowed to call Stella Grandma yet?" she asked, leaning her head out the passenger side window as I grabbed my backpack from the back of the truck bed.

"Watch it," I told her.

"Too early?" she said.

Dylan rolled his eyes as he backed the Ford out the driveway, and I headed to the porch.

"Hey, kiddo," Mom said when I reached the front steps.

Pace lifted his head and looked up at me, so I dropped my bag and squatted down to scratch the spot between his ears he liked to have rubbed. There was a small watercolor drying by the door, an abstract painting with quick slashing brushstrokes flung across the canvas with seemingly no pattern or purpose. I imagined that if I looked at it too long, the sharp angles and lines of chaos might kick open a migraine or another round of nausea.

It was a Friday, and Stella seemed a little more boozed than usual as she told me about Simon buying the new car and about the celebratory dinner she was planning on cooking that night. Tacos and margaritas, fresh guacamole and salsa. It should have sounded good, but by then I was sick of having dinner with Simon and Stella. I was tired of watching another guy fall for her, knowing that eventually she'd screw it up. I liked this one more than I'd liked most of them, and I could tell how much he liked us back. Simon was complicated since he was Stella's boss, and I worried that in another month or so, when the relationship turned to shit, we'd be broke again. She'd lose her job and make us move to another small town where we'd have to start over. There was a formula, and Simon was one of the good guys, one of the men who'd be stunned when Stella woke up one morning and just walked away because she was bored or jaded or in a bad mood. Guys like Simon, the nice ones, were better than guys like Denny and Rocco, the not-nice ones, but by then I knew none of them ever lasted.

"I thought I might go out with Emmy and Dylan for dinner," I said even though my mother had unofficially grounded me since she caught me with Johnny Drinko that day back in Virginia. She never actually said I wasn't allowed to go out at night, but I knew not to ask. It was clear I couldn't do anything fun once I was pregnant.

"Give me a break, Lemon," she said just before she asked Simon to top off her glass. He poured her a drink as I geared up for a fight with my mother.

"You can't hold me captive," I said. "I want to go out." In truth, I'd been going out to the spillway every afternoon, but I'd recently decided that didn't count. I wanted my nights back. I wanted to drive around with Emmy, to drink beer, to get out of the house where I was beginning to like the man my mom was pretending she'd keep around.

"You've been out enough," she said, bringing the glass to

her lips and peering at me over the rim of her third or fourth vodka tonic. I noticed Fire Engine Red paint on her fingertips. "You smell like cigarettes, Lemon, Jesus Christ."

I knew my mother had smoked Marlboro Reds the entire time she was pregnant with me. In fact, she smoked them the entire time I was a kid and quit smoking only when the relationship with Rocco fell apart. I also knew that the night before she left him, Rocco put his cigarette out on Stella's arm when he was piss-drunk and jealous, something she'd tried hard to hide from me. So when we left the Jersey Shore, she left her smoking habit with Rocco back in the pool hall he managed for the woman he was screwing on the side. Denny was the con in Philadelphia, Rocco was the rite of passage in New Jersey, and I suppose Johnny Drinko was the one who knocked up her kid in Virginia.

"Emmy and Dylan smoke," I said. "What do you want me to do?"

She put her glass on the porch, by her chair, and leaned forward toward me, perching her elbows on her knees.

"Look at me, Lemon," she said. So I did. "I don't *want* any of this. But now that it's happening, what I *want* is for you to take some responsibility, to take care of yourself. To take care of—"

"Mom." I stopped her and looked at Simon, who was leaning in his chair, calm and curious, ready.

"You should tell him," Stella said as she picked up her glass and leaned back. "He should know."

Simon moved his hand to her knee and squeezed. "Be cool, Stella," he said. "We're celebrating tonight."

I guess by then he figured my mom and I fought in the way most teenaged girls fight with their mothers—provokingly and intentionally—but he didn't know yet about Johnny Drinko. He didn't know he was dating a woman who would be a grandmother soon. I guess I had hoped I wouldn't have to tell him, since the whole thing was pretty humiliating. Plus, part of me worried he might take off if he found out what a loser his girlfriend's daughter really was, that he might disappear and leave us on our own again.

"Tell him," she said. "He should know."

I looked down at Pace and up at the rotting wood of the windowsill above us and over at the weeds creeping up from the lawn and onto the front porch. "I'm pregnant," I said. "I guess I'm having a baby in July." And before he got the chance to ask, I lied, "The dad is a boy from my school in Virginia. He doesn't know, though."

Stella liked to say her favorite thing about Simon was that he was really good at rolling with the punches. So when I told him about the baby, he was calm and collected and told me, "Sometimes the best things that happen to us are the ones that aren't planned," and then he took a long swig from his glass, draining it, before he looked up and winked. And I thought that might be the end of it, but the vodka must have hit Stella all at once then, because her cheeks flared up red just before she rose to her feet and started yelling. Yelling at me for being an idiot and yelling at Simon for being so apathetic, yelling at no one in particular for this being the life she had not imagined. A knocked-up daughter, a shit hole in the middle of West Virginia where she couldn't even buy a bottle of booze on a Sunday. She kicked over her glass by the chair, which startled the dog, who popped up and bolted down the stairs and into the front yard, where he rummaged behind a bush and started rolling on his back.

"Jesus, Stella," Simon said. "Chill out."

Stella started in on him about his mangy dog he cared more about than her and how she felt like she was running a boardinghouse with him and his mutt staying at our place all the time, with Simon's dishes in the sink and the dog's toys all over the floor. But I couldn't watch her yell at him, watch him take it just like I did when she turned on me that way. It made me sick to see her treat him like a child, so I picked up my backpack, slid inside through the screen door, and headed to my bedroom.

CHAPTER FOUR

THAT NIGHT, I TALKED MY MOM INTO letting Emmy come over, so the two of us sat on my porch and talked about her dad, who had left the week before.

"He always left," she said as she slumped back into the camping chair and crossed one leg over the other. "One weekend a month he'd train in Preston County at Camp Dawson, but he always came back. He'd be tired and sunburned and he'd cuss more at first, but eventually the training would work its way out of him," she said, and she reached down into her bag and pulled out her cigarettes. "He always came back," she repeated in a way that meant she knew this time there'd be no guarantees.

Emmy's dad and the butcher at the grocery store and the guy who changed my mom's oil down at the gas station had all left town, and a whole slew of kids like Emmy became what I had always been: fatherless. Thinking about it too much made me wish I was still allowed to smoke and drink.

She lit the Marlboro Light with a pack of matches and told me she and Dylan were thinking of having sex, next weekend maybe, or the weekend after.

"How come now?" I asked because part of me was surprised they hadn't had sex already, and part of me was jealous they might have sex soon. Mostly I was just glad to talk about something besides her dad and my pregnancy.

She said she was pretty sure Dylan might love her and that she was absolutely sure she liked him better than the other guys she had slept with, so it made sense to do it with him. She said she liked the way he wore his hair messy instead of sculpted with product, or worse, cut short and buzzed at the neck like the other boys from school. Dylan wore black high-tops and slim-fitted T-shirts with rock bands on the front, and he read poetry during his free time instead of four-wheeling through the muddy trails out in the country like the kids we knew in town. I nodded when she told me she thought Dylan might be the most interesting boy she knew.

"I love how he doesn't give a shit about fitting in. Plus," Emmy said as she cocked her head to the side and smiled, "I like the way you can see his hip bones nudging out from under those stupid corduroy pants. So cute and rocker. I don't know if I'll ever be able to date a boy who wears jeans again." She ran her tongue across her lips and groaned.

I rolled my eyes. "Well, just be careful," I said, and pointed to my stomach.

She laughed, but I think she was pretty sad and restless then. I think she needed to feel important and safe and beautiful.

"Just be careful, Emmy," I repeated, that time serious since I wasn't sure anymore what I thought of sex or what I thought of Emmy giving herself away like that, even if Dylan was a good guy.

Stella was painting in the living room, and I could smell the fumes leaking out the window screens when Emmy reached into her bag and pulled out a flask, unscrewing the top and tilting the silver bottle back. It was easy to imagine the liquid burning down her throat as she sucked on the lip until her eyes began to water.

"I swear this town is eating me alive," she said. "You know, I've never been farther away than visiting my grandparents in Miami. Who the hell wants to go to Miami?" she said. "I want to go somewhere great, you know? I want to see the Mississippi River and the Grand Canyon and that place with all those guys' heads carved on it."

"Rushmore," I said as I waved her smoke away from my face.

"I need to see Mount Rushmore," she said. "Shit."

It was hard to imagine what it would be like to have stayed in one place growing up, to know the same town and the same group of people for so many years that things became predictable. Stella never let us stay in one place for longer than two or three years before she'd pick a new destination and announce we were moving again. I never got a say about where we went: Each uprooting was always nonnegotiable. I figured I would be a different kind of mother than Stella, and I thought about the way she was still trying to control me even though I would be a mother myself soon. But then I heard Emmy breathe in wet and heavy, and I realized she was crying, so I took her hand and leaned over to rest my head on her shoulder.

"Did you hear about Bobby Elder?" she asked when she pulled away. She leaned down to put the flask on the floor.

I nodded and said, "Yeah, I heard," because everyone in Morgantown had heard about Bobby Elder by then. Emmy and I just hadn't talked about it yet.

Bobby was a twenty-three-year-old kid who'd worked on cars down at Ervin's Auto Repair on Kingwood Street and gotten killed by a roadside bomb near Kabul a week earlier. The local paper did a feature story about his family and his childhood, about how he was supposed to play football at WVU but lost his scholarship after a knee injury. He joined the Army Reserve instead to help pay his tuition. He wasn't a soldier, the paper wrote. He was a kid. A linebacker and a mechanic. He was a college student who was studying physical therapy. It was the most miserable thing Morgantown had been hit with in a while, and everyone was talking about it except for me and Emmy because I wasn't sure what to say to her about Bobby Elder.

"He was, like . . ." She turned her head away from me, so I could barely hear her say "so young."

I nodded and looked at the shadows being thrown around at our feet by the porch light on the wall behind us. It had rained that afternoon, so the air was thick with the smell of mud and bugs and water, and I couldn't catch my breath. I couldn't look at Emmy either, sitting next to me feeling so shitty and depressed. It made me crazy because I didn't have the words to turn the conversation into something good.

"My dad and Bobby were at Camp Dawson together." She turned her face to look at me. "I think he helped my mom out once when her car broke down on Interstate Sixty-eight."

We sat there for a while, but eventually I found the nerve

to ask her if she'd heard from her dad since he left.

"Just an e-mail," she said as she ashed her cigarette on the wood-slatted floor of the porch.

"How'd he sound?" I wanted her to tell me that he sounded good. I wanted her to say he made some jokes and wrote about how the war wasn't really that bad after all. I wanted her to say the e-mails were light and cool and easy, just like I remembered her dad being.

"Hot," she said instead. Emmy took a long, hard drag from her smoke. "He sounded hot and thirsty. I guess there's a lot of sand."

Her dad was a thick-necked man I'd met a handful of times when I'd gone to her house to avoid Stella after she found out about the baby. He was a sunburned, T-shirt-wearing kind of man who smelled like wood chips and drank Budweiser after he got home from work at the landscaping company. He liked to watch *Dirty Jobs* and *This Old House* and another show about fishermen in Alaska risking their lives to catch crab in the Bering Sea. He also liked to tell knock-knock jokes that weren't very good. I remember him saying once that Emmy's mom's homemade spaghetti sauce was the best he had ever eaten.

"Ever," he said, and then he winked at me over his bottle of beer as he raised it to his lips.

"I don't think he'll be able to get to a computer very often," Emmy said, and she tossed the cigarette over the railing. "Dylan wants to write a poem about it for the spring issue of the lit mag." The butt hit the ground and sizzled on the damp grass. "He wants to title it 'Sandstorms.'"

My stomach got all fluttery then, and I wondered if the baby could hear me and Emmy talking about the things that were closing in around us.

"What if he never comes back, Lemon?" Emmy asked. "What if he's gone? I can't stay here for the rest of my life and take care of my mom and my sister."

And she was right, she couldn't get stuck in Morgantown, stagnant and sad forever, just like I couldn't get stuck inside Stella's world, running and restless, endlessly unhinged.

"I'm going to take you somewhere amazing," I told her, and I took her hand and lowered our entwined fingers to my knee. "We're going to take a trip over Christmas break, and when we get back you'll be happy again," I promised. "And I bet your dad will be home safe and sound soon, Emmy," I said, even though I wasn't sure he was ever coming back, wasn't sure safe and sound was really ever possible.

My first official prenatal appointment was scheduled for that Monday, and Stella took off from work early and picked me up from school so we could go to the hospital for the exam.

"If you go, I go," Stella said, which I was glad for. I always got nervous around doctors. I think it was the white coats: The clean, stiff fabric made me feel like they were hiding something. The white coats and the smell of all that sanitation.

Dr. Stines asked a ton of questions about my medical history and decided to do an ultrasound to check for the heartbeat of the baby and to figure out exactly when my due date was. I lay on a table, eyes closed while the technician did the test, and all the while Stella stood next to the bed waiting for good news or bad, we weren't sure yet.

The tech tilted the monitor toward us. "Look."

And then the image showed up on the screen, and nothing mattered after that because I finally saw the thing I'd been so worried about, this tiny lump of shadow flickering on the monitor. The technician was talking about the fetal heart rate and the amniotic fluid volume, but all I could think of was this child I'd made in a tattoo parlor with a guy I'd probably never see again. This child who would be with me forever.

I thought of Johnny Drinko, of how he'd probably never thought of me again after that day at the shop and how his life was probably no different now than it was before. And then I thought of my own dad, a man I'd never met, living somewhere far away in California, not thinking of me or Stella or the little heartbeat thumping in my stomach.

But mostly I thought of my mother doing the same thing over seventeen years earlier all the way in San Francisco. I reached over and took her hand, and in the dark like that it was easy to imagine her just like me, laid out on a table watching the screen as her entire life changed, as she realized, just like I did, that nothing would ever be the same again. For her it was the moment that the vision of her life and what she thought she would become transformed into an unrecognizable image.

I cocked my head a little and looked her up and down in her tight blue jeans, her low-cut shirt and high-heeled boots. I remembered our shitty house with the stained carpet and the worn-out couch waiting for us on the other side of town, and I realized I'd spent most of my childhood being angry at her for making us live like that, for not having enough money for us to rent a nicer home, and for refusing to pick a place to settle down in. I looked at Stella's face, the wrinkles and tired eyes camouflaged by the darkness of the room, and I wondered if she would go back if she could, wondered what she would change and how things would go the second time around if she had a chance to fix the choices she regretted.

And before we left I found out that I would be having a baby the first week of July. Just like that. A person unlike all the other people who had drifted in and out of my life with my mother. A person who would stay. A child who would be bound to me in the same way I was bound to Stella.

CHAPTER FIVE

WE GOT OUT OF SCHOOL EARLY the day before Thanksgiving, so Emmy and I sat on the porch at my house, enjoying the freedom of our mothers being stuck at work. Stella was at Simon's studio taking calls and organizing his portfolio, while Emmy's mom served coffee at a diner near the mall. We complained about the weather turning too cold too fast and about finals just around the corner and about our mothers and the way they still treated us like children.

"I miss my dad," Emmy said as she fingered her four-leaf-clover necklace. "Mom never paid as much attention to me and Margie before he left. It's like she's worried if she's not careful, we'll up and disappear too."

She was smoking, and I was watching the road in front of our house where the neighborhood kids played: two brothers on dirt bikes in matching black sweatshirts, a little sister who couldn't keep up on her red and white scooter as her brothers sped out of view. On the other side of the street a woman in slippers walked to her mailbox and yelled for her dog, a honey-colored mutt that had jetted next door to rummage through a pile of trash bags tossed on the lawn.

"I swear if she asks me one more time if Dylan and I are having sex, I'm going to say yes." Emmy flicked her butt over the railing and pulled her hands into the sleeves of her shirt, shivering. "I can't imagine why she keeps asking."

"Because your best friend's knocked up and she wants to make sure I'm not rubbing off on you," I told her. "Hello."

She nodded, reached into her purse, and lit another cigarette as we talked about our trip, picking the departure and return dates as if everything was planned even though neither of us had bought a ticket and neither of us had told our mothers yet. The semester started the second week of January, so if we left two days after Christmas, we'd have ten days out of town, which sounded like a lifetime as we sat on the porch.

She said, "Let's go west," and I said, "Obviously."

"I hear Lake Michigan's pretty badass," she told me.

"In the winter? Way too cold," I said, shaking my head. "Plus, I want to see the Mississippi River."

"Fair enough. What about those big heads?" she asked. "I think they're in Nevada?"

But I was pretty sure they were carved in a mountainside somewhere in South Dakota, and besides, even though I hadn't told Emmy yet, I was hoping we'd head all the way to California.

"We should pick a day, a time that we both have to tell our mothers by, a deadline," she suggested, since we still hadn't figured out how to talk Stella and her mom into letting us go.

"It doesn't matter when I tell her," I said. "Stella will have a shit fit. She'll try to stop us. I want to tell her when Simon's around," I said, thinking he could balance out her anger with all that calmness he always had. "And I think I'll buy the bus ticket first. If I use my own money, she won't be able to do anything about it," I said, because in addition to my allowance and the fives I'd been sneaking from her purse, Simon had started slipping me ten-dollar bills after he found out about the baby, and I hadn't spent a dime of it, just in case.

Next to me, Emmy nodded. "I like the way you think, Lem." Emmy had her own money too. She had worked that summer babysitting a couple of kids who lived in her neighborhood, and she said she wanted to use every penny of it to get the hell out of Morgantown, even if it was just for a week or so.

"It's like they don't understand we're not kids anymore," I told her. "I mean, I may not have a license, but I'll have a baby and a diploma this time next year," I said, and I meant it as a joke, a way to lighten the mood and verify my adult status, but once the words were out of my mouth I got a sick-to-my-stomach feeling that settled heavy in my lap.

"I want to know about the dad," Emmy said after a while.

"My dad?" I asked, but she shook her head.

"The baby's dad. Does he know?"

I thought of Johnny Drinko still in Virginia and how easily I let him have me in the back room of the tattoo shop that day. I'd never done it in a chair before, and I hadn't been able to figure out where to put my legs, one foot hanging down toward the floor, searching for leverage, and the other awkwardly folded between Johnny's knee and the armrest. He told me to bring both legs up to the seat as he reorganized my body, and I ended up squatted above his lap like I was digging in the dirt. Burying treasure, or searching for it, maybe. He put both his hands on my waist then, pulling me onto him as he tried to find a rhythm. Eventually my leg fell asleep, a bloodless limb dangling.

"He doesn't know anything about me, really." I sank down into my chair. "He was older. Twenty-seven, I think." I imagined Johnny Drinko spending the rest of his life in that small town in Virginia inking big-boobed women with frizzy yellow perms and drinking beer with his buddies at dead ends in the county. "He tasted like cigarettes, and we did it in a chair where he worked. I sat on top," I told her. I could feel Emmy looking at me, but I kept my eyes on my fingers as they traced circles around my belly button. "It didn't feel very good," I said finally.

"Jesus Christ, Lemon," she said, and I tried to decide if she thought I was disgusting, if she thought I was a slut, but then she said, "He sounds like such a scumbag," which made me feel a little better. "So you're not going to tell him, then?"

"I wouldn't know how to get a hold of him if I wanted to," I lied. If I had decided to tell Johnny Drinko about the baby, it wouldn't have been that difficult to track him down at the tattoo parlor, but it was easier to pretend the option didn't exist. Stella had worked hard to talk me into believing my father would have made things worse for us, in the same way I was working hard to convince myself Johnny Drinko would make things worse for me, and by that time he lived in a world far too detached from mine to bridge the gap.

In the morning I found Stella in the kitchen: Pop-Tart in the toaster, coffee in the mug, black with half a packet of sugar.

It was Thanksgiving Day, and I still had sleep in my eyes as I pulled on a sweatshirt. She stirred the mug and then used the spoon to check her lipstick in the reflection. November was the month of Fire Engine Red. She first discovered the color in lipstick form, and she kept a tube of it everywhere important: one in her purse, one on the bathroom counter next to the bars of hotel soap she always took when we traveled, another tube on her dresser top, the tip blunted from use.

"Fire Engine Red just sounds good, doesn't it?" she said to me a few weeks earlier in Walgreens.

We were waiting for her birth control pills prescription, her in the makeup aisle, and me in the school-supplies aisle running my fingers over perfect five-subject notebooks and rolls of Scotch tape, boxes of paperclips, and scissors still shiny and sharp with newness.

"Get over here, Lemon," she said. I stood by her as she took the tester, swiped the lipstick over her mouth, and looked in the little square mirror stuck next to the sale rack. "It's good, right?" she said, and I nodded and told her she was beautiful just like I knew she wanted. Sometimes it was easier that way. "Fire Engine Red," she read from the bottom of the tube.

The lipstick made her teeth look white. White like light-bulbs or the laces on new tennis shoes, white like the sugar she put in her coffee. "Your teeth look like snow," I said, which I guess she liked the sound of because she reached over, pushed my hair away from my eyes, and rubbed her nose across mine, Eskimo style.

"This is the month of Fire Engine Red," she announced, and then she took three tubes off the shelf. Afterward we went to the art supply store and found a matching paint for her canvases.

But with the sun slicing lines into the kitchen through the blinds that morning and my mom standing there in a cream-colored sweater and black miniskirt, with her hair pulled back off her face, Fire Engine Red was so bright and brilliant, it almost hurt to look at her. She squinted into the spoon again and wiped a smear from her teeth with her finger as I sat down at the table and opened my book to the dog-eared page I'd left off at the night before. I was working through a list of Tom Robbins novels and was anxious to find out what happened at the Rubber Rose Ranch to Sissy Hankshaw, the small-town heroine of *Even Cowgirls Get the Blues*. Stella dropped the mug in the sink, and on her way out of the room she stopped at the table where I sat and placed the hot Pop-Tart in front of me, its strawberry jam bleeding onto the paper towel. She bent to kiss me on the forehead, and she smelled a little like paint and a lot like hotel soap.

I thought of telling her then. I almost grabbed her hand so I could explain it was my turn to go west. I had practiced it in my head enough times that it should have been easy to start with the I-know-you're-not-going-to-like-the-sound-of-it-but-I-promise-it's-going-to-be-okay part and to end with the I'm-almost-eighteen-and-you-were-my-age-when-you-left-for-San-Francisco part. I wanted it over with before I lost my nerve, but it was a holiday, a bad day for picking fights, so I let the moment pass.

"I'm heading out to grab the bird and the fixings," she said. "I expect you to be here to help when I get back," and then, "I'm fully prepared to admit your apple pie kicks my apple pie's ass, which makes you in charge of dessert."

For Thanksgiving, Stella, Simon, and I invited Emmy and her mom and her older sister, Margie, over to eat turkey and drink wine and pretend we were thankful for all the things we had, when really I think we were all hoping to distract one another from the things we were missing. I was feeling pretty nauseous all the time by then, and Emmy's family hadn't heard from her dad in almost a month, but I guess the wine was pretty good because everyone seemed to get along okay, and everyone thought of something decent to say when we went around the table before dinner to name one thing we were glad about.

"I'm thankful my boss finally taught me how to give high-lights, so I can make more money now," Margie said as she swept her bangs away from her face.

"I'm thankful that I'm healthy," Simon said. "And that we could all be together today. I'm thankful for the people I love," he said, and he reached for Stella's hand.

I thought it was sweet, him looking at her like he believed in them, but Mom shifted her eyes to the floor and pulled her fingers away, which reminded me of the bartender she told me about from Gibbie's Pub, a man she'd met recently with her friends on a girls' night out.

"I'm thankful for this food," she said quickly, reaching for her glass. "And for Lemon," she added when she put the wine back down. "For Lemon being safe and healthy, even if she is, you know." She shrugged one shoulder, a new habit she saved for times when we talked about the baby.

When it was my turn, I said something lame and predict-able about being thankful for having a family and food to eat and a house to live in, which was fine because I was pretty grateful for those things, but when it was Emmy's turn, she froze, silent and shell shocked and gaping into her heap of mashed potatoes like no one else was there.

"You're up, baby girl," her mom prompted, nodding at her.

I thought maybe it was the joint she'd smoked in the back-yard before dinner, but when I kicked her under the table and she looked me in the face, I could tell she might puke or might cry, sitting there thinking about her dad in Afghanistan a million miles away, imagining him eating sand and drinking warm water on Thanksgiving day.

"Emeline," her mother said.

"It's okay, she doesn't have to go," I said, hoping we could just skip over the whole thing and start eating, but I guess she snapped out of it when she heard my voice, because she looked down at her plate and said she was thankful Stella and I had invited them over for dinner since her mom burnt the hell out of the turkey the year before.

I thought that was pretty smart.

Afterward, Margie left to meet her boyfriend at the bowl-ing alley, and the grown-ups went to the living room with another bottle of wine, so Emmy and I headed out for a walk around the neighborhood. Emmy had knitted a beanie for Dylan that week in home ec class, and she wanted to slip it into his mailbox and leave it for him as a surprise. He lived about a mile from my neighborhood, so we planned to sneak over and drop it off that night.

"It's good for me to exercise," I reminded Stella when she hesitated to let us leave the house together. "It's good for the *baby*," I said, just so I could watch her squirm.

"Just around the block," she told me. "And make sure you wear your coat."

It had rained that afternoon, so it smelled like water and roasting turkeys and maybe even snow, which made me feel better about it being Thanksgiving and Emmy being so depressed. Snow would be clean and fresh, and I wished for the sky to split open and cover everything in white.

"I saw Tony Adams yesterday down at the grocery store with his wife," Emmy said as we walked down the hill past the house with the yellow shutters, and I knew she was thinking of her dad because Tony had worked with Bobby Elder at Ervin's Auto Repair.

And Bobby Elder had just died in the same city Emmy's dad was stationed in.

"He's in the reserves too, you know? But there he is the day before Thanksgiving picking up a can of cranberry sauce and a box of mashed potatoes with his wife like nothing's changed. Like all his buddies didn't just get sent away on a school bus." She kicked a stick out of the road, and I watched it disappear into a neighbor's overgrown lawn.

We were in front of the house with all the ironweed then, so I picked one out of the yard, which made Emmy smile as she tucked it into her hair. She looked a little less angry with the purple flower peeking out from behind her ear.

"How come he's not there?" I asked.

"I guess he enrolled in the motor pool unit, since he worked at Ervin's and all," she said, which didn't mean much to me because while Emmy had been researching the military during our library period once a week, I'd been alternating between Tom Robbins and childhood development books.

"Motor pool?" I asked.

"They work on the war trucks. Bobby Elder and Tony Adams did the exact same thing down at Ervin's, but Tony joined the motor pool and Bobby was in infantry like my dad."

The dogs behind the house with the half-moon driveway

were going nuts by then, so we turned on Ashland Avenue and headed into the dark toward Dylan's neighborhood.

"Motor pool is a support unit, but they needed boots on the ground, guys like my dad. It's chance, I guess. They called for infantry and left Tony Adams at home. It's the luck of the draw," she said, which reminded me of something Stella told me once when I asked her about my father.

I was five years old and upset and wanting a normal family like all the other kids in my kindergarten class had: two parents, a child or two. I didn't understand why some kids had dads and I did not.

"It's the luck of the draw, kiddo," Stella answered. "You got a bad pick." She said some boys were made to be fathers and some were not, which stopped me from asking about him for a little while. The stories she gave me about my dad were thin and detached anecdotes, sketches of a man who wasn't good enough or smart enough to be a parent, and back then I didn't know I had any other option but to accept whatever she told me about him.

The light was on in Dylan's room when we got to his house, and we stood in the side yard and threw rocks at his window. Emmy had the beanie rolled up in her back pocket, and when she pulled it out she told me she had kind of screwed up the edge. "I messed up the pattern here," she said, and pointed to the line where the blue fabric alternated to green.

"I think it's perfect," I told her, and then Dylan appeared at the window.

"Looks like trouble," he said when he got the window opened. He smiled at Emmy, and she smiled back and told him she was leaving him a present in the mailbox.

"I'll come down," he said. "Don't move." But Emmy told

him we couldn't stay and that we'd see him at school on Monday. And then she blew him a kiss.

I loved the way he looked at her when she did that, and I figured that was the kind of look I should have waited for before I gave myself over to the pothead in Virginia or to Johnny Drinko in the tattoo shop. I wondered if that was the way my father used to look at Stella.

On the walk back to my house I promised to start researching bus routes, and Emmy agreed to look up the place with the faces in the mountain just to be sure we knew where it was, and when we stopped in front of my front porch I told her, "Your dad's going to be okay, Emmy. And screw Tony Adams anyway. Your dad'll be back before you know it, and I bet he shows up with some kind of medal," which she must have liked the sound of, because she told me I was beautiful all pregnant and glowy, and then she flicked me on the belly before we headed inside.

CHAPTER SIX

THE WEEK BEFORE CHRISTMAS BREAK, someone called in a bomb threat after lunch, and we all got sent home from school. It turned out to be a prank call from some guys who had graduated the year before and were home from college for winter break, but at the time the school had to follow procedure and move all the students to the football field, where we stood for over an hour freezing our asses off. They literally went through the list of the entire student body and released us individually onto the buses, double-checking all the forms to see who was allowed to drive home and who needed to have their parents called.

"Everyone must be accounted for in an emergency," they told us.

"I cannot wait to get out of this town," Emmy said when she found me in the crowd. Her small shoulders were shaking, and I could see her breath in the air when she spoke.

We were supposed to stand in groups based on the first letter of our last name, but the whole thing was a catastrophe, and kids were pretty much doing whatever they wanted while the vice principal stood in the announcers' booth at the top of the bleachers and called our names out one by one, directing us to the parking lot, where the school buses were and the parent carpool line had started, or releasing us to drive ourselves home.

Dylan had left by then to spend the vacation in Asheville, North Carolina, with his grandparents, and she hadn't told me yet, but I was pretty sure Emmy had slept with him before he took off. For me, sex was inadequate and ugly then, so I hadn't asked her outright. I didn't want to know if it had been better or worse for her than it had been for me. I knew she wanted it to be important, and I was worried that if they'd done it already, it might have been a disappointment.

I recognized some of Emmy's old friends standing in a huddle near us, but she didn't wave them over, so neither did I. There was a new girl with them I'd never seen with their crowd, so I asked Emmy who the brunette was.

"A robot," she said. "Their new recruit. They won't hang out with Emily Curtis anymore because rumor has it she had an abortion over Thanksgiving break," she told me, and shrugged.

I was born just months after the Supreme Court affirmed its *Roe v. Wade* decision in the *Planned Parenthood of Southeastern Pennsylvania v. Casey* case. I only asked about it once, back in the eighth grade, when we were studying the justice system at school. We'd spent the week debating women's rights, so it was on my mind. Stella and I lived in the apartment in Philadelphia with Denny then, and there was meatloaf in the oven and a vodka tonic in her fist while she waited for him to come home. That day, a girlfriend from work announced she was pregnant, and Stella was reminiscing about what it was like when it happened to her, how frantic she was when she bought the pregnancy test and how scared she'd been when she decided to leave California and move back east to live with her mom.

"Did you ever think of getting rid of it?" I asked. I had wanted to know for a while, and it seemed as good a time as any to finally say it out loud.

She turned toward me, dropping the glass in her haste as her cocktail splashed across the cheap linoleum floor. Her eyes flashed like headlights, angry and spinning, and I wondered if she might have slapped me had she been standing closer.

"Don't you ever talk to me like that," she said. "Have you lost your mind?"

I watched the Preps' newest addition and wondered how they'd picked her. She was pretty enough, but she looked kind of blank faced and starstruck while she listened to the rest of them talk.

"She's a freshman," Emmy said, "but her dad works in TV. Used to write for the CW network or something awesome like that," she said sarcastically, and rolled her eyes with a grunt.

Mr. Holton was only up to Sheri Anne Coleman, and I eyed the football equipment lying on the side of the field. "I'm pretty sure I might stab myself with one of those orange flags before he gets to Lemon Raine Williams," I told Emmy.

"Hysteria?" she asked.

"Boredom," I said. "Seriously, can't they just let us all go?"

She bounced in place and blew into her hands. "Entertain me, Lemon Raine Williams," she said. "Tell me about our trip."

"Well, obviously there'll be superheroes and time traveling machines and gruesome battles where we're the only ones with the magic powers to survive," I told her, and then immediately wished I had left out the part about battles and survival, thinking of her dad, but it didn't trip her up a bit.

"And don't forget the rock stars that are actually vampires who suck our blood and talk us into riding on their wings all the way to Paris."

"Naturally," I said.

Next to us, Jenny Myers and the new robot were whispering. Some of the boys had sat down on the grass, lined up their textbooks in a square, and begun playing football with a folded piece of paper they flicked back and forth. Jenny and Allyson Cooper stood behind them, watching.

"Hey, Emmy," I said.

"Let me guess." She shifted her eyes away from them and back to me. "You're starving. Jesus, Lemon, I know you've got a kid in there, but it's only a few inches long. It can't eat *that* much."

Mr. Holton was up to Andrew Lynn Dexter, and a low hum of laughter erupted throughout the football field when someone yelled, "Homo." Evidently, Andrew Lynn had never told anyone his middle name.

"I'm not hungry," I lied. "I've got a new idea for our trip," I said, and she said, "Mermaids in Mexico?" but I shook my head.

"It might be a little expensive, but I've been doing some thinking, and I figured I might as well throw it out there, just in case," I rambled, and she said, "Jesus, out with it already," and flicked me on the belly, her newest habit I'd fallen in love with.

"I think we should go to San Francisco," I told her.

My mother lived in California when she got pregnant, and according to her, my biological father worked in a movie theater on Fillmore Street and won her over with free films and supersize boxes of Milk Duds. For a long time this was the only story I knew about her life before me, and later, when I was old enough to ask questions, she said her years in San Francisco were pretty hard to remember.

"It was a different life, baby," she told me once. "If it weren't for you looking back at me the way you do, sometimes I would think I imagined the whole thing."

Emmy's face was hard to read since her lips were turning purple and she was shivering so hard, so I kept talking. "It'll take forever and the ticket's more expensive, but Greyhound goes from Wheeling to San Francisco in about three days." We'd talked about spending a week at the beach in Corpus Christi or at the mountains in Fort Collins, but she didn't know anything about Stella's life before me, and I figured she was wondering why I'd picked a place so far away. "But it is San Francisco," I said. "A real city. West coast."

The Preps were all crouched on the grass by then and laughing as if everything they said to one another was the most magnificent and hilarious thing they'd ever heard, begging us to watch them. It was like a car crash. Something about them made it hard to look away.

"That is a brilliant idea," Emmy said, and moved her eyes to mine. And then she smiled bigger than I'd seen her smile since her dad left town on that bus.

I didn't tell Emmy right away that the Greyhound route wouldn't take us by Mount Rushmore, and I also didn't tell her about knowing my dad lived in San Francisco, because I wasn't sure she'd want to be part of a trip that might get me closer to my father while hers just kept getting farther away. None of it really mattered, though, because once we decided to go she couldn't stop talking about the snow on the Colorado Mountains or the view of the Pacific Ocean, or how big and hopeful the Golden Gate Bridge was going to look when we pulled onto it. We each bought our tickets that night. Emmy used her sister's credit card and gave the cash to Margie, and I used cash to get a money order at the grocery store and bought my ticket by mail. We'd depart December 27, and even though we agreed to leave California on January 3, I bought a one-way ticket. I didn't know how long it would take to find my father, and I decided nothing could limit my trip. Not school or Stella, not even Emmy. It was the most impulsive thing I'd ever done, but once I made the purchase I realized I'd been planning it ever since Emmy and I first started talking about going away, maybe even before that, weeks or months or years earlier even, maybe since I first found out Stella had left my dad back in California before I was born.

I'd been hoarding details about my father for as long as I could remember, though the information came in clips and fragments.

"He hated getting haircuts," Stella whispered once as if offering up an essential piece of information. "He was allergic to mangos and strawberries," she told me. We were curled on the couch watching *Full House* reruns together when she said, "He used to say we'd move to Mexico. He used to say he'd buy me a hundred striped bikinis," and then she put her mug of chamomile down on the carpet. I was nine and wondered why my father had a preference for stripes and if she could remember his favorite color, or whether he preferred stripes that ran from head to toe or side to side, but Stella's eyes were closed before I had the chance to ask.

I kept each detail planted in my head, hoping one day she might slip and say something monumental, might confess he sent me letters when I was a kid or might tell me he had, in fact, called on each of my birthdays. But of all the things my mother was, she never was a liar. She may have left things out when she wanted, but she never made them up.

That weekend, Stella decided we would spend the day at the mall choosing gifts to mail to various friends she'd kept in touch with over the years. Laura Sanders in New York, who worked as a catalogue model and a waitress. Tony Neilson at the Jersey Shore, "my boss with the tattoos," she reminded me as we got into the car and headed for Morgantown Mall.

"Julia Reeves was the dancer in Maryland who helped us pack when we decided to leave," she said as we stood in Victoria's Secret and searched through a sale bin for bras and underwear. "Don't you remember?" she asked. "Julia, with the fingernails," which brought it all back, the long red press-ons she used to slice through the tape as we sealed up our belongings in big cardboard boxes.

In J.C. Penney we picked out a new watch for Simon, and Stella flirted with the guy behind the men's jewelry counter, testing to see if she could get a discount on the Seiko, but all J.C. Penney made me think of was her job back in Virginia and the smell of witch hazel and skin at the tattoo shop.

Eventually we stopped for lunch at a small grill and pub in the mall, so I could eat again.

"I'd swear you just downed two eggs and a quarter pound of bacon," she said as she flagged down the waiter.

"Yeah, like, three hours ago."

After she ordered a vodka tonic, I shot her a you've-got-to-be-kidding-it's-only-midafternoon look, but she shrugged and said, "What? It's happy hour a few hours east of here," which was true, plus I figured she might take the news of my trip a little better after a drink or two. This was the day I had to tell her: I was running out of time. Emmy had broken the news to her mother earlier that week, and even though she flipped at first, eventually she caved. I think she knew how depressed Emmy had been about her dad, how badly she needed to get out of town, to do something exciting. I also think she was too distracted by the holidays and too worn down by having Emmy's dad stuck in Afghanistan to argue with Emmy for very long.

I used my thumb to push the last of my mac and cheese onto my fork, a habit I knew Stella hated.

"Don't use your fingers when you eat, Lemon. It's trashy."

She talked for a while about her and Simon and how he thought it'd be good for her to take an art class at WVU, and then I talked for a while about how bizarre the last week at school had been, how obvious it was the students were cashed and the teachers were too burned out to care.

"Cliff Granger brought his iPod and a docking station to the cafeteria last week and blasted the Yeah Yeah Yeahs the entire lunch period," I told her as I pushed my plate out of the way and reached for the dessert menu. "No one batted an eye," I said, and wondered if she would call me out if I ordered a piece of chocolate cake *and* a slice of apple pie. "Our whole class has senioritis. It's like we're all just waiting to get out."

And then I put the menu down, took one deep breath, and finally spit out the news I'd been practicing. I'm not sure exactly how I started, but I remember the words coming quickly once I began.

I told her about the bus route and about how sad Emmy had been before we started planning the trip, which was true, but it didn't help to change that angry look pressed on her face when I admitted I'd already bought the ticket for the Greyhound. "I'm practically eighteen, a legal adult," I said, which was nine months short of being the truth.

She waved away the waiter when he came by to take our dessert orders and finished her cocktail as she measured me, silent and listening.

"I promise we'll be safe," I said, but she narrowed her eyes as if imagining all the trouble Emmy and I could get into in a place like San Francisco, maybe remembering all the trouble she got into herself. "And we've already picked out the hotel," I told her. "Travelocity gave it five stars," I said, which wasn't even close to being true, but we had a budget and had agreed not to splurge on a fancy room since we wouldn't be spending much time at the hotel anyway.

I worried she might start yelling before I gave all the excuses as to why we'd chosen California, but she didn't say a word, not until after I told her how I had wanted to go to San Francisco since I was a kid, since I knew that's where she'd been when she found out she was pregnant. Finally, I ended with a line about having roots in California, about feeling connected.

"It feels important," I said. "I have to see it for myself. I have to go."

She said, "No way in hell," which I had heard before. And then, "You're pregnant, Lemon," which was obvious. "You're just a kid," she said, which I didn't agree with, and finally, "You don't have any money," which wasn't true at all.

The last time I counted, I had almost four hundred dollars left after I bought the bus ticket, and I figured Simon would slip me a bit more for Christmas.

And then we sat there for a while and didn't say anything. I never mentioned my father, and I never told her how long I was planning on staying, but I guess she probably knew anyway, because eventually she put her drink down, pushed her chair back, and walked to my side of the table. She tugged me to my feet even though there wasn't much space in the restaurant, and she hugged me tight, tighter than she did at my grandmother's funeral ten years earlier, tighter than the time she thought she lost me at the pool hall back in New York, tighter even than the night she finally snapped out of the depression after Denny and realized I'd been taking care of her all those days at the hotel.

I knew everyone in the restaurant was watching and that they probably thought she was drunk or crazy, but even though I could feel their eyes on us it was nice to settle into her arms and let her hug me like that. It felt good and familiar, like bare feet in the summertime.

She held on for a while and whispered, "Tell me you're coming back before school starts again."

"I'm coming back before school starts again," I said even though I'd bought a one-way ticket.

Eventually she pulled away and repeated it as a stipulation.

"You're coming back before school starts again," she said, and I nodded, smiling like a kid stoned off a Halloween sugar high.

But then I looked at her face, really looked that time, and I realized her skin seemed looser than before, that her mouth was slack and worried and her eyes were glazed under tears.

I asked if she was mad, but she said, "I should have seen it coming. You are your mother's daughter," and then she put her palm on my cheek just for a second before she returned to her side of the table, pulled herself together, and slid into her seat. "Fine," she said. "It'll be fine."

And eight days later Emmy and I boarded a Greyhound and headed for California.

BOOK TWO
Landscape of Strangers

Nothing we do is inevitable, but everything
we do is irreversible. How do you propose to
remember that in time?
—Joy Williams, *The Quick and the Dead*

CHAPTER SEVEN

I WAS DETERMINED TO MAKE LEAVING my mother a remarkably easy process. I folded and stacked my clothes, neatly packed the travel-size soap and toothpaste and miniature shampoo bottles into various pockets of my backpack. I chose a list of songs about road trips and freedom, and Emmy downloaded them onto the red iPod her mom gave her for Christmas. Dylan loaned us a copy of *On the Road* even though I told him I'd already read it a million times, and Stella gave us her credit card for emergencies only, which I thought was pretty generous.

We'd booked evening-departure tickets, and the day I left for California Stella and Simon took off from work and milled around the house while I finished packing.

"Hey, kiddo," Stella said as she watched me from the hallway, halfway in my room, and halfway not. "Anything you need help with?" she asked, but I shook my head.

I'd washed my backpack with a load of laundry, organized my wallet and purse, and carefully chosen which books to take with me. We'd be reading *Lolita* in class next semester, so I checked it out from the library along with *The Red Tent*, a novel my English teacher recommended before school let out for break.

"It's a good fit for you, Lemon," Ms. Ford said after the bell rang the last day of class. Earlier that week I mentioned needing some recommendations for the vacation, so she hovered by my desk citing titles while I loaded up my backpack. "Now that I think of it," she said, and cocked her head to the side, waiting for me to pay attention, "it's the one that you should read most. Scratch the rest if you don't have time."

Chloe Ford was one of the youngest teachers in school, a slow talker and a published author with willowy limbs and long dark hair she kept pulled back in a loose knot. I'd noticed the thin lines of tattoo ink on her wrist as she handed out a test earlier that semester, and when she caught me eyeing it as she placed the paper on my desk, she shrugged and winked. Quick and stealthy, a secret exchange. Afterward, I Googled her and tracked down a story she had published in *McSweeney's*, a hip little magazine I'd never heard of before. She was by far my favorite teacher, and I would have read anything she recommended. Emmy joked that I had a girl crush on Ms. Ford, but really I just liked the books she picked for us to read and the way she cocked her head and nodded when I had something interesting to say in class. She was one of the few teachers who actually listened when we talked— this and the fact that she had a tattoo and that I knew about the tattoo even though she had to hide it at school made me feel like we shared something significant, common ground.

"It's about this amazing woman, about her family and her struggles," Ms. Ford said. "About a voice that almost was forgotten." She tucked a loose piece of hair back behind her ear.

All around me kids gathered their books and moved toward the door, but a few Art Kids and English Nerds lingered, watching us. Maybe they wanted book recommendations too, or maybe they just wanted one last chance to talk with her before they left for break. She was known for making you feel like you mattered, like what you did and said made a difference.

"*The Red Tent*," she said again, and she took my pen off my desk and produced a yellow Post-it notepad from the back pocket of her boot-cut corduroys. She bent over and scrawled the title and author onto the paper before handing it to me. "You'll love it," she said.

I also packed *Into the Wild* because I still hadn't read it even though Emmy and I were mildly obsessed with Eddie Vedder and had been listening to the film sound track incessantly since the movie came out, and then I threw in *Dharma Bums* to round off the group with my favorite Beat writer. The books were in a pile next to the stack of sweaters and pants on the floor, and Stella frowned at them as if they'd just come to life and said something wildly offensive. She and Simon had sprung for a cell phone for me for Christmas, and she nodded toward my night stand, where it sat hooked to an electric socket, charging.

"You can call whenever you want. It's free," she said. "Not free but, you know, included in the plan." They'd paid for limitless minutes for calls between my number and theirs but had refused to set up a text plan.

December was the month of Byzantine Ceiling Blue, so

while I was surprised by the gift and happy to finally have a phone of my own, the cell was the kind of shiny blue that made you see spots if you looked at it too long in the sunlight. I would have liked a black or a red one better, but I didn't complain.

She was in the room then, and she sat on my bed, hovering while I pulled on my black Converse, left foot, then right. She tried not to look at the backpack and the bus ticket resting on top. "I was seventeen when I left for San Francisco, too," she said, and I nodded because I'd branded every clip of info I knew about her past into my brain like a scar, like a tattoo.

Stella left my grandmother for California the year my grandfather died, and she departed Pennsylvania after his funeral and never looked back. That's how I imagined it, at least. She said she filled one red suitcase and left her mother behind because she believed grieving alone would make them more strong and independent. When I asked my grandmother about it as a child, she never called Stella selfish or neglectful, words I thought of later when I pictured my grandmother newly widowed and on her own. Instead she told me that, just as she imagined I would be when I was older, my mother was a woman who always followed her instincts.

"She's a wanderer," she told me, "a restless explorer. Your mother is who she is. I could never ask her to change." But that was back when we still lived close by, back before it became clear Stella's wanderlust would not dissipate just because she had a child, a fact that became a source of tension between my mother and my grandmother in later years.

Stella fidgeted and smoothed out the wrinkles in my bedspread while I pulled on my hooded sweatshirt. "The thing is . . . ," she started, and I glanced at her, waiting while she looked for words. "It's just that there's a risk every time you leave home."

I put my hands in my pockets, eyes to the floor as I waited for the moment to pass. I figured she thought I was repeating her mistakes, but I thought I was changing them, attempting to reorganize her past into compartments I could manage and investigate. I believed finding my father would help me understand Stella and the choices she had made for us and would help me discover what kind of person I wanted to become. Maybe she understood why I needed to go or maybe she didn't. I can't say for sure what she felt, because I never asked her. It was easier that way.

But she kept talking. "There's a risk of never seeing things exactly as you did before. And a risk of not going back, of forgetting what you left behind," she said, and I nodded, wondering if we were running late and if we'd get to the bus station in time to get good seats. I didn't want to get stuck in the back near the bathroom. "There's the risk of forgetting who you are and who you are not," she said, but then she must have recognized my distractedness, because she didn't say anything else after that. She stood up, shrugged, and almost reached for me, a slight lurch forward, but then she stopped herself and turned away, leaving me as she moved down the hall.

She and Simon drove Emmy and me to Wheeling, West Virginia, to catch our bus that night. Emmy had overpacked, so we took Simon's Tacoma, and Pace sat curled on top of our luggage in the back. The drive was easy and fast up Highway 79, and when we arrived, Simon unloaded our suitcases, and I gave Stella a copy of our itinerary for the next few days on the road.

"Thanks for the ride," Emmy said to them, and then to me, "Let's hit it," and she moved away from the car and lingered in the parking lot.

Simon gave me a hug, leaned in close, and told me, "I'll take care of Stella, you take care of you," and I realized I would miss all the late-night television and the quiet energy he gave our house when he was there. I hugged him again, and then he stood by Emmy to give me some space, so I could say good-bye to my mother.

"Lemon," she said, "I just . . ." But she stumbled on her words.

I half listened to her stammer as I glanced over her shoulder at my friend and the long Greyhound bus in the background that would move me away from everything familiar.

"Thanks again for the phone," I said. "And thanks for the painting."

Besides the cyber-blue cell, Stella also had given me a small four-by-six-inch painting of an ocean-colored house. There was a fence in front, a blue tree in the yard, and four sky-colored shutters lined up above the front door. It looked like a nice home outside of all that blueness, but I couldn't place it and wasn't sure if it was a painting of a place we had lived before or of a place she hoped we might live eventually. Either way, I liked it best out of all the other paintings I'd seen of hers and planned to use it as my bookmark on the road.

"I brought it with me," I told her, and she nodded.

I said something about being excited to see her artwork when I got back, since Simon had paid the tuition for Stella to take a painting class at the university as his Christmas gift to her. And I said something about being sure to call as soon as we got to California.

I did not say "Thank you for letting me go," and I did not say "I'll miss you."

My mother was never good at saying good-bye either, so she hugged me quickly, awkwardly, and then whispered that she left me something tucked into the pregnancy book I had packed in my purse. I hoped that it was money.

"Be good, and don't do anything stupid. Take care of each other," she said.

I smiled widely so that later, when I didn't come back, she'd think of me as being beautiful and brave. As someone she wished had stayed.

I guess I should've realized she must've felt that not only was she losing me, she was losing the baby as well, the long months that remained of watching its development through the series of ultrasounds, of witnessing the growth of a child from a tiny sack of cells. But all my life, all around me, people had been leaving, moving, and trading spaces: strangers at rest stops when we were on the road; families at the Amtrak station when we headed down the coast; men and women at hotels checking in and out of rooms with paper-thin walls, with stained carpet and X-rated television channels. It's startling how frequently people shifted in and out of view, the addition and removal into and out of one another's lives. I'd witnessed it for as long as I could remember, had watched Stella nonchalantly pack our lives into boxes more times than I could count, and at the age of seventeen I discovered I was an excellent mimic.

The bus driver came out of the station and started calling for the passengers, so I told Stella I should get going.

"Don't forget where you came from, Lemon," she said in a way that made me wonder if she already knew I'd bought a one-way ticket. "Take all of that in," she said, nodding toward all the things that lay beyond my view, "but don't forget where you came from."

And then it was over and she was back in the car running her fingers through her hair when Simon leaned over and kissed her on the cheek. As the car began to move away, they became silhouettes, mere lines of shadows shaping out the frame of strangers, two people I may or may not have known. And they were out of the parking lot before I had the chance to tell Stella the reason I was going to California was to see where I had come from.

Emmy brought two disposable cameras, one for the road and one for the city, and she made me pose in front of the bus before we boarded and picked two blue recliners we'd call home for the next three days. We started north, skittering along the highway until our first transfer in Pittsburgh, our dinner-stop layover before we drove west through the night. In Pittsburgh the buildings were checkered with rows of windows, the roads lit by cars and the streets lined with lampposts as we headed downtown toward the station. Snow draped the city from a storm that'd hit the week before, and the air looked heavy.

I hadn't been in Pennsylvania in a long time, not since we left Denny in Philadelphia, so when Emmy said, "Didn't you used to live around here?" I looked out the window and tried to decide what I wanted and didn't want her to know.

"We lived in Harrisburg when I was little, before New York," I said. "Stella moved us back to Pennsylvania when I was eleven, though, Philadelphia that time," I told her.

We pulled into the terminal, and Emmy started putting

away the deck of cards, gathering the books and magazines scattered on the floor, and returning them to my backpack at our feet.

"It's weird, right, having lived in so many places? I mean, I bet in some ways it's cool to have had all those different experiences, but sometimes, when you talk about it, it seems exhausting," she said once the bus was parked.

I thought of the Denny years in Philadelphia, when Stella worked day shifts processing Tastykake orders and night shifts bartending at Whiskey Tango on the north side of the city. I was in the sixth grade, and Stella was having a hard time taking care of us, when Denny showed up, a big guy with big plans and a big appetite for Stella and the life she was trying to make for me and her.

"Some of it was good," I said, thinking of how my mother would pick me up every day after school between her shifts at work. On a good day we'd stop at a coffee shop and drink hot chocolates, or she'd take me to a playground. Sometimes we'd just drive around watching the city and listening to music on the radio, swapping stories about my day at school and her shift at the baking company. "My mom and I used to go to a great park in the city, and we'd rent bikes sometimes or hang around the fountain throwing pennies in the water before her bartending shift at the nightclub," I told her. "But some of it was bad, too," I said, thinking of the day she met Denny.

She was waiting for me in the parking lot by her old Geo Metro just as he came out to his truck to get a sheet of metal for the air duct. He'd been hired to fix one of the heating units at my school, and he took one look at her in her tiny white miniskirt and her big hoop earrings and knew, just like that, that he saw something he wanted. His next project, his next scam.

Three weeks later Stella moved us into Denny's two-bedroom apartment in Levittown. I shared my bedroom with all the boxes of the things he never made room for, the items he decided we didn't need anymore, like photos from our life before him and toys he said I was too old for. Stella liked that Denny lived outside the city where she thought things would be safer for me. She liked that he didn't drink, that he drove a big truck, and that he took a job at the club to keep an eye on her. And she loved the gifts. He'd show up at the apartment with lingerie and jewelry and perfume, presents he bought her on South Street when he went to Philadelphia for work. We lived with him for almost two years, moving again just weeks after my fourteenth birthday.

"I liked my sixth-grade teacher in Philadelphia," I told Emmy as we waited for the other riders to move through the aisle, "but I hated the winters up north, the way the days were so short in December. The darkness seemed longer there than anywhere else," I said.

I didn't tell her about the time Denny sold Stella's car without asking, about the bills he forgot to pay or all the cash he took from the bank account Stella had opened for me with the money my grandmother left when she died. And I didn't tell her about the black eye the night we left, the hotel room, and our escape to the Jersey Shore, where things got even worse when she met Rocco. I kept waiting for the memories to fade away, but they were threaded into me like DNA, fixed and permanent, consequential to the person I'd become.

It was almost six thirty when we stopped, and I made Emmy pose for a photo in front of the station, her arms and legs stretched out into the shape of an X, and then we headed through the doors. Inside the bus station we ate peanut butter sandwiches Emmy had brought from home and drank warm Pepsis from the vending machine. We slumped against the wall and watched the other riders move around us. The station was loud and smelled like sweat and winter wetness, the whole thing so overwhelming I didn't notice when Emmy pulled a small square box out of her backpack. She had wrapped it in newspaper, and she handed it to me.

"I know we said no Christmas presents since we're blowing all our money on the trip, but I couldn't help myself. Open it," she said.

I unwrapped the gift and pulled out a small ornament, a wood carving of a naked woman swollen with pregnancy. "I love it," I said, holding it up and inspecting the curve of her stomach, the peaks of her nipples, and the wave of her hair that was carved to her waist.

"I think it's great, Lemon. I know it's hard and weird and not what you planned," she said, and she looked at the tan and cream checkered floor. "But I think you're going to be a kick-ass mom," she said, raising her eyes to mine. "And this way, every Christmas you'll have to think of me and this trip when you and your little boy or girl decorate your tree."

And I knew then that Emmy didn't think any less of me for what I'd told her about Johnny Drinko, about the rushed and rude sex that got me into so much trouble. Emmy was a better friend than that. By then I could have told her about Denny and Rocco and everything else, too, and she would have loved me anyway.

CHAPTER EIGHT

WE TRANSFERRED TO A DIFFERENT BUS in Pittsburgh, and Emmy said, "Smells like cat piss," when we got on, but I nudged her down the aisle and tried to not think of clogged shower drains and musty basements, tried to ignore the smell seeping out from behind the bathroom door in the back of the bus.

She stopped in the middle, said, "This okay, boss?" and then we settled into the pleather blue seats we stayed in while we moved through our next two stops: Columbus, Ohio, at midnight and Indianapolis at three in the morning.

"Hungry?" Emmy asked, and she opened her fist and revealed two little white tablets, Ambien sleeping pills she'd taken from her mother's medicine cabinet. She popped one in her mouth and threw her head back, but I wouldn't take one because of the baby.

I felt swollen and couldn't get comfortable enough to sleep, so I watched the miles move by us while the sky turned dark and then light again as day broke. For the most part the bus was quiet from Ohio to Illinois, but around five in the morning, Poplar Street Bridge sprang out of nowhere from the maze of twisting roads, and if it weren't for the nausea that kept me awake as we crossed through the turns of the up-and-down stretches of highway, I might have missed my first sighting of the Mississippi River. The bridge was a narrow shred of concrete, and the water lay still and resting under a film of gray-blue ice. In the distance, I could see St. Louis's Gateway Arch standing silver and tall on the other side of the Mississippi, and above the city the sky began its slow transition into early-morning dawn. It was fast, a hundred or so feet of water that passed in less than a minute before the bridge dumped us into downtown. I didn't have time to wake Emmy so she could see it, and I never mentioned it after.

The sun rose over Missouri as we moved into St. Louis for our second transfer, and I nudged Emmy awake so she wouldn't miss the view of the arch.

"What'd I miss?" Emmy said. She rolled toward me and took *The Red Tent* from my lap, where I'd been clutching it since I'd finished it over an hour earlier.

"A long-haired kid with a guitar and dimples," I said. "A nun passing out plastic glow-in-the-dark rosary beads."

"No shit." She turned the book over in her hands. "How's the book?"

"Completely kick-ass," I told her. I'd devoured *The Red Tent* before we got to Effingham and was already thinking of reading it again.

"Because . . ." She waited for me to fill in the blank.

"Because the main character is this incredible girl who endures all these horrifying things."

Emmy rolled her eyes. "That's original."

"Some seriously horrendous stuff happens to this girl. But," I continued, "even in the worst circumstances, after all her grief and her anger and pain, she survives. It's—" I hesitated. "It's kind of amazing, actually."

She opened the front cover. "Lesson learned," she said.

Outside, the sky had shifted to the light blues and oranges of morning, and long patches of snow were scattered along the highway, but inside, the bus windows were sweating.

She pulled her glasses from the crevice between our seats, where she'd been keeping them when she slept, and she read the first sentences out loud: "We have been lost to each other for so long. My name means nothing to you. My memory is dust." She mouthed the last sentence a second time. "That's depressing," she said finally. "Like eventually we all just get forgotten? Our stories just get lost?"

"Or maybe just that it's impossible to really know another person's story," I told her. "That our stories and memories are misinterpreted, and mangled, by time."

"Or maybe she means our past doesn't matter," Emmy said. "That eventually it becomes unimportant."

"But her story *was* important. The character's voice needed to be heard, her past needed to be acknowledged."

Emmy closed the book. "And not all do?"

"It'd be nice," I said, "if you could pick and choose which parts to leave behind. The stories to forget and the memories you want to keep."

Emmy shrugged. "Just doesn't work like that, though."

It was almost seven by the time the Greyhound moved

into the lot of the station, a large scaly building in the heart of downtown. We had forty minutes to stretch our legs, and Emmy and I each bought a cup of coffee from a vendor in the food court even though I wasn't supposed to have caffeine.

"I need oxygen," she said, so we drank our coffee outside under a wall of multicolored windows and waited to board the bus that would take us through Kansas City and Junction City, the bus we'd stay on all the way to Denver later that night. The area was vacant and seemed weighted down by a winter of snowstorms and wind.

Emmy lit a smoke and asked, "Think I have time?" while I stretched my back and checked out all the other riders. "Tell me a story, Lemon Raine," she said, so I told her about the old lady on the bus who yelled at a little girl for taking too long in the bathroom. "I swear she called the kid a 'snot-nosed brat.' The girl couldn't have been more than six years old."

"No shit?" Emmy said. She bounced in place to keep warm. "What a hag. It must be miserable to be old," she said, and then we promised never to get old and crabby. "I will never let you get wrinkles," she said.

"What about stretch marks?" I asked, and she said, "Life is what it is."

"Worse things have happened, I guess," I said, looking down at the new curves of my body. My chest was twice its normal size, and my belly felt a lot fuller even though the pregnancy book said the baby was only the size of a jumbo shrimp.

Eventually Emmy flicked her smoke on the ground and said, "Let's go, fat lady," as she headed toward the bus.

The transfer landed us with a redheaded boy sitting across the aisle, and while I half expected Emmy to ask to change seats with me, so she could spend some time flirting, she mouthed, "He's all yours," kicked off her Chuck Ts, and rolled toward the window after we ate another peanut butter sandwich for breakfast.

Nelson was nineteen and wildly talkative, all zipped up in his blue North Face jacket and on his way to San Diego to start basic training for the marines. He smelled a little like chicken wings and wore a St. Louis Cardinal's baseball cap pulled low on his head. He paid a lot of attention to his cell phone, texting and taking pictures of all the things that we drove past, which made me think he might have left someone important back where he came from in Missouri.

We coasted up I-70, and all around us the land was dull and vacant, the power lines strung above us linking the cities and towns.

"You know what I-70 is really called?" Nelson asked. "The Mark Twain Expressway, Mark Freaking Twain, right? All the way up through Columbia and Kansas City. Missouri's so wild," he said, though I wasn't sure I believed him as I looked at the blunt, flat setting moving outside our window.

We passed Motel 6s and IHOPs and gas station signs that read BUY OLD STYLE BEER. We passed small roadside diners advertising award-winning cherry pie, pork barbeque, and homemade apple cobbler, and Dairy Queens that had closed down for the winter. The farther we moved from St. Louis, the larger the patches of snow became, until eventually it felt as though the highway were an island stretched through a sea of white foam.

I asked him about living outside St. Louis, and he asked me about West Virginia, a place, he said, he imagined was dry and slow and hot.

"We're in it for the long haul," I told him, "all the way to San Francisco," then I slapped my palms together and swooshed my right hand out fast like it was taking off for flight.

He told me he'd never been farther west than Kansas, where his sister had moved with her boyfriend. "Took the Greyhound out a year ago, and if it weren't for her and the baby, I wouldn't care if I never went to Kansas again. All that flat space and nothingness during the ride almost made me crazy," he said, which made me worried for the seven hours ahead. "I brought a book for this time around." He winked at me and pulled a paperback out of his coat pocket. John Green's *Looking for Alaska.*

We played Uno and gin rummy and War and a dice game called Farkle, and eventually I told him about the pregnancy, but I never caught him staring at my stomach like the kids at school did once news of the baby had gotten out. I told him about some of the great books I'd been reading, and he told me about his older brother who worked at a cemetery a few blocks from his house, how they didn't talk much anymore even though they both lived at home. He said he wanted to be a snowboard instructor one day, wanted to own a German shepherd and move to Colorado.

"One day I'll have my own farm where I can ride horses and grow grapes, maybe even rhubarb," he said. "You have any idea how many different things you can make with rhubarb?" he asked. "It's like a vegetable from the gods. There's nothing like a crisped rhubarb tart." He also said he wanted to be sure he never had to live in St. Louis again. "There's just some people that never want to go back home," he said, and I realized if I had said the sentence myself, I wasn't sure what home I would have been referring to. There'd been so many, and really there'd been none at all. "I want trees and mountains, and towns with log houses, wildflowers and vegetable gardens," he said. "The air is too heavy in St. Louis."

I told him about Pace, my mom's boyfriend's mutt, and that one day I wanted to find a place where I could settle down and get my own dog, that Stella had moved us around so much those last years all I craved was standing still. "I feel like I've been tired for the last year and a half," I said. "My mom is impossible to keep up with."

Nelson said he'd never lived anywhere but St. Louis, and he couldn't believe he'd finally gotten out.

"I'm getting off in Reno. Bought a fake ID and plan to have some fun before I head out. No one stands still in Reno, I bet," he said with a smile.

When I asked him about training in San Diego, he said he was worried he was going to miss the change of seasons so much it might make his heart stop, and that he'd never been much of an ocean swimmer because he didn't like not being able to see what was underneath him.

"San Diego graduates more than twenty-one thousand marines a year," he told me in a way that made me think he'd practiced saying the sentence out loud. "I'll be there thirteen weeks, then maybe four more of combat training in North Carolina. Who knows where I'll be stationed after that, but I'm betting I'll end up in Afghanistan," he said, and I could tell he figured he wouldn't be back for a while.

Someone from the recruiting office told him San Diego had sand dunes the size of mountains, which I'd never heard of, but I didn't say anything because he seemed to like the sound of it.

"My dad says the sunsets there are always red. That red in

San Diego is so bright it hurts to look at sometimes, fire red. Bloodred in the sky." He pulled an apple out of his duffel and took a bite. "In the wintertime you can see whales swimming south," he said, spewing bits of the fruit into the aisle between us. "I'll miss the seasons of the Midwest, how different each month makes the land look, but whales are pretty damn cool." He held out the apple so I could take a bite.

"So, how'd you get knocked up?" he asked.

"Well, there's really only one way, Nelson," Emmy said as she rolled toward us and swung her arm over my stomach, groggily nestling her head on my shoulder.

I didn't know how long she'd been listening to us, but I hoped she slept through the talk about Afghanistan.

"I mean, you're so young and all. Are you scared?" he asked.

It was the first time anyone had really asked me about it like that. I was scared when Johnny Drinko and I had sex in the tattoo shop, and I was scared when I stole the pee test from the gas station on the road to West Virginia. Most of all I'd been scared to tell my mom, and then pretty scared about the first appointment with the baby doctor. But once Stella knew about the pregnancy and the doctor made sure the baby was okay, I'd stopped being so scared. I had tried to focus on staying healthy and getting through the end of the semester, so Emmy and I could go away. Now that we'd officially gone away, all I could think about was my dad, and maybe I used that as a way not to think about the baby because thinking about meeting my dad kept me scared enough.

"Are you scared about the birth? All that blood and goop? Are you scared to be a mom? I know I'd be scared shitless, being so young and all," he said as he tossed the apple core into his bag and looked up, staring.

Next to me Emmy shifted in her seat, pulled herself up, and leaned across me toward him. "Are you scared, Nelson?" Emmy asked. "To leave the Midwest? To go to California? To go to war?" She narrowed her eyes at him. "You're pretty young too."

I don't think she meant to be a bitch, and I don't think she wanted to sound so rude. Maybe she just wanted to shut him up so she could get some sleep, or maybe she really wanted to know what it felt like to be where Nelson was, to be getting ready to do something that seemed so foreign and far away. Maybe she was trying to understand what her father might have felt too, but I think most likely she'd been listening all along to me and Nelson talking about his training, that it had probably eaten her up, had been tying her stomach in knots as she sat there pretending to sleep. So even though I wished she hadn't sounded so sarcastic and snobby, I knew she was doing it intentionally because she wanted him to stop talking, because she was tired and was ready to get the hell to San Francisco, because she was strung out on sleeping pills and too many cups of shitty coffee, and mostly because she was scared about her dad even if she wasn't talking about it much, which I couldn't blame her for. She'd probably been sitting there all that time thinking about her dad and Bobby Elder and all the other men from Morgantown who'd gotten sent away, and that's enough to make anyone a little pissed off.

So maybe that's why her voice sounded the way it did when she looked him in the face and said, "Are you scared you might not come home?"

Either way, Nelson didn't give me a chance to apologize for her acting like such a bitch, because he didn't talk to us much after that, and he switched seats when we stopped in Boonville. When I thought about Nelson later, I always regretted the way things ended. I forgave Emmy, but I always hated the memory of her words and the way she'd put her anger in the wrong place, forced it onto Nelson even though it didn't belong to him.

CHAPTER NINE

AROUND NOON WE PULLED INTO KANSAS CITY, where a small woman about Stella's age replaced Nelson across from us.

She fussed over a wide-eyed boy dressed in Superman pajamas under his puffy blue snow coat and eventually leaned over and said, "You look starved," before producing two packs of peanut butter crackers from her backpack. She split the food between me and the child, introduced herself as Marni and her little boy as Jonah, and then launched into a story about the bull statue we were about to pass by, a landmark in Kansas City that, she said, had been a source of controversy since it was placed on top of the American Hereford Building in 1953.

"I guess a lot of people viewed it as an icon, but most folks hated it, figured it detracted from the natural landscape and all that," she said. "Look." She hoisted Jonah into her lap and then tugged me from my seat into theirs and scooted over so I could look out their window to see the giant bull perched in the skyline, solid and serious, a massive hunk of a thing. "Doesn't suit my taste, but to each his own," she said with a shrug. "They moved it to Mulkey Square in '02, but to me it doesn't matter where you stick it, it'll always just be a bull with a huge you-know-what."

She licked her palm and tried to flatten the cowlick that curled at the front of Jonah's head, and then he looked at me, said, "I'm only allowed to wear costumes on Mondays," pulled a Superman mask out of his pocket, and slid it over his face before he turned to look out the window.

"We're on our way to visit my sister in Denver. You like to travel much?" Marni asked after I'd moved back to my seat and settled in next to Emmy.

"I like the forward movement," I told her and popped the last peanut butter cracker into my mouth. "I like the sound of the asphalt hissing under the bus," I said, and she nodded.

Emmy leaned on my shoulder and said, "I like not having to do anything," before she closed her eyes again.

Marni laughed, but I agreed. "It's like we know we're going to end up exactly where we want to be but we just get to sit here. I like that, not being responsible, getting to relax."

Marni asked where we were headed, and I told her Emmy and I were going to visit colleges in California. I didn't mean to, hadn't been thinking about colleges at all since I hadn't even applied, but it just kind of came out since I knew that's what most kids our age were probably doing over winter break.

"You girls sure are brave to want to go so far from home for school. I didn't leave home like that until I was married," she said, and I had to look at the floor because I was starting to feel crappy about all the lies I'd been telling: the lie to Simon about the baby's father, the lie to Emmy about not knowing how to reach Johnny Drinko, and the lie to Stella about my plans to return when school started.

And even worse, we had only another thirty hours or so left before California, and I still hadn't told Emmy about my one-way ticket or my dad living in San Francisco. I worried the lies would spin out of control and get so knotted together I might get lost inside them, so I promised myself I wouldn't let us cross the California state line without coming clean.

Kansas was as flat and vacant as Nelson had made it sound, with nothing but small towns and big grain elevators and dark dirt fields that I imagined Stella would have liked to paint, and when we hit a snowstorm along the way the land turned white and the bus got even colder. Eventually Jonah and Marni nodded off. Outside, the trees were thin and frail, and I watched the sky move into late-afternoon colors of diluted blues and grays, the brake lights in front of us guiding the bus into the evening. By Hays, Kansas, we'd been on the Greyhound for twenty-four hours, and I still hadn't slept.

Marni and Jonah woke up around eight that evening as the boy sat up suddenly, stating, "The day before the day before yesterday was Christmas." Marni turned toward him, still half-asleep, and kissed him on the forehead, and just like that I knew she was the kind of mom I wanted to be.

"Wanna know a secret?" I asked Jonah, and he nodded and took off the mask. I pointed to my belly. "There's a baby in here," I said.

Jonah was somewhere between three and four years old, with eyes the color of night and skin the color of coffee with a splash of cream, so I wondered if his father was black since

Marni was fair skinned and redheaded. He squeezed his face into a tight set of skeptical wrinkles, and it was easy to imagine what he would look like when he became a man.

"In there?" He looked at Marni as if to ask if he was supposed to believe me or not.

She smiled. "Like Miss Lisa at school," she said.

"Can I touch it?" he asked.

I turned my body and leaned forward, taking his hand in mine and bringing it to my stomach. At first I thought he might cry, but instead he took a deep breath, closed his eyes, and waited for the baby to do something that might prove itself.

His hand was small and soft resting on my stomach, and I willed the baby to move, tried to imagine the kicking I'd read about that would start around the eighteenth week, but nothing happened. The book said there would be a distinct and forceful moment when I would finally feel as though my swollen stomach was actually my child, a person all its own, and with Jonah sitting there in his pajamas pressing his palm to my belly, with the land moving by us outside, the weight of my body finally became more than just a heaviness. It became a warm and undeniable evidence of life.

After a moment or two Jonah pulled away, opened his eyes, and said, "I think he's happy in there, Lemon. You might want to leave him be," before he slid back into the seat next to his mother and began playing with a pair of Matchbox cars.

I nodded. "You wanna see a trick?" I asked him. "Switch seats for a second?" I said to Marni, and she double-checked Jonah's face for permission, then traded places with me, so I sat next to Jonah. He smelled like little-kid sweat even though it was freezing out.

"Wanna go walking?" I asked him, mimicking a phrase Stella used to say when I was little and bored in the car.

He looked at his mother and then shrugged. "Whatcha mean?"

The window was fogged over with all that cold air outside and our breath and heat inside, so I squeezed my hand into a ball and reached past him to press the side of my fist against the glass. Then I used the tip of my finger to make five toes. I did the same with my other hand and pulled back.

"You are here," I said, and drew an arrow to the footprints. "Now you decide where you're going next."

Stella had played the game with me millions of times. She could always tell when I was getting restless in the car, so she would wait until we hit a red light on the road, lean across me, and make the first prints, and then I would take over, marking my own feet up and down the passenger-side window with my tiny hand as I narrated an imaginary journey.

I looked at Jonah, waiting.

"Like, I could go . . . ," he started slowly, hesitant.

"To never-never land to play hide-and-seek with the Lost Boys," I said. "Or to Papa Smurf's house to help him outsmart Gargamel."

He was nodding then as he put his fist to the glass and pressed. "Or to Batman's cave?"

"Absolutely. Walk on over. Tell me what happens when you get there," I said, so he did and I sat with him for a while, playing the game for almost an hour while Marni flipped through a magazine, occasionally nodding off.

Sometime after Colby, Kansas, and before the Colorado line, I remembered the money Stella slipped into my pregnancy book. I was back in my seat by then, so I pulled out my purse and flipped through the pages, hoping for a twenty, or a fifty if she was feeling especially sad about me going away. But there were no bills at all. Instead I found a piece of yellow paper torn from the legal pad she kept in the kitchen, folded and tucked into the page that began the chapter titled "Your Fourteenth Week of Pregnancy," which surprised me because I'd had no idea Stella was counting.

Emmy was awake by then, so when I unfolded the paper, she said, "What is it?" and put on those little black reading glasses. She was there looking over my shoulder when I read the name Ryan Cooper followed by a street address in San Francisco. Below it my mother had written one sentence: "I promise this is all I know," scrawled above a sloppy *X* and an *O*, in Byzantine Ceiling Blue ink.

"Who's Ryan Cooper?" Emmy asked, and she took the paper and squinted at my mother's handwriting. "Is it someone you know in San Francisco?" she said.

But I couldn't really hear her anymore because my mind was wobbly as I realized Stella knew all along, that even though I'd stopped asking about him years ago, she knew I'd never stopped wondering. She probably knew before I did that my trip with Emmy would end up being all about my dad. I guess sometimes that's how mothers work.

"Is it someone we can stay with?" Emmy asked. "Because I don't think this babysitting fund's going to last long," she said. "I don't mind spending it, but I'd rather not sleep in a shit hole." She stopped then because I guess she noticed my hands were shaking. "Hey," she said. "What is it?"

And then I finally told her about my dad in San Francisco. I told her about Stella leaving my grandmother for California, about her living out west for a year and a half before she got pregnant, and about the way I imagined her and my father falling in love in a city that always seemed so energized and full of possibilities.

"She was nineteen when she found out she was pregnant, so she moved back to Pennsylvania, which is where I was born. She left him there and decided we didn't need him." I folded and unfolded the piece of paper as I spoke. "I'm not even sure he knows about me."

"I guess I never thought to ask about your dad," she said. "I just figured you were one of those kids who only had a mom. I just figured Stella wasn't sure," she said, and I tried to decide what would have been worse, having a mother who didn't know who my father was or having a mother who knew and just wouldn't share him, wouldn't give me any of her memories.

Emmy said something about history repeating itself, but I told her it was different, that I never really knew Johnny Drinko, and that I believed Stella and Ryan had been in love before she left him. I started to cry a little when I told her how tight-lipped Stella'd been when I was a kid, how little I knew about my father.

"He was the only thing that made her quiet."

Jonah got out of his seat and came over, put one tiny hand on my knee, and held his other fist out, opening it to reveal a red Matchbox car.

"Take it," he said, and patted my leg. "This always makes me feel better when I get sad." And then he crawled into Marni's lap. "Mommy says when you're sad you have to cry to get it out of you. That once it's out, you'll feel better," he said. "It'll be over soon," and he turned away and began drawing letters in the condensation on the window.

Emmy was a good listener while I complained about writing my father letters when I was kid and finding them tucked under magazines and food scraps in the trash.

"That's so after-school special," she said, shaking her head. "Jesus, Lemon, that really sucks."

"She never gave me any answers, and I was little, you know? I didn't understand," I said as we finally crossed out of the flat expanse of Kansas and into Colorado.

She took off her glasses and squished her eyebrows into a V. "But you're not little now," she said, and she pulled her hand into her sleeve and used it to wipe my nose. "She doesn't get to decide anymore. You're in control," she told me, which I liked the sound of even if I didn't believe it yet. "Maybe that's what this trip is all about, about taking responsibility," she said. "You're actually doing something now."

"I wanted to believe she made the right choice for us," I told her, "but I just couldn't help being pissed off. It's like sometimes I blame her for not making a family out of us, but then sometimes I know it was probably better that way," I said. "He never came for me, so I figured he was a loser, the kind of guy who couldn't handle being a dad."

I thought of Johnny Drinko and how similar he and my father must have been, and I wondered if Stella had recognized similarities too, if she had wanted Johnny Drinko because she'd seen pieces of Ryan in him.

"But as hard as I've tried to write him off, I never stopped wondering," I said as the bus motored us through the first miles of Colorado. "I just need to see for myself. To know she was right, that we're better off without him."

And Emmy said, "Or even that you're not," and I nodded.

I slipped the piece of paper back into the book and took

a deep breath. I apologized for not telling her the truth and for thinking of myself and my father even though he'd been gone all along and I should have been used to it by then. I also apologized for not being able to change the fact that her dad had just gotten taken away.

"I know this trip is supposed to be about escaping our families, not chasing them down," I said. "But I was worried it would be my only chance to go, now that I'm pregnant. I just want to find him before the baby comes. I need to see if knowing him would make anything different." I told her I was an asshole and a crappy friend for lying and dragging her along.

"But this isn't about me," she said, and I couldn't tell if she was mad or not. Mostly I think she was just glad I'd come clean. "I mean, yeah, you're a shithead for not being honest, but I would've come anyway, even if you had told me." She moved her hand into mine and left it there, rubbing my fingers with hers. "My dad being gone has nothing to do with you," she said. "And maybe you're selfish a little, but it's still California." She shrugged. "I'm in," she said. And then I burrowed down into her lap and shut my eyes, finally falling asleep as the bus moved us toward the mountains, the gears of the Greyhound kicking back and forth.

CHAPTER TEN

IT WAS DARK WHEN WE DROVE INTO DENVER, but it didn't matter, because the mountains had so much snow on them that it seemed like they were glowing when they exploded in the distance, so I took a photo of the Rockies out the window even though I didn't think it would turn out. It was late, eleven or so, but I nudged Emmy awake to see the backdrop of the snowy peaks as I-70 carved a path into the city.

"Jesus," she said, "is that for real?"

"You got it," I said. "The Rocky Mountains, full on." And we pressed our noses up to the window and leaned our foreheads against the glass.

Marni and Jonah's trip ended in Denver, and Emmy offered to grab some snacks and sodas from the terminal when we stopped so I could stay on the bus, and I watched as Marni packed up all their toys and books and empty food wrappers.

"Put your coat on, muffin," Marni said to Jonah. "Looks cold as an icebox out there."

Jonah told me I could keep his red car for when I got sad again.

"I don't know the story," Marni said, eyeing my belly. "But sometimes the decisions we don't make for ourselves are the decisions we need the most." She smiled. "And from where I'm standing, it looks like you'll be a wonderful mother," Marni said, and then we showed Jonah how to use the camera so he could take a photo of Marni and me before they got off the bus and headed toward an old minivan waiting for them in the parking lot.

When we left Denver for Salt Lake City, where our next transfer fell, Emmy ate another Ambien, and I must have nodded off too, because when I woke we were parked in the lot outside the Rock Springs, Wyoming, terminal. There was a man on the other side of the aisle staring so hard across the space between us that his eyes felt like fingers poking me awake. In his lap he clutched an old army-green sac—not a duffel or a backpack but a lumpy, stained bag with a black cord tied in a knot at the top. I could smell whiskey and sweat, stale bacon grease and dampness, as he leaned over toward me. He was older— older than Johnny Drinko, older than Simon, too—and his face was pitted and pocked with acne scars, his voice jumbled and slurred when he narrowed his eyes at me and said, "Hey, girl."

I looked at Emmy, who was heavy with sleep, and checked the floor to make sure our purses and backpacks were still there.

"Hey, girl," he said again, "you too young to be traveling alone."

I elbowed Emmy, but she didn't budge, and all around

us the riders were sleeping; the ones who were awake were stretching their legs outside near the snow banks in the parking lot or getting snacks in the terminal. Below my window a woman in a black ski cap and a puffy white coat smoked a cigarette. Next to her the bus driver talked on a cell phone. I turned to look in the back of the bus for Nelson, but he was gone.

"Hey, girl," he said again, but then I felt him on me, his hand squeezing my knee as I looked down at his knuckles, which were covered in wiry black hair.

Maybe he was harmless. Maybe he thought I was someone he knew, or maybe he wasn't really touching me at all and I was stuck inside one of those nightmares I couldn't make myself wake up from. But then he was there again, pressing his thumb into my thigh as he moved his hand up my leg, his body leaning closer and his fingers like spiders crawling across me.

"Little girls need chaperones," he said.

I knocked his hand off, and he slipped and tumbled into the aisle. And that woke Emmy up, the sound of body hitting rubber floor, but no matter how much braver and stronger than me I believed she was, she couldn't stop him when he hissed, "Teenage whore."

He scrambled to his feet and hovered above us, looking.

Emmy said, "What the hell?" and rose to stand, but it was too late. He spit at me, a white and bubbled glob that landed on my shoulder. And all the time I didn't move. I sat there looking at his chest breathing heavy and fast, at his eyes glossing over. I sat there and let it happen.

"Get out of here, you freak show," Emmy said.

And then he leaned forward and rubbed his thumb over my

cheek and down to my shoulder, where he wiped the spit away.

"You should take better care of yourself," he said. He pulled the bag into his arms and added, "This is my stop, baby," and then he left the bus.

It was a long time before I could shake the feeling of him, the stripped and simple disdain just because we were girls traveling on our own. I was glad to see him fading from view when we finally pulled out of the parking lot.

Emmy said, "He was crazy, Lemon, a nut job," and she nuzzled against me and closed her eyes. "Every road trip is bound to have one—don't take it personally." I tried to believe her but couldn't help thinking it wouldn't have happened if I wasn't pregnant, if my body hadn't been begging for attention with all those new curves and slopes.

I never did get any more sleep after that. We left Rock Springs around six in the morning and drove right through to Salt Lake City. Utah was a quick state covered in snow summits and rolling hills, and soon after, images of Nevada began to fill the windows as the land alternated between wide-open country and white-capped mountain peaks. We passed industrial dumps with cargo trucks lined up out front, storage warehouses set in front of small and spotless mountain crests with flat plains of open land cut into their sides. The buildings in Nevada were squat, square objects that contrasted with the peaks of the mountains, and all along the ground, brittle plants jutted out from under a thin carpet of snow.

And then Reno finally appeared, all lit up and loud beneath the evening sky, the neon signs and flashing lights, the gold and green and red lit casinos, and the advertisements for keno and stage dancers, buffets and poker tables. The bus stopped around eight o'clock, and as I watched Nelson gather his things and make his way up the aisle I wanted to grab his arm, say, "Ditch boot camp and come to San Francisco with us instead."

I didn't want to imagine him with a buzz cut in San Diego, so I almost stopped him on his way off the bus and told him to bail on the war and wait for something safer to do with his life, something that would move him closer to that dream of growing grapes and rhubarb, but I didn't say a thing. I watched him get off the bus, zip up his jacket, and head toward a revolving hotel doorway under a blinking gold sign that read THE BIGGEST LITTLE CITY IN THE WORLD.

The trip from Reno to California passed quickly, and we crossed the state line around nine thirty that night. Emmy celebrated by pulling up her shirt and pressing her boobs against the window at anyone on Highway 80 who wanted to look, and then she took out the disposable camera and tried to get a shot of the WELCOME TO CALIFORNIA sign.

"Smile," she said, so I squished against the window and did as she said. "You'll never forget this exact moment."

I imagined the image: blurry, words in motion, a rush of lines moving behind me in the background.

Truckee and Soda Springs were gorgeous covered in snow late at night like that, but Donner Pass slowed us down and pushed us off schedule by a few hours when we had to pull over onto a snow bank and wait for the driver and a crew of men in Carhartts and ski coats to put chains on the bus tires. There were two men in flannel shirts with matching bushy beards sitting across from us by then, and even though they said they'd seen worse coming into Tahoe, I was pretty sure the snowstorm qualified as a blizzard. I looked out my window and saw all the cars that had pulled off the road, all the people who decided to wait out the storm.

"I'm pretty sure we'd get there sooner if we walked," Emmy said, but I was glad the bus driver had decided to keep going even if we had to drive super slow.

All I could think of was the Golden Gate Bridge and the city I'd been waiting so long to see. I thought of Ryan Cooper too, a man in San Francisco not thinking of me, not knowing how close I was to him, how soon I'd find him. I imagined Valencia Street, him opening the door and seeing me on his front stoop, his daughter, a stranger he wouldn't recognize.

We had twenty minutes in Sacramento, so we found a quiet corner in the parking lot where Emmy could smoke while I squatted on the curb and called Stella with my new blue cell phone. It was almost two in the morning there, but I wanted to call because I missed her and suddenly felt like I knew my mother a little better than before just for having crossed the state line. She answered after the third or fourth ring, but it was hard to hear her over the bar on her end and the bus terminal on mine.

"Stella, it's me, it's Lemon. Can you hear me?" I yelled.

She was at Gibbie's Pub with a girlfriend, and she sounded high on booze and the feeling of being out on a Friday night. I imagined her in the red miniskirt she liked to wear, her hair soft and curled around her shoulders, her eyes smeared with black liner.

"Baby," she said. "Where are you?" she asked before she leaned away from the phone and said, "It's my kid calling from California."

I asked if Simon was with her, but she said something like, "Don't get me started."

"Are you two okay?"

"We're fine," she said. "He's just busy, that's all, working on the deadline for The North Face and submitting his new photos to galleries."

I could tell she didn't want to talk about Simon, so I filled the air with details from the trip.

I told her the ride was long, that I wanted a shower and clean clothes, that I hadn't gotten much sleep. "I like the looks of California already," I said even though I'd only been there for an hour or so.

"I remember that," she said. "It just feels different, doesn't it? It changes you as soon as you arrive." She sighed, and I wasn't sure if she thought that was a good thing or a bad thing for me or for her all those years ago.

"How are you feeling?" she said to me, then, "Hang on, I can't hear a thing."

There was a rustle, the noise level dropped, and I heard the hum of a hand dryer and women's voices in the background before she asked again, "How are you feeling?" Her voice sounded warm through all that distance even though I figured she was probably still mad that I left.

"I feel fat," I told her. "And obtrusive. Like a road sign. Like an advertisement for birth control or condoms," I said, which made her laugh.

"You're barely even showing yet, Lemon," she said. "Just wait. Give it a few more weeks, and then you can tell me about feeling fat." Behind her I heard water running.

"Are you in a bathroom?" I asked.

"It's fine," she said. "Good God, at least it's quiet. It's amazing how loud drunk people are."

I told her I'd found the paper in the pregnancy book.

"Listen, Lemon, don't get your hopes up," she said. "I don't even know if he's still there. Ryan . . .Who knows where Ryan is now. What's done is done."

Behind her voice I heard the flush of a toilet, and then she mumbled, "Sorry," and I imagined her tucked in the corner of a stall, her cell phone cupped between her ear and shoulder as she hid from the sounds of the bar.

Emmy was beside me then and whispered, "Two minutes, boss. It's colder than a witch's tit," and she moved onto the grass and began bouncing on the balls of her feet to keep warm in the snow. On the other side of the parking lot, passengers were climbing onto the bus.

"Does he know"—I paused, held my breath—"about me, about . . ."

"We didn't speak much after I left California," Stella said, and I hoped she'd offer some kind of significant excuse.

I wanted her to take responsibility, to say she loved him too much, that it hurt too bad to keep in touch once she left him behind. Or maybe I wanted her to say it'd been his decision, that he asked her not to contact him because he didn't want to be involved.

But all she said was, "I called a few times after you were born to tell him we were okay, but it's been years since we've talked."

"So he knows," I said, not sure which would have been easier, him knowing and never looking for me, or him not knowing at all.

"Just don't get your hopes up," she repeated.

But I'd read the city was seven miles wide by seven miles long, and after seventeen years without him, forty-nine miles seemed like nothing, the last simple and conquerable distance that separated us. I was determined to find him.

Then Emmy was back by my side again, the camera raised to her face. "Say 'California,'" she whisper-screamed, so I smiled and mouthed the word before she took the shot.

We left Sacramento, and the bus was packed with stringy men and women with bloodshot eyes, snagged leather sneakers, and baggy sweatshirts. We rode into the city on the Bay Bridge, which wasn't the same thing as the Golden Gate, but Emmy and I were happy all the same because even though it was the middle of the night San Francisco looked like magic when we drove over the water and into the lights, the sound of the metal bridge clicking beneath the tires of the bus.

"Look at all that movement," Emmy said as we stared out the bus window at the lights of cars and flicks of lampposts and blinks of signs too far away to read. "It's like the city's dancing."

The skyline was jagged and quick, buildings that burst out of the ground and sat stacked and pieced together like a puzzle. We moved toward the Transbay Terminal, and I was nauseous the whole way in, my palms sweating. We were there. And suddenly all the things behind us felt truly far away.

The bus driver announced we were heading into SoMa, which I'd read was a neighborhood near the Embarcadero, by the water, and he said the next terminal would be our final stop, that everyone must exit the bus once we arrived.

"Please collect all your personal items," he shouted over the murmur of the passengers. "This is our final destination."

The Transbay Terminal was a multistory bus depot, and the area around it was filled with brick buildings, high-rise condos, and small chain-link-fenced parking lots scattered along the streets. The driver told us the 6 and 31 bus lines ran just out front and that we could catch the Muni train a few blocks away, but we picked up our luggage and nudged our way out of the station to hail a cab. We didn't really know where we were, and we decided we deserved a taxi after the last three days on a bus, three days of having to smell the chemical blue liquid from the bathroom, of substituting hand sanitizer for hand soap because we didn't have running water on the Greyhound.

Eventually a cab slid up to where we waited under a NO STOPPING ANYTIME sign, and we told the driver, Ari, to take us to the hotel address where we'd booked our room. He took us down Howard Street toward the Mission district, and from the window I could see warehouses and tattooed kids in tight pants leaning on lampposted corners, bars and restaurants and signs advertising stores and happy-hour specials, sales on used CDs and books. In the Mission, the streets were littered with people, and everyone—the homeless slouching by cardboard boxes, the artsy kids in beanies and brown leather jackets, and the women in slim dark jeans and ballet flats—they all looked distant and unfamiliar as we headed through the neighborhoods. We drove past flea markets and taco stands and nightclubs while the cabbie talked nonstop about the city and the Mission and the bacon-wrapped hot dogs he swore we could smell from the street if we'd only roll down our window. He said he didn't know where we came from, but it was a cold winter in the city that year. He hoped we brought jackets. He hoped we had hats and gloves. I lowered the window, and the smell of cheap, hot meat hit us hard as we watched swarms of people stumble out of the bars and hover in front of Mexican men grilling hot dogs on flat burners right there on the sidewalk.

"With the bacon wrapped around them and the onions and mayo like they do, I was pretty sure I'd died and gone to heaven first dog I bought on Valencia," he told us. "I'll never forget it. Was the week me and my partner found our apartment down on Folsom Street. Been almost thirteen years now," he said, and shook his head like he could hardly believe it.

Emmy took a slow, deep, dramatic breath of air. "I could eat nine of those. Right. Now."

"It's drunk food, girl," Ari said. "The bars are letting out and the cats are starving."

He said our hotel was a good spot for two kids who weren't sure what was up yet, that most of the people there were transits and hipsters passing through town with not a lot of money but not a lot of reason to leave the city. When we pulled in front of a pink slot door squished between a café window and a storefront advertising burritos and sangria, I wished we'd sprung for a place with a higher rating on Travelocity.

But Emmy said, "Looks like home," and opened the car door.

The cab was inexpensive, and even though the hotel entrance didn't look like it led to much, we got our stuff out of the trunk, paid Ari the fare plus a five-dollar tip, and headed into the hotel.

CHAPTER ELEVEN

OUR FIRST FULL DAY IN SAN FRANCISCO opened with rain and wind rattling the window panes, and Emmy muttered, "I feel disgusting," and stumbled into the shower before I had the chance to remind her that we were, in fact, in San Francisco for the next four days with nothing to do but whatever we wanted and no one to keep tabs on us, no one to answer to.

I lay in bed listening to the couple staying next to us thump and groan on each other on the other side of the wall while I waited for Emmy to finish in the bathroom. I was grimy from all the time on the bus and my head was pretty groggy, but I also felt the particular sense of freedom that comes the first time you leave home.

It was almost noon by the time we left the hotel, so we ducked into a small café on Valencia Street and bought coffee and scones and small cups of fruit. We sat by a window and watched the sidewalk wanderers while we created a plan of attack. We had about seven hundred dollars between the two of us, but we were confident that a city like San Francisco could be explored cheaply, so we planned to be extra frugal. And I knew I needed some of my share to get the bus ticket back when I was ready, so we made a list of all the things we wanted to do that wouldn't cost much. We wanted to see Alcatraz and ride a trolley, and we wanted to take a bus up to Muir Woods to see the redwoods. We wanted the nude beach and Golden Gate Park and the shopping we couldn't afford, the food we had never tasted and the music we had never heard of and the museums we had read about in books. We wanted all of it.

"I want to eat sourdough bread and Ghirardelli chocolate," Emmy said, and she plucked a red grape from her fruit cup and forked it into her mouth. "I want to see the Japanese Tea Garden and the place where all those rock stars used to eat acid."

"The Fillmore," I told her, remembering the pages she dog-eared in the travel book we bought before we left.

We watched the weather outside turn from rain to sun to rain again, the back-and-forth tug-of-war that happened in a matter of minutes.

"I know you'll be distracted until we look for him," she said. "And I'm okay with that." She picked at the oatmeal chocolate-chip scone on the plate sitting between us. "We should get it over with, though. In case it doesn't go well. We should try today," she said, which seemed okay to me.

I figured it was hard for Emmy to think about my dad while hers was so far away. Plus, if we didn't find him immediately, I would have time to keep looking once Emmy left.

We stayed in the Mission for the day and planned to find Ryan's house around five o'clock, when most people would be heading home from work. We window shopped and people watched and walked from one end of the neighborhood to the other, stopping to rest in Dolores Park and again at a small hole-in-the-wall eatery where we bought green tea and homemade granola bars. The air was wet and cool, so we both picked out new scarves at a used-clothing store: Emmy chose one that was a deep purple, and I picked a knitted green one with silver specks that Emmy said matched my nose ring. We shopped at secondhand stores, and I dragged her to the pirate shop that fronted the office where they made the literary magazine Ms. Ford had been published in. We roamed past bookstores and nightclubs and more taquerías than I could count.

According to Stella, Ryan lived on Valencia Street down near Twenty-first, and it was almost dark when we found the building, a tall, skinny house the color of eggplant that sat across the road from a Laundromat and an all-night pizza shop. We tried the doorbell, but it didn't work, so we parked ourselves on the front steps and huddled together to stay warm, inhaling the smells of marinara and car fumes and something dank and wet seeping from the street drains. Emmy slung her arm around my shoulder, and I rested my head on her chest, tugging and twisting the fringe that lined the bottom of my scarf.

"Tell me this won't ruin our trip. Tell me that if he's not here or if he's a total asshole or if he doesn't want to see you . . ."

"Emmy, stop," I said.

"Tell me it won't ruin our trip," she repeated.

"It won't ruin our trip."

"Are you scared?" she asked.

"I don't know," I said. "I'm excited. And worried. But I've got nothing to lose, I guess."

She squeezed me tighter while the wind pushed brown, damp leaves around our feet. Five o'clock came and went, but we stayed on the stairs because I'm not sure we had anywhere else to go. I must have nodded off for a while, tucked under Emmy's arm like that, because she nudged me around six thirty to ask if I was hungry.

"We can go," I said groggily. "We can leave."

I was thinking of food and warmth, somewhere dry and bright. I wanted fajitas or those bacon-wrapped hot dogs or maybe even a beer. My head hurt, and my stomach was gassy and nauseous. I wanted to sleep. For a very long time. But just as we stood up to leave, I heard the door behind us open.

I froze, stopped breathing, still and scared on the front steps of the house I'd hoped was my father's, but Emmy took my hand in hers and said, "Three. Two. One." Then we turned around.

The woman pushing her bike out the door was tall and slim and had skin the color of chocolate caramels and a perfect black afro framing her face. She wore snug bell-bottom jeans with red leather boots, and a tight white T-shirt under a small brown leather jacket. She was beautiful. After leaning her bike against the wall, she pulled a set of keys out of her bag and locked the door behind her. When she turned to carry her bike down the stairs, she noticed me and Emmy standing on the sidewalk staring up at her.

"You're not Ryan," I said, and I scanned her face, the

pointed nose, the long black eyelashes thick like caterpillars, and the shiny red lips. Her eyes were brushed with shimmery gold makeup, and her lids were lined with thick black strokes that made me think of the Chinese symbols we'd seen written on the signs of so many restaurants that day.

"I'm not Ryan," she said back. "He picked up a shift and won't be home until three or so." She stopped halfway down the stairs with her bike hoisted over her shoulder. "Who's asking?"

I scanned a list of possible responses. I was Stella's daughter. I was a friend, a friend of a friend, maybe. Finally I settled on, "I'm Lemon. My mom used to know him." And then, "A friend of the family."

She shrugged. "He won't be home until late." She was on the sidewalk by then, and she swung her leg over the bike and propped herself on the cracked leather seat as she adjusted the red bag slung across her chest. "I'm Cassie," she said, and next to me Emmy mumbled, "Sassy Cassie," right before I turned my head and shot her a shut-the-hell-up look. Emmy lit a cigarette and stared at Cassie parked on her bike in front of the purple house.

"I like that," Cassie said, and then she reached over and took the cigarette out of Emmy's hand to take a drag.

I thought that was pretty cool.

"You want to leave a message? I'm heading there now. We're working together tonight—it's a sold-out show," she said.

I wasn't sure what to say to that, but it didn't matter because she looked us up and down again, and then she said, "You can come back around three thirty if you want. It takes a while to unwind after work, so we'll be up." And then she took one more drag, handed the smoke back to Emmy, and pedaled down Valencia.

Afterward, Emmy and I sat at the pizza shop across the street and split a large pie with green peppers and sausage.

"They must work at a bar," Emmy said, and she reached for her second slice and covered it with parmesan cheese and red pepper from the glass shakers on the table.

"Do you think they're roommates?" I asked.

She raised an eyebrow. "I don't think grown-ups have roommates," Emmy said.

It was a wish, something I should have known better than to say out loud.

"Right. Stella never did," I said, and she nodded.

I thought of the different men my mother had brought into our homes over the years, the one-night stands before I knew what one-night stands were, the losers like Denny and the drunks like Rocco who thought using women as ashtrays made them strong and cool. I wanted to ask Emmy if she'd seen anything like that before, if her mom had brought any men home since her dad got deployed, but I figured I already knew the answer, so instead I said, "She might have been the most beautiful woman I've ever seen up close," and I tried to wrap my head around the fact that Cassie was, most likely, my father's wife. And that made her better than my mom and me. She had something Stella did not, something worth working for, which made me feel sorry for myself and pissed off at Stella that she wasn't smart enough or pretty enough or confident enough to have stayed in California with Ryan and made a family out of the three of us. "I bet he loves her, you know? Like, long-term loves her. I bet they're the kind of couple that—" But Emmy cut me off, shaking her head.

And for the first time since the pizza came, Emmy looked up from the food. "Let's get one thing straight," she said, pushing her plate away from her and leaning over the table toward me. She looked me straight in the face. "You don't get to do that now, Lemon," she said. "You don't get to make him something different than he is." She leaned back and shrugged. "Maybe he's a good guy and maybe he's not, but you don't get to decide. He gets to show you—that's why you're here. You quit that game when we got on the bus." And then she tapped her finger on the table and said, "Quit."

And I knew she was right. None of the versions of Ryan that I created through the years would turn out to be him. Being in California made him real, and I wouldn't get to make-believe him into someone different if he wasn't who I wanted.

"Your dad," Emmy said with slow, careful words. "He's white, right?"

"He's white." I nodded and nudged a piece of pizza crust around my plate. "His mother was half-Mexican, but that's all," I told her, remembering Stella's explanation one summer at the shore when I asked why my skin tanned so much easier than hers.

When I was a kid back in Philadelphia, I'd sit in my mother's closet while she was at work, hiding from the empty house, maybe, shutting out all that vacancy. Eventually I found two photos jammed inside a pair of black chunky shoes with leather straps and towering wedge heels. They were tattered and blunted from wear even though I never once saw her wear them. They were artifacts she used to hide the only images of Ryan I had ever seen, and once I found them, I'd sit beneath her clothes, her pants and skirts draped over me like curtains, and spend hours studying the pictures tucked inside the heels. The first was a Polaroid of my mother during what I assumed was the summer she arrived in San Francisco. She was laughing behind purple sunglasses that were too large for her face, and next to her a man with shoulder-length hair stood with his arm slung around her waist, his finger hooked into one of the belt loops on her blue jeans. The two of them stood on the street, below a movie-theater marquee, and it looked cold and windy, Stella's long blond hair flapping around her face in wild strings and knots.

The man—my father, Ryan—wasn't looking at the camera. In fact, it looked like he didn't know the photo was being taken, because he seemed so distracted by my mother. He wore a white T-shirt and pants with a black leather belt, and he was leaning in toward Stella's neck, maybe whispering. When I was a kid the photo made it easy to imagine he loved her very much. It made it easy for me to blame her for ruining whatever it was they shared. And though the photos were dulled by distance and time, Stella seemed brighter in that picture than I'd ever seen her. It was difficult to equate the image of that girl with the mother I had grown up with. The restless woman who yanked us from town to town, an impulsive mother bound by bitterness, a woman boarded in by secrets, or regrets.

The second photo was of Ryan alone. He sat on a blond hardwood floor with a drum between his legs, and he wasn't looking at the camera as he hunched over the instrument, but it was a clear shot of his body: the shaggy brown hair that hung over his face and the narrow shoulders, the tan fingers blurred with movement as they banged out the rhythm to a song.

"My sister dated a black guy once," Emmy said. "My dad flipped his shit." She reached over and pulled a green pepper off one of the two remaining slices of pizza.

I'd never imagined my father with a black woman, though when I did imagine him with Cassie, I realized I'd never envisioned him with anyone but Stella, which only proved how limited I'd been in my imagining. Of course he had someone. A woman with silver hoop earrings, a red smile, rich skin.

"I thought my dad might kick Margie's ass when he first found out about it, but the relationship didn't last long. The guy was a football player, and he ended up dumping my sister for some girl at WVU who ran track. The whole thing was cli-chéd and dramatic." Emmy looked down at the table. "It was back when we had to worry about getting my dad's approval if we liked a boy," she said, and I did the math and figured it had been over a month since Emmy's dad left.

I tried to think of something encouraging to say, but a man with honey-colored dreadlocks entered the pizza shop, dis-tracting me, and the moment was polluted and lost. He car-ried a green plastic bucket filled with books, and his thick beard matched the shade of his hair and the chaos of his knot-ted mustache. His blue T-shirt had a topless mermaid printed on the back and read CATCH OF THE DAY, and a plastic cof-fee cup hung from the belt loop of his black jeans by a big metal hook that looked like it could be used for rock climbing. Emmy shifted in her seat and reached for one of the slices of pizza as he moved from the door toward the counter in the front of the restaurant. I couldn't see the man's eyes behind the dark sunglasses, but I imagined them to be blue. Blue like a swimming pool lit up at nighttime.

"Homeless," Emmy said before she took a bite. "I can smell him from here."

At the counter the kid working the register said, "Hey, Jared, let me check in the back to see what we've got."

The man put the bucket on the floor and began digging in his ear.

"I wonder how long they've been together," I said, and I tried to imagine how many women had moved in and out of Ryan's life since us.

"She looked pretty comfortable coming out of that house. If you ask me, I bet they've been together for a while," Emmy said.

Which meant Cassie knew what kind of soap he used in the shower, how he liked his coffee, and which T-shirt was his favorite. She knew if he put the cap back on the toothpaste in the mornings or if he left it lying by the side of the sink. She knew his habits, while I hardly knew what he looked like.

At the register the homeless man took a paper plate with two slices of pizza from the boy, said, "Jah be with you, little brown-haired man," and bent down to pick up his bucket of paperbacks.

"Are we really going back tonight?" Emmy asked, which was the obvious question neither of us had said out loud.

The dreadlocked man walked toward us then, mumbling words I couldn't understand, but when he got to our table he spazzed into a coughing fit and had to stop to catch his breath, wheezing, before he pulled himself together and headed out the door.

Once he was gone I looked at the boy behind the register, who shrugged and said, "The neighborhood regular. Owner gives the throwaways to Jared, burnt and misorders." He shook his bangs away from his eyes. "He mops for us some-times, takes out the trash or sweeps the back stairs in exchange for slices of pizza."

I thought of the man tucked inside a doorway with an awning or camped out in Dolores Park on one of the wood benches we saw that afternoon. I tried to imagine what it would be like to live in a place where people slept on side-walks, the differences between real cities and the small towns Stella had stuck to after we left Philadelphia. I looked up and noticed the boy behind the counter again. I looked, and he looked back.

"We'd better get out of here," I said. "Head to the hotel and take a nap? I can't remember the last time I stayed up until three in the morning."

Emmy tossed the rest of her pizza onto the metal tray. "I'm in."

And then we left to wait out the small slice of space that separated the time before and the time after I met my father.

CHAPTER TWELVE

I DIDN'T KNOW WHAT CASSIE TOLD MY FATHER that night at work, but when Ryan opened the door he had a joint in one hand and a sloppy smirk slung across his lips. "You're the kid Cassie told me about," he said. "Come on in."

He was taller than I expected, but the wavy hair was the same from the photo, and he still wore it long, tangled and hanging down to his shoulders. His eyes were dark and wandering as he looked at the street behind me. I had his nose, the perfect slope I'd always liked, and his cheeks were warm and tan, weathered with fine lines. I figured he was somewhere in his midforties, a little older than Stella. His lips were full and wide when he smiled and turned to head inside.

I'd decided to go to Ryan's alone, but Emmy had promised to wait at the pizza shop across the street, since I figured I wouldn't stay long. She'd brought the San Francisco book so she could read through the section on Muir Woods, where we planned to go the next day.

Cassie and Ryan's house was a duplex, so he led me up a set of carpeted stairs, past a hand crank that opened the front door from the landing on the second floor. At the top I could see a kitchen down the hall, but we turned in the opposite direction and moved past a row of matted concert posters and into a small living room, where Cassie sat cross-legged on the floor with an old camera that had been stripped and gutted, the pieces spread out between her bare legs like toys. I noticed she wasn't wearing a wedding ring after all.

"Hey there," she said.

She wore a pair of frayed and torn cutoff jean shorts that were splattered with green paint, but I saw traces of the gold eye shadow, and her lips were still carefully painted red. The room was decorated with framed black-and-white photos, and a world map spanned an entire wall on the far side. A fall-colored quilt made of rich purple and orange and red squares was draped over an old leather couch, and the overhead light was off, the room lit by candles scattered on furniture armrests and along the floor. I eyed a fishbowl on a bookshelf, set among stacks of hardbacks and magazines, framed photos and odd pieces of pottery and rocks, seashells and stones.

Ryan said, "So," and he looked at me standing in the door frame while he took a seat on the arm of an upholstered La-Z-Boy in the corner. But then no one said anything for a while after that. I looked at them, and Cassie looked at the camera, and Ryan grabbed a pack of matches from the coffee table and lit the joint he'd been holding all along.

Eventually Cassie said, "Where's your friend?" which was

a good excuse for me to tell them that my best friend, Emmy, and I had just come into town on a Greyhound.

"She was too tired to come along," I said, which wasn't the truth, but it worked to break the quiet while Ryan sucked on the joint, the smoke filling the room and reminding me of Dylan and the lake and Emmy's truck all the way on the other side of the country, a place that didn't seem so bad as I stood there staring at my feet. Of all the scenarios I created in my head over the years and all the different ways I imagined the scene might go, I failed to remember any of the words I'd planned as I stood there face-to-face with the man who had been kept a secret for so long.

Somewhere down the hall a stereo played electronic music without words, and it might have been the secondhand smoke going to my head, but it seemed that Ryan's voice synched with the rhythm of the bass when he leaned down to ash into a mug on the floor and said, "So you're a friend of the family? Which family is that?"

Cassie had a photo lens in her hand, and she wiped it with a ripped piece of an old stained T-shirt. She looked at me still standing in the door frame, halfway in the hallway and half-way in the room, and asked, "What'd you say your name was? Lemon?" but her words were muffled things rumbling below darkness, a shadow closing in.

Ryan's jaw slacked open for a moment before he said, "No shit." He put the joint on the table, stood up, brought one hand to the back of his neck, and stuck the other in his pocket as he looked at me, really looked hard and long at me for the first time. "Lemon?" he said, squinting. And maybe he saw his lips or his nose strung up on my face, maybe he recognized the dark eyebrows Stella always said I got from him, but maybe he didn't. I couldn't tell, because all he said was "no shit" again, his voice strained and sounding far away when he sat back down.

"Do you know her?" Cassie asked like I was somewhere else. "Who is she, baby?" she said, and she pulled a cigarette out from behind her ear, a white tube tucked into her afro. She leaned forward for the matches on the coffee table.

"Lemon," he said again, "Lemon," as he sized me up, his gaze unwavering, searching me out. His eyes started at the floor before gliding up and back down again, moving over the lines of my body. Eventually he stopped at my face, exploring, looking for him in me, looking for Stella maybe, for pieces of them merged into a girl he'd never met before.

It felt like the entire world stopped then, with his eyes on me as I tried to catch my breath. I felt stretched thin by those eyes, my image shapeless, floating, as he watched me watching him back.

"You?" he said, a question, and then just "You."

But the room and the music and the smoke of the joint started to fall out of focus, and I had to lean against the wall to stop from falling over. I was nauseous and sweating a little, the heat of the candles and his eyes pushing on me. The darkness kept getting bigger, diluting the smell of the pot and the incense, shrinking the light of the room down to a pinpoint of whiteness. There wasn't time to make it to the couch, and the next thing I knew I was on the floor with my back against the wall as I pulled my knees to my chest and tried to make myself smaller.

"Jesus, Ryan, help her to the couch," Cassie said, so he did, which was embarrassing, it being the first time my father had touched me as he hoisted me up, his hands under my armpits.

"She's white as a sheet," Cassie said when he dumped me on the couch.

"I'm fine," I mumbled. "I'm pregnant, that's all." All the movement stopped then as their eyes locked down on me. "Pregnant," I said again.

"Jesus Christ," Ryan said before he went to the kitchen, where I heard him turn on the faucet. I tried to pull myself together, but then he was back, handing me a glass of water and asking, "You wanna tell me what this is all about?" He stood with his hand stuck to the back of his neck again.

With him squinting down at me, frowning like that, I figured he was pissed I'd shown up on his doorstep, and I imagined him asking me to leave, abruptly pulling me off the couch and shoving me through the hallway, nudging me down the stairs and using the hand crank to open the door because he couldn't be bothered to walk me to the stoop. I imagined him telling me he wanted no part of whatever it was I hoped to find there. I figured he was too worn out to deal with me.

And I guess I was pretty close, because next he asked, "Did Stella send you for money?" which I suppose was a valid question, but it hurt my feelings, so I shook my head and looked at the wood floor, my voice stuck somewhere between my chest and my throat.

Cassie was on her feet, asking, "What the hell is going on? Who is she?" but Ryan didn't look at her, his forehead creased and confused.

He stared at me and said, "If she wants money, she'll need a lawyer. She's screwed if she thinks she can send you here like this after all these years." His eyes were red and glassy, sharp and pointed things.

"Jesus, Ryan," Cassie said. "Stella your ex, Stella? Shit," she said, flustered.

The whole thing was slipping away from me, and I couldn't find the words. All the things I'd imagined I'd say to him were disappearing below my feet, disintegrating somewhere between the bus ride to the city and the little purple house. I wanted to tell him I didn't need any money, which wasn't really true. I wanted to say Stella didn't know I'd come to find him, which wasn't true either, but mostly I wanted to tell him that I came because I'd decided to have the baby of a man who would never be a father. And something about that made me need to find Ryan first, to find some kind of closure. But even though it made sense in my head I knew I would never get the words right, so I didn't say anything at all. I let Ryan and Cassie argue about who I was and why I was there, about where I had come from and whether or not I was who I said: his daughter, Lemon, the kid of a woman he loved when he was young.

And then the pieces of the camera slid across the floor in all directions as Cassie jerked her foot at the fragments, the glass slipping over the wood toward Ryan. She hissed, "You're such a dick, you know that? This is huge, Ryan. A kid? You never said a word."

And I knew then that in all those years he'd never thought of me. I wasn't a part of him or his life at all.

I stayed quiet as long as I could and stared at the candles set on saucers along the floorboard, wondering how long it would take the whole place to catch fire if one of us knocked over a flame. She was sucking on the cigarette and ashing on the floor, asking questions he wasn't answering, not really, and under all the noise, the sound of him stumbling on words and her trying to piece things together, I heard the music down the hall. I tried to focus on the thump of drums and the space of keyboard riffs that didn't fit together, the endless drone of sound that could be found in bars and underground nightclubs across the city.

The yelling stopped when Cassie put her hand up, silencing Ryan with the gesture. She looked at me and said, "Are you okay?"

I guess she asked because of the sweating and the way I almost fainted, my skin flushed and hot as I sat on the couch and watched them argue. My hands rested on my stomach, the small bump that had recently budded from my body, and I didn't realize it until she asked, but I was crying too, a subtle and quiet kind of moan children make when they're scared or lost.

After that everything settled down. Cassie sat next to me on the couch and asked about the pregnancy, while Ryan relit the joint and watched us from the recliner, evaluating. I didn't say much except that I should get going because my friend was probably worried that I wasn't back yet. I stood up, and Cassie stood up, but Ryan stayed in the chair, looking down at the floor while I tightened the green scarf around my neck.

"I'm not here for money," I said. "I just wanted to meet you, to see San Francisco." I nosed the toe of my tennis shoe on the floor. "Stella doesn't say much about living here, and I wanted to fill in some of the gaps before the baby came." Which sounded pretty good to me, and I was glad I finally found something worthwhile to say before I left. Something he might think of after they closed the door behind me.

Ryan stared at his fingers, the fingers I studied as a kid, in the photo in the shoe, the same fingers from the picture of my father playing a drum, and I realized I was standing on the exact floor he'd sat on when someone snapped the shot. This had been his space with Stella, the home they made before she got pregnant and took off back east. Before Cassie, this house was my mother's.

"Look, I'm sorry I flipped. I'm sorry I said that thing about the money, but it's just a little crazy, man," he said before he looked at me. "You showing up like this. It's been a long time since me and Stella—" But he stopped and lost his words somewhere among the candles and the butt of the joint that sat dead in the bottom of the mug. "It's just been a long time," he said, and shook his head.

Cassie walked me out, and when we got to the bottom of the stairs she took a pen out of her back pocket and asked me where I was staying. She wrote down the address, the letters printed neatly in blue ink along the inside of her maple-syrup-colored wrist, and under it she wrote my cell number.

"Give us some time. Shit," she said. "It's been a long night."

I agreed and opened the door, then made my way back down the front steps of the house. Across the street the boy with the bangs had been replaced by a woman with long red hair, and Emmy was nowhere to be found.

It was almost five in the morning by the time I got back to the hotel, and my eyes burned dry and aching when I put the key in the lock and opened the door, expecting to see Emmy splayed out on her bed, her shoes probably still on, and her scarf still slung around her neck as she slept. The room was empty, but next to the bed the window was open, and I could hear Emmy laughing outside, could smell her cigarette smoke seeping down into our room. I climbed up the grid of the fire-escape stairs and found her and the boy from the pizza shop sitting on the rooftop, a small square space littered with beer cans and cigarette butts.

Emmy told the story. "I swear I was waiting at the pizza place forever, but Aiden—this is Aiden, you remember," she said, "Aiden finished his shift and asked if I needed a ride. He doesn't have a car, though. He drives a blue Vespa. *Blue*, Lemon. Isn't that some shit?" she smiled.

He'd told her it'd be safer to take a lift from him than to wander through the Mission.

"God, and have you seen this neighborhood at night? So yeah, I believed him. Jump on the back of that Vespa or wander home alone? No-brainer," she said, and I realized her words were slurring together. "And check this out. We grabbed some beers and found these plastic chairs on the roof. Right here where we needed them to be so we could get some fresh air and have a quick smoke. And OhMyGod, look at this. Look—we smoked almost an entire pack of Marlboros," she said, staring into the box of cigarettes. "Shit. Shit, are there stores open at this hour? What hour? What time is it, anyway? Jesus," she said.

I eyed the empty beer cans at their feet and guessed Emmy had also swallowed a pill or two since her eyes were so glassy and red.

She waved her hand as if swatting a fly and added, "I told him about you being knocked up. I told him about your dad and stuff."

I looked out at the street when she said it, and I wished to be skinny and drunk and self-confident just as Emmy was in that moment, but then the air shifted and the feeling passed when I thought of her going back to West Virginia the next week, to a home she didn't want anymore, to a family with a dad serving in Afghanistan.

Aiden said he was twenty-one and he wrote music reviews for *SF Weekly* but he didn't get paid much so he worked four nights a week at the all-night pizza place.

"I also pick up extra cash managing my friend's band," he said. "They're basically launching the jamtronica movement," he told us, and Emmy and I nodded like we knew exactly what that meant.

He didn't say anything about going to college or having any parents nearby, and I could tell he and Emmy had been trading stories for a while when she reached over and put her hand on his knee, laughing at a joke I didn't catch. He looked at me when she did that and shifted his leg away. Eventually Emmy asked how things went with Ryan, but I didn't feel like talking about it while she was so boozed and distracted, so I told them I was tired.

"I can't even see straight," I said. "I'm going to bed."

"Don't do that," Aiden said, and he stood up. He wasn't tall or short, really, just in the middle, and I noticed the edge of a tattoo on his bicep when his T-shirt sleeve rode up as he brought his cigarette to his mouth. "I remember you from earlier," he said. "Stay up. We'll get breakfast."

I was hungry, but my back hurt and my head was throbbing in pulses again, tiny thumps I couldn't quiet down. I looked at Aiden, the smooth skin and the dark hair and the emerald eyes that I swore could look through me if they wanted to. He had the kind of eyes that made you want to believe everything he said. I ran my hand through my hair, straightened out the V-neck of my sweater, and grazed my finger over the stud of my nose ring. Aiden and I looked down at Emmy, who had her head resting on the back of her chair, her eyes tilting up to the sky, and then he looked at me.

"I think we're about to lose her," he said, and when I looked back down, she'd fallen asleep.

I shut my eyes and wished myself not-pregnant. I wished myself lighter, less tired. A seventeen-year-old girl wanting a boy who wanted her back. I imagined myself before the tattoo shop or the move to West Virginia, before the bus ride to California. I wanted pink Trident gum, perfect tiny bubbles flirting from my lips. I wanted to meet Molly-Warner at the park and worry whether or not anyone else at school knew about me losing my virginity to the pothead, the time when that was as complicated as it got. I wanted my old body back, and tank tops from the summertime, pants that fit on my hips, that didn't feel so tight. I imagined that I was who I was before I thought that I was using Johnny Drinko and not the other way around. Before I thought he'd be a way to get back at my mother for all the things I'd never put into words. But when I opened my eyes and looked down, nothing had changed.

And then Aiden said, "I remember you from earlier" again, and, "We'll get breakfast," so we did.

We put Emmy to bed, and then he took me to a twenty-four-hour diner on Church Street near Market. And I knew it was stupid to leave the hotel with a stranger like that, but something made me trust him anyway, those green eyes or the sound of his voice, the way he touched my elbow when we turned the corner. Safe, that's how Aiden made me feel, even on the first night. It's just like that with some people—it had been with Emmy, too, that first day at school.

CHAPTER THIRTEEN

Aiden and I sat across from each other in a booth at the diner and ordered eggs over easy with bacon and sourdough, but he wouldn't let me drink coffee.

"Even I know you're not allowed caffeine." He nodded toward my belly.

He didn't ask about the father or about the due date, but as I smeared grape jelly across my toast I said, "I guess this week, if I could see the baby, he'd be making facial expressions," remembering what I'd read in the pregnancy book that morning. "Frowning and squinting his eyes. Some babies start sucking their thumbs around this time," I said.

"That's so badass," he said.

The diner was quiet except for the muffled sounds of the cooks in the back washing dishes and cutting food, getting ready for the morning rush as Aiden and I moved through conversations strangers typically have when they first meet. He talked about his job writing for the paper, and I told him I was worried about finding work to make money for when the baby came. I had never needed money like I needed it then.

"I've never had a job," I said, "not really."

"Jobs are overrated," he told me. "You'll be fine, though. You're a smart girl, smarter than lots of people I know with jobs. It's amazing how many morons land nine-to-fives with decent pay."

A man sat down in the booth across from ours and ordered a cup of coffee. He opened a copy of the *New Yorker* while he waited and eyed the curves of the waitress when she bent over to pour him his mug of caffeine.

"The trick is to find something you actually like to do. Find a place you like to hang out, a place with interesting people, and then work there," Aiden said in a way that made it sound simple.

Afterward, Aiden walked me back to the hotel while I rambled about the Greyhound trip and about the couple staying in the room next to Emmy and me, about the endless sounds of sex drifting through the walls. I said I was planning on trying one of those bacon-wrapped hot dogs the next night even though I'd had some pretty bad luck with onions and mayonnaise since the pregnancy. I told him I'd read about the Palace of Fine Arts in our travel book and that I wanted to see those cracked columns, those ruins, while we were in town.

When we got to the skinny pink door of the hotel, he interrupted and said, "You're adorable. You know that, right? The way you talk, the way you see things."

I was quick to reply, the words streaming out of me as

though I were a leak. "Actually, I'm not. I'm selfish and judg-mental." I looked at my feet, the tips of my Converses shuf-fling on the sidewalk. "I judge people all the time. I judged that homeless guy tonight at the pizza place."

He nodded.

"And I judged you too," I said.

"You're honest," he said. "That's endearing."

But I kept going because I'd evidently misplaced the brain-to-mouth filter in my exhaustedness or maybe just because it felt so good to talk to him, to talk to someone who didn't know me yet. "I judged my father, too, before I even met him."

"That's not judging," he said. "That's just imagining, I bet."

"I'm judging him right now. For being so absent. For smok-ing pot. For never coming for me, for never looking."

Next to us a taxi sped by, the light on top turned off.

"As I'm standing here with you, I'm deciding things about him. It's disgusting, really. The opposite of adorable," I said.

"Shh," he said. "Stop." And then he kissed me on the fore-head before I went inside.

Emmy was knocked out cold when I got in, so I ran a bath and climbed into the tub, soaking for what felt like hours and studying the body that had become mine through pregnancy. My skin was tight and stretched smooth over the small mound of my belly, and I ran my hands over the new curve of my abdomen and up across my nipples, now tender and hard. I leaned my head back against the rim of the tub and breathed, relaxed. And I thought again of Aiden before lowering my fingers to the V between my thighs. Afterward, I dried off and slid into sweatpants and a T-shirt before get-ting into bed.

Emmy rolled over around two in the afternoon, checked the clock, and announced, "We are the laziest freaking vacationers *ever*," before reaching for the glass of water on the nightstand. "Jesus, what happened? My breath tastes like shit." She took a long gulp and flipped onto her back to look at the ceiling tiles shadowed with stains. "Seriously. It's like a little man climbed into my mouth while I was sleeping and took a dump. God," she said, "gross."

"I met my dad," I told her, "and you met a boy with a blue Vespa," and she smiled at the thought of Aiden, which I didn't blame her for. "But then you fell asleep, so I went to breakfast with the boy before I came to bed."

"Big night," she said, mulling it over. "No wonder we're so tired."

I'd been awake for an hour or so trying to decide how to tell Emmy I didn't have a bus ticket back for Sunday like she did. It was time. It was past time, really, and I felt terrible about planning to stick her on a Greyhound by herself even though I knew she would have done the same to me if we'd been in opposite places, if it'd been the other way around. I knew Emmy would forgive me, but it didn't make me feel any better when I imagined her in those crappy leather seats, using the liquid hand sanitizer, fending off the crazies on her own while she traveled back to West Virginia. But she would love me anyway, even after I told her I wasn't going back when she was. It's a wondrous and rare thing to have a friend who knows about the skeletons—the tattoo shops and the wreckage of your family—and who likes you anyway. Emmy was my first, and I was feeling pretty awful about lying to her for that long.

"I want to hear about Ryan, but I won't be able to

concentrate until I feel less filthy," she said, and then she was in the bathroom taking a shower.

Afterward, I threw on some jeans, and we left for a little café near Van Ness Avenue, where we stopped for breakfast.

"It's New Year's Eve, you know." I smeared cream cheese across my everything bagel and watched a woman in a blue cocktail dress and sweatpants push a grocery cart down the sidewalk. It was drizzling again, and I wondered if she was cold in those high heels and silk spaghetti straps.

"New Year's is overrated," Emmy said irritably, which was true, but I could tell she was just pissed about missing breakfast with Aiden, and about being hungover.

"Whatever, Buzz Kill," I said. "You know you're excited to spend New Year's in a city. A real city, Emmy. Come on, don't be an ass."

"It's inevitably disappointing, and you know it." She dunked her spoon into a cup of yogurt topped with perfect red strawberries. "New Year's is never as good as you want it to be. Over. Rated."

"Not necessarily, not always." I was determined to be optimistic. I would pull her from her funk and refuse to let her waste a whole day sulking. "There's a party if we want to go," I told her when I squished the top and the bottom of the bagel together, the cream cheese oozing out the sides just how I liked it. "Aiden told me about a music thing, something at the Regency. He said it's a pretty great event."

But Emmy didn't want to talk about Aiden anymore and changed the subject to Ryan, so I told her about the house and about Ryan thinking I wanted money, about Cassie walking me out and taking my phone number.

"It all happened really fast," I said, leaving out the part about the sweating and the room spinning, about me crying on the couch. "We didn't talk all that much. Mostly I just told him who I was, and then they argued for a while. I also told him about the baby, but I left after that."

"Sounds like it could have been worse," she said right before she asked if it was all right with me if we didn't talk about our dads for the rest of the day, which I thought was fair enough.

So we acted like we hadn't planned to go to Muir Woods that morning and spent the day window shopping in Union Square and walking around the city instead. We took a trolley ride downtown, then hiked up the hills of North Beach to see Coit Tower before we grabbed a bus out to Baker Beach to watch the sunset. Eventually we headed down to the water at Fisherman's Wharf, where we ate sourdough bread bowls filled with clam chowder for dinner. But it was only when we made it back to our hotel in the Mission that we were allowed to talk about New Year's again, because there under the door Aiden had left an envelope with two tickets to Anon Salon's New Year's festival.

The tickets read A COSTUMED ART & MUSIC SPECTACLE and listed three bands Emmy and I had never heard of. I rubbed my thumb over the silver letters, printed on the pink and aqua paisley design. We stood in the doorway of the room and read the note from Aiden: "Meet me at 11:00 in line." A wave rolled from one side of my stomach to the other as I thought of seeing Aiden again.

And Emmy must have been feeling good by then too, because she shrugged and said, "I'm in if you're in, boss."

That night we scoured through our suitcases to see if we could find anything New Year's Eve–worthy to wear.

"I miss being skinny," I told Emmy while we tried on clothes in the hotel.

Everything felt small, my body shoved and squished into cotton that didn't stretch enough. I missed being able to get away with not wearing a bra, and the perfect way my jeans had hugged my hipbones just months earlier. Emmy tried to talk me into wearing a silver sequined tube top she'd brought in case we went out to a club, but I was having a hard time imagining spending the night stuffed into the tiny piece of stretchy fabric.

"You look hot," she said, and she moved behind my back and adjusted the back hem of the sequins before beginning to comb through the knots of my hair. "Your boobs look amazing."

"I look bloated is what I look." I eyed myself in the mirror in front of us, the silver fabric stretched tight over my curves. "Like a sausage in sequins," I said.

"Please. It's just a little belly pooch. If I didn't know what you normally looked like, I wouldn't even notice." She tugged the hairbrush gently. "You look hot," she repeated, and she parted my hair down the middle before twisting each half into a tight little bun at the base of my neck. "The only place you're showing is your boobs and that teeny tiny belly bump. It's beautiful, really," she said, and our eyes met in the reflection. She smiled. "I like running away with you, Lemon Raine. You know that?" but then the phone rang, and the moment was lost as I thought of Emmy's dad, instantly thought of bad news, of her mom calling to tell us something loud and crashing.

And I guessed Emmy was thinking the same thing, because she dropped the hairbrush on the floor and scrambled to find the phone.

She sighed and said, "Thank God, it's Dylan," when she grabbed it from under the bed and flipped open the cell. She sank to the floor, smiling when she heard his voice on the other end. "Happy New Year's, baby," she said as she pulled her legs in crisscrossed. She began twirling her hair with her fingers, as if he could see her in her underwear and tank top all the way from West Virginia.

I looked at the clock and realized it was after midnight where Dylan was. It was New Year's for Stella and Simon three time zones ahead, too. I slipped into the bathroom to do my makeup and found Emmy's gold eye shadow in her toiletry bag. I carefully swept it across my lids and decided to be brave and wear the tube top and black mini stretch skirt. I told myself she was right, that I looked good with flushed cheeks and dewy skin, with full perky breasts I never had before the pregnancy. It wasn't so bad once I had on some makeup and black knee-high boots. I checked my nose ring, put matching silver studs into my ears, and vowed to learn from Emmy, to practice her self-confidence and steal from her the traits I wanted for myself.

From the other room I heard Emmy whispering before she broke into laughter, and I felt good about being in California and about meeting Aiden later at the concert. Last year's New Year's was a disaster, an evening that ended with Stella on her knees puking in the hall bathroom, the splash of liquid on liquid as I held her hair back and looked away.

Molly-Warner had watched us from the doorway, said, "Smells like pineapple," and rolled her eyes.

But I knew it was pomegranate martinis, Stella's drink of choice that winter, and I also knew the man in the living room in the sports coat was an insurance salesman my mother met when he went to J.C. Penney to buy a pair of earrings for his wife for Christmas. Stella helped him pick them out during her shift: white-gold dangles that shimmered from Stella's ears when her head jerked forward as she vomited again.

"I'm sorry," Stella mumbled between heaves. "I'm sorry, baby," she said, and I realized she'd begun to cry.

I'd never seen her that drunk before, and I'd wondered if she'd remember it in the morning, or if all that booze flooding her body would wash out her memories during the night and she'd wake up guilt free. I wondered if she'd be embarrassed or if the hours of sleep would rinse away the humility.

"How can a woman that small be filled with so much stuff?" Molly-Warner said and headed for the kitchen as I used my fingers to pull Stella's hair tighter.

I could tell she was sleeping then by the weight of her head, the final spew having kicked her out of consciousness. It was the month of Pine-Needle Green, and she was spilling out of a jade-colored minidress that hugged her curves, while Molly-Warner stood at the counter eating chips and salsa, and the married man sat on the couch in the living room looking nervous. I caught him watching me.

"Go," I mouthed, and he did, shutting the door carefully behind him.

And then I plucked the earring from Stella's left earlobe and watched it hit the water, bobbing in the filmy bile before I moved her to the floor and left her slumped and sleeping against the bathroom wall. I flushed.

As I looked at myself in the mirror in San Francisco, a

million miles from Stella, I knew this New Year's would be nothing like last year's.

The Regency Center, a massive rectangular building set on the corner of Van Ness and Sutter, was lit up and glowing when we parked in front in the taxi and dug in our coat pockets to pay the driver. The first floor was made of oatmeal-colored stone, and we looked up at the rows of huge arched windows and white crown molding, all bright and shining gold. The eaves atop the building were intricately sculpted into complicated shapes and designs.

"This is amazing," I said as we got out of the taxi and joined the line of people stretched around the corner and down the street.

Most of the crowd was masked or winged or adorned with sequined pants, furry leg warmers, feathered headbands, or intricate jewelry. People poured out of cabs, and we found ourselves in line behind a tall woman in white leather pants and a blue tank leotard. A sparkly scene of jellyfish and seaweed had been stenciled on her arms and chest, and small plastic octopuses and glittering sea creatures were scattered throughout her hair, a teased nest of long blond curls. I heard her say she was freezing, and the man standing next to her offered the feather boa wrapped around his neck.

"Now, *she's* got great boobs," Emmy whispered, and she slid her hand into mine and squeezed, sensing my insecurity, maybe, sensing my hesitation.

One girl had tied red balloons to the ends of her pigtails, the helium pulling her hair into the air as if her head might float away. Another dressed as a flamingo in a bright cotton-candy-colored miniskirt with black fishnet tights underneath. Her hair was dreadlocked into short tubes and spray painted

Pepto-Bismol pink with black stripes, her stomach bare and muscular and camouflaged under paint designed to look like feathers. Men wore dresses or cowboy chaps and leather boots, furry vests and sunglasses in the shapes of fish, belts that worked as bottle openers and bright blue sweatbands around their heads. Camera flashes sparked and people yelled, and I smelled pot and booze and cherry-flavored lip gloss, sweat and cigarettes and spray paint. I couldn't imagine how Stella had left this city behind.

We waited for almost an hour on the sidewalk, and I was pretty certain it'd be midnight before we even got inside, but then Aiden showed up out of nowhere and smiled as if he'd been searching for us all along.

"You shouldn't be in this line," he said, his mouth like a smokestack as his breath turned white in the cold. "Come on," and then he took my hand, and I took Emmy's hand, and she handed the joint back to the girl in the leather pants and the boa, and Aiden led us around the corner to the front, where he nodded to a woman with a clipboard. She smiled and moved out of the way so we could pass between two black poles that had been marked off by a sign reading VIP.

Once we were inside, Aiden led us up a set of stairs, where we checked our coats. He leaned in and whispered something about me looking perfect when I straightened out my sequins and checked my hair in a mirror at the top of the stairs. Emmy wore tight red bell-bottoms and a lacy black tank top, and she told Aiden he looked "very Jim Morrison" in snug dark jeans and a white tee. Someone had rubbed silver glitter into his hair, and he had huge star-shaped sunglasses pushed back on top of his head, holding his bangs out of his eyes. He produced two matching pairs from who knows where, one red and one gold.

"For you," he said as he slid the red pair onto my face and kissed me on the cheek. "And for you," he said to Emmy, repeating the gesture.

I eyed him and felt the bewilderment that comes in the early stage of a relationship when everything the other person does seems significant and extraordinary.

Under the glasses the room seemed more manageable, the lights dimmer and the disco balls less intense as he took my hand and maneuvered us back down the stairs to the front hall, where the heat of the crowd went straight to my head. The walls looked like they'd been frosted with vanilla icing, and I studied the intricate door frames, the sconces that helped light the room, and the massive gold chandeliers that made me feel small. From the foyer, the noise of the mob echoed off the walls and bounced inside my head. Above us a disco ball hung in the center of the ceiling, and I looked down and realized my tube top was throwing rainbows across the walls.

"There's a DJ playing in the ballroom on this level, and some kind of fire-dancing troupe through those doors," Aiden said, nodding down the hall. "The bar closes at two, Emmy, but it'll reopen at six a.m.," he said, and I realized Aiden had no idea how old we were. "The late-night show is a techno theater thing with painters and belly dancing, but the band you want to see, my friend's band, just started. They're play-ing in the Lodge on the third floor, up those." He pointed to a marble spiral staircase on the opposite side of the room. "It's a little confusing, but you'll figure it out," he said, and then he told us he was going to get some drinks and check backstage. "I'll meet you upstairs once I make sure everything's set for the countdown. The band wants sparklers and fire sticks." He shrugged and rolled his eyes, and then he was gone, melting into the crowd so quickly I almost wondered if we'd imagined him.

"Good God, is it me, or is there something so supersexy about that kid?" Emmy pulled a tube of lip gloss out from her bra and swiped it across her mouth. "You would never find a boy like that in West Virginia." She handed me the makeup. "Onward," she said after I'd applied the gooey red gloss and she'd stashed it back between her breasts. She took my hand to lead me toward the stairs.

CHAPTER FOURTEEN

THE BAND AIDEN WANTED US TO SEE was playing in a long room with crimson walls and blood-colored carpet, dark wood ceiling beams and teardrop-shaped chandeliers.

"Now, this is what I'm talking about," Emmy said. "High class."

The stage was decorated with giant papier-mâché conch shells and blue and silver foil streamers that glowed under black lights. Near the bar at the entrance, a topless woman dressed as a mermaid sat inside a large glass bubble resting on a small makeshift stand about three feet high. Her black hair was tied up with white and blue and green ribbons, and her breasts were dusted with silver and gold glitter. We stood at the foot of her glass globe and stared at her as she mimed combing her hair and doing her makeup.

"Does everyone in this city have amazing ta-tas?" Emmy

asked. "Talk about claustrophobic," she said. "How does she breathe in there?"

I looked at the mermaid's silver-dollar nipples and the blue scaly skirt that had been cut into the shape of a fin, the thick silver paint swirled across her skin. "She looks sad," I said. "And trapped."

She stood up, stretched her arms above her head, eyes wide, lips slack and slightly parted. The drone and buzz of Aiden's friends echoed inside the vaulted ceiling and seeped into electronic jams intensified by drum solos and bass riffs while I adjusted to the room.

"Which one of those boys you think wants to buy me tequila?" Emmy said, and then she sauntered to the bar.

The mermaid moved to the front of the globe, where she pressed her hands against the wall, looking out at me and at all the motion and chaos in the room that she couldn't get to, and I thought of Stella. I figured that was how having a baby in San Francisco would have been for her: a tease and a trap. She'd be surrounded by the energy of the city, but she'd be fenced in by a child she wasn't sure she wanted, stifled and tied down in a place that should have been full of possibilities, and I thought maybe that was why she left. The limits and sacrifices of motherhood would have been exaggerated in San Francisco, and the life she gave up would be easier to forget if she placed all those miles between her and Ryan.

Three shots of Jose Cuervo later, Emmy made her way with me toward the stage, where Aiden stood next to a skinny long-legged girl in white ankle boots and fishnets, a black leather bathing suit with a low-cut V in the front, and a gold belt cinched around her waist. They clutched cocktails in small plastic cups, and Aiden bobbed his head to the music while she swayed and smiled at the boys onstage. I slipped in next to Aiden discreetly, but the tequila must have been moving fast, because Emmy came up behind him and grabbed his ass.

"Hola, amigo," she said. "So these are your friends? Not bad." She eyed the four members onstage dressed in matching yellow jumpsuits and red helmets, with dark sunglasses masking their eyes. They were construction workers or firefighters, maybe, musicians zipped into costumes that made me think of sci-fi books.

Aiden introduced us to his sister Sophia, the girl in the boots and the bathing suit, who was visiting from Seattle.

"She's in the middle of a divorce," he whispered. She looked like she couldn't have been older than nineteen. "She couldn't stand to stay in Washington for New Year's," he told me, and I couldn't imagine being so young and married, let alone divorced, but then I remembered I was seventeen and pregnant, the setting mixing it all up in my mind.

Aiden got another round of drinks for them and a bottle of water for me, and we danced for a while down front, a crowded space of all ages, the noise of the speakers filling my head and shifting my body to the beats of the music. Aiden had his arm around my waist by then, and next to him Sophia swayed her hips in tiny figure-eights in front of a rock-star-looking black guy with dreadlocks to his shoulders, and everything felt right in that crowded room with red walls.

But when the band started gearing up for the countdown, Emmy slid in next to me and said, "I know I'm sloshed, but is it me or is that your dad's lady friend over there in a bug suit?"

Emmy had spotted Cassie, who was with Ryan on the other side of the stage, in front of the keyboardist. Cassie was wearing wings, and her afro was tied into a hundred little braids spiked out from her head. Ryan was shirtless under a fringed leather vest and was wearing an Indian headdress that framed his face with red and brown and white feathers. He was sweating and dancing, and Cassie was glowing beside him as she bounced to the music. They looked happy, happy like Stella on the porch with Simon drinking vodka at sunset. The drummer was counting down to midnight, but I didn't hear much, because the room started spinning under all those strobe lights and spotlights and the fog machine, the darkness moving in again. Next thing I knew I was slumped against the wall by the stage, with Aiden squatting over me, rubbing my cheek with his thumb as I sat straddled between his knees.

He pushed a strand of hair from my face and said, "It's good to have you back," and next to him Emmy nodded and tried to catch her balance, swaying. He told her, "I'm going for more water," before he disappeared into the crowd.

"I'm so humiliated," I said, and remembered losing my balance and grabbing Aiden's arm as the silver and black spots filled my eyes and wiped out all the lights.

Emmy said I blacked out supersudden and hard, which she thought was very hip of me, since half the crowd was on drugs, and in a way, fainting made me blend in a little better. "Well played," she said.

"That doesn't make any sense," I told her when she sat down on the carpet beside me and closed her eyes.

"I'm drunk," she said.

I nodded. Next to us, onstage, the band began a patterned song that looped inside the same ten beats of music. My head throbbed in tiny pulses, pounding, and I became acutely aware of how absurd it was to be at a music festival pregnant and sober in some club full of hippies and hipsters and adults who partied like kids, kids costumed as adults.

"I don't belong here," I said to Emmy. "Not now and not ever, with this whole motherhood thing trailing me."

"Chin up, Lemon Raine," she said, but her voice was muddled as it stumbled out of her mouth.

The whole thing made me sad as a headache moved in behind my temples and settled there with fierceness. Next to me Emmy leaned her head against the wall and breathed heavily, the smell of booze puffing out of her with every exhale.

"You can have Aiden, by the way," she said. "Tonight Dylan told me he loved me." She smiled. "I kind of believe him, you know?"

I was glad she had something good to go back to when she left San Francisco at the end of the week.

"Did they see me?" I asked, thinking of Ryan and Cassie dancing by the stage before my vision faded. I wasn't sure what I wanted—for them to have noticed me or not have noticed me.

"I don't know. I was a little distracted when your knees buckled and your face turned all white and pasty," Emmy said. "You're a drama queen, you know that?"

"And you're a drunk," I said back.

"Agreed," she said. "But it's temporary, I promise." She looked me over. "Are you okay? I mean, I've never seen anyone faint like that," she said.

"I'm just tired, I guess. I probably should be eating better. And getting more rest."

Across the room a computer was hooked up to a projector and was casting screen-saver images above Emmy's head, her hair shifting from the light, swirls of pink and yellow and blue that brought back the nausea. "Want to make a beeline for the door before your hipster honey comes back?" Emmy asked, and I agreed, so she helped me off the floor and led us past the bar and the mermaid and down the stairs into the front foyer.

"Coats," I said, remembering our jackets we'd checked upstairs.

"I'm on it," she said, and I waited while she went to get them.

And we almost made it out, but then I turned and saw Cassie coming from the bathroom door in the hallway. She adjusted her tight yellow miniskirt and straightened out her black tube top just before she looked up and our eyes met from more than ten feet away. By the time she was next to me I realized she was dressed as a bumblebee with two yellow antennas glued to the top of a headband resting between the braids.

"Hey there," she said, and then, "You're here? I mean, I didn't expect you to be . . . here," she stammered. Her eyelashes sparkled with silver dust, and with her legs stretched long and thin under the miniskirt and black fishnets, she reminded me of a peacock, of an ornate and brilliant bird. I tried to imagine what this dark-eyed woman could possibly be doing with a loser like Ryan, a stoner and a deadbeat dad. "You're not alone, are you?" she asked.

"I came with a friend," I said, and thought of Aiden upstairs probably wondering where the hell we'd gone to.

"We work for the Fillmore and the Warfield, so we got free tickets," she said. "We've been thinking about you, you know? We want to get together."

The way she used the word "we" made it seem like it belonged there coming off her lips, stamped on every sentence like a little copyright.

"We're still at that hotel," I told her restlessly as I looked up the stairs for Emmy, wanting badly to get out of there, wanting to make our escape before Ryan or Aiden saw us.

I wanted my bed, my body heavy from the music and the heat. And I wanted to call Stella, to hear her voice on the end of a phone connecting us from opposite sides of the country. Suddenly the memory of hovering over the toilet bowl with my mother the year before didn't seem so terrible. At least with Stella I knew what to expect. Her unpredictability was predictable. At least with her there was a sense of familiarity. I wanted to hear her say everything was going to be okay, just like she always said when bad things happened to us, that none of this really mattered.

"Tomorrow will be better than today," she liked to say. "That's the beauty of time. It's always moving forward."

I wanted to call my mother and hear her say that she was waiting for me to come home.

"We've got tomorrow night off." Cassie looked straight and focused, concentrating. Behind her a woman on stilts with green glow-in-the-dark pasties moved by us. "Can you come for dinner?" she asked.

I tried to imagine sitting at a table eating a meal with Cassie and Ryan, relaxing on their couch afterward, asking them questions about San Francisco and being comfortable with my father and his girlfriend. But I couldn't imagine it at all. They were strangers with stories I didn't know, people navigating the landscape of a city I wasn't comfortable in yet.

"Come tomorrow for dinner," she said. "We have to get

together before you leave." She assumed I was there for a quick visit, an adventure during my vacation from school. "Six o'clock," she said just before I spotted Emmy heading down the stairs.

I nodded, slipped away, and left her in the foyer with the bass of the DJ down the hall rattling the floor beneath us.

Outside, Emmy and I attempted to walk home, weaving our way through a New Year's Eve city crowd. We walked the streets for almost an hour and suddenly found ourselves in front of the Regency Center again.

Emmy said, "I told you New Year's was overrated," and then we hailed a cab.

It was nearly two o'clock by the time we pushed the door of the hotel lobby open, and the woman behind the counter looked at us and asked, "You two the girls from 546? Some woman with a southern accent's been calling here all night for a kid named Emmy."

And the lights fell away again, the floor shifting underneath me, quaking. It was faster that time, and I was seeing blackness when I stumbled, as the weight of my body tipped over and dropped to the ground.

Later, when we were back upstairs and I lay on the bed listening to Emmy moving around the room, she asked, "Is this fainting thing your new trademark? Because I have to be honest: It's a little too much for me to handle."

I rolled onto my side and tried to focus my eyes, my vision strained under the fluorescent lights of the hotel room. She was a blurred figure bending down, a hazy shape moving around the bed, squatting on the floor and rising again as she packed her things. I waited and watched her shadow become the shape of my friend when she finally came into focus.

"He's coming back," she said, and even though she was turned away from me, I could tell she'd been crying. "It's his leg. They're sending him back next week. I'm leaving today if I can get a flight."

The night before, while we were eating clam chowder bread bowls and exploring the city, Emmy's dad was on the road to Bagram Airfield north of Kabul, a base for U.S. troops in Afghanistan.

She stripped off the red pants and folded them. "It was an IED," she said. "I guess it's pretty common." She put the bell-bottoms into her duffel and pulled a pair of jeans off the floor. "His SUV hit a roadside bomb," she said, shaking her head back and forth quickly. "How does that happen?" She was facing me then, one hand on her hip, her cheeks wet, eyes red and tired. "He lost his leg, Lemon. He's in some hospital in Germany, but he'll be at Walter Reed by tomorrow."

"Shit, Emmy," I said, which was a pretty lame thing to say to a friend who just found out her dad had been wounded in Afghanistan. I could have said, "I'm sorry," or maybe, "I'm glad that he's okay."

She sat at my feet. "My mom sounded pretty wrecked. I mean, he's going to be one of those people with a plastic stick for a leg. With a—" But she choked on the words and started crying again, so I moved down beside her and pulled her into my arms. And we must have stayed there for a while, because by the time she moved away, the front of my tube top was stained with tears, stripes of black dampness trailing down the sequined fabric.

"I'm sorry I fainted," I said even though it wasn't important anymore.

"I'm sorry I got drunk," she said back.

Outside, the sky was turning the colors of early morning, and when I looked at the clock it was almost five.

"What else did your mom say?" I asked.

"She was sleeping when I called, so mostly she just told me what happened. I guess she'd been trying my cell phone all night, but I'd forgotten to charge it," she said. "I'm supposed to call when I figure out my flight. She's going to pay for my ticket, which kind of makes me feel like an asshole for coming here in the first place, but she wants me home as soon as I can get there."

I told Emmy we would get a cab to the airport and that I'd wait with her until she got on the plane.

"Do you want to come home with me?" she asked from the bathroom, where I heard her toss the eye shadow containers into her makeup bag. But then she glossed over the question and added, "I know the bus ticket will be cheaper, though. When you buy one," she said, and my heart fell into my stomach as I realized she'd known all along that I wasn't planning to leave with her on the Greyhound. Back in the room she tossed the makeup bag into her duffel and said, "I saw your one-way ticket on the way out here. It's okay, I'm not mad." She started opening the drawers to the dresser and searching through the piles of clothes inside, stacks of her stuff and mine that we'd thrown together when we first got there. "I mean, I was at first, but now"—she stopped and held up a red long-sleeved shirt, assessing it before she realized it was mine and tossed it back into the drawer—"now it doesn't seem so important."

"It was before Stella gave me the address, back when I thought it would take weeks to track him down," I told her.

"I couldn't lock myself into a return date. I was going to tell you," I added.

"But then you didn't," she said.

Somehow the information had gotten lost once we made it to California. It was easier that way, maybe because telling her would have made it real, when actually I was scared shitless to be in the city on my own.

Emmy finished packing, and I changed into jeans and a hooded sweatshirt so I could go with her to the airport, but just as I was searching under the bed for my sneakers, there was a knock at the door.

I looked at Emmy, and she looked at me.

I couldn't imagine who'd be waiting in the hallway, until I heard Aiden's voice say, "Tell me you're in there. Tell me you didn't get kidnapped by mermaids or fairies or Smurfs. I just can't be held responsible."

Emmy rolled her eyes, and I went to the door to let him in.

Aiden eyed the mess, the clothes strewn across the floor and the empty containers of take-out food on the dresser top. First he said something about how shitty it was that we left without telling him, and then he looked at me in my jeans with no makeup and at Emmy with her face streaked with tears, and her hair swept into a knotted ponytail. He eyed my backpack on the floor and the copy of *Lolita* on the nightstand, the SIGG bottle on top of the TV and next to it Emmy's retainer, a plastic and metal mouthpiece she wore at night to avoid getting braces. "How old *are* you two, anyway?" he asked.

"Nineteen," I lied, but Aiden raised an eyebrow.

"I'm eighteen," Emmy said. "And she's seventeen." She looked at me and shrugged, "Come on, Lemon. Who gives a shit how old you are?"

Emmy picked up her duffel and said something curt about him needing to leave because we were on our way out the door, but Aiden offered to call his buddy who drove a cab, and he waited in the lobby while I told him about Emmy leaving town but about me deciding to stay for a little longer. He didn't ask why she was going or how long I'd stay, but when the taxi pulled up he borrowed a pen from the front desk and wrote his cell phone number on my hand.

"I'm sorry I didn't tell you about my age, that I'm only seventeen," I said while he wrote.

"It's just a number, right?" he said. He stamped his writing with his thumb so the ink wouldn't smear and told me to call him when things settled down. "Don't disappear this time." And then he kissed me on the cheek before we got into the taxi.

Emmy booked a flight to Charleston, West Virginia, where her sister would have to pick her up to drive her home, but she got a one-way ticket for about two hundred and fifty bucks, which didn't seem so bad to me, and when I walked her to the security gate I hugged her and told her that I loved her.

"Take care of your dad," I said, and she said, "Take care of yours," and then she leaned into my neck and whispered, "Call Stella, Lemon. You need your mother." I tried to brush it off, but she wouldn't let me. She pulled back and put both hands on my hips, looking me in the face hard and serious. "You. Need. Your. Mother," she said. "And she needs you, even if she doesn't admit it."

Next to her a man pushed by with a big black suitcase. The intercom announced a departing flight. Last call for boarding.

"He may be your father, but she was your family first. Don't forget that just because you're distracted by this," she said, and then she kissed me on the cheek. "Life's too short to walk away from people who love you. Even if that love is flawed and complicated and screwed up," she said, "it's still love. And that makes it worth finding a way to hold on to it."

And then she moved away from me, took off her shoes, and crossed through the metal-detector.

It was hard to watch her go, because losing Emmy felt like being stripped of the brave piece of me that wasn't scared to be so far away. She made the city safe, and it seemed impossible to stay there without her, so I almost called out to her when she began to move out of sight. I almost asked her to stay, but it would have been selfish because there was nothing more important to her then than being with her family, and thinking about it that way made me want to get in touch with Stella. I watched Emmy go and decided that even though we'd be separated, a little bit of her would stay with me—that bravery and independence. Which I guess is exactly what family is: the pieces of you that you never realized you had.

CHAPTER FIFTEEN

I SLEPT ALL AFTERNOON, DREAMING OF WATER too thick to swim through, and when I woke sweating and breathless, I called my mother on my Byzantine Ceiling Blue cell. It was around three o'clock in California, just about the time Emmy was making her connecting flight in Dallas.

Stella picked up on the third ring and began with a hurried, "Yep, I'm here." Behind her I heard the rattle of pots and pans in the kitchen. "I was just thinking of you," she said. "I'm up to my ass in casserole for the Prestons. Everyone's talking about what happened to Tony. Do people really eat casserole when they're sad?" she asked, and I listened to her pause for a sip of something with ice cubes clinking against the glass. "It's awful, right? Who the hell wants food that's all melted together like this? It's like baby food for grown-ups," she said. "All lumps and mush."

"You're home? I thought you'd be heading out for happy hour."

"Not me. Tuesday night's my painting class. Club soda, on the rocks. I've got an hour to turn this casserole into something good, and then I'm out the door. Class starts at seven thirty," she said, and I realized I didn't know what color she'd picked for January, but before I got to ask, she said, "Is Emmy okay?" and then, "Shit, I forgot to preheat."

"She's on a plane heading back east," I told her, and I sat down on the bed and pulled open the drawer in the nightstand, rummaging out of nervousness.

I listened to her take a deep suck of breath and then a huge puffy-cheeked exhale, her dramatic version of a sigh. "And that means that you're where?" she asked, slowing down. "You're alone out there, aren't you?"

"I'm still in San Francisco." I pulled the phone book out and flipped through ads in the yellow pages. Taxis and dentists and churches. Bookstores and nightclubs and AA meetings.

"Uh-huh. You're in San Francisco. By yourself," she said, and I imagined her eyes making the squinting face she used when she was pissed. "Brilliant. That's genius, Lemon. Jesus Christ."

I closed the phone book and eyed the Bible in the drawer. I couldn't figure out why hotels bothered to put them in all the rooms; the only time I'd ever seen someone use one was back when Stella'd hand roll her cigarettes on the hard surface of the cover when we slept in motels between towns.

"And you're planning to stay there for what, another week? A month? What, Lemon? What?" she said, her throaty voice laced with anger, heavy and thick through the telephones connecting us.

"I'm not really sure anymore." I reminded myself she was too far away to do anything about the choices I was making. That she loved me and her anger was rooted in that.

"Here's the deal. You're coming home at the end of the weekend because school will be starting, because that was our agreement, and because I'm not letting my knocked-up kid hang out alone in the city for more than three—no, make that two—more days," she said. "Your ass is on that bus on Sunday. Done." Stella didn't believe in negotiations, so she added, "No ifs, ands, or buts," and I imagined her stamping her bare little foot on the kitchen floor. "I'm the mother. I'm in control," she told me, and I wondered if she said it to remind herself or to remind me.

"School doesn't start until the fifth," I said.

"It's a three-day trip, Lemon, don't screw around. Sunday is the third of January, which means you'll still miss two days of school," she said, which surprised me because she was right even though I never considered her to be the kind of person who knew exactly what the date was. I actually couldn't remember ever having a calendar in any of our houses.

But I felt like being honest. "I can't make any promises. It just feels too soon."

"Lemon," she said.

"Stella," I said back.

"This isn't your decision to make," she said, and I had to bite my tongue to keep from saying the exact same thing. "You're just a child."

"Not really," I told her. "Not anymore."

I heard the pots and pans again, the open and closing bang of the oven door.

I told her I found the house on Valencia Street, and I lied

and said Ryan was happy to see me. "I want more time with him. I want more information."

There was a slamming of glass against countertop in the background, and I imagined the ice cubes airborne, landing on the floor and sliding across the linoleum, drops of club soda splattering on the oven top. Pace began barking somewhere in the house.

I waited and listened to her suck one deep breath after another as she tried to calm down. "You've got to move on, baby," she eventually said softly.

"But I'm not ready to leave, and school's not a problem because Emmy'll be there to take notes and give me the assignments when I get back." School seemed completely insignificant. It'd be a miracle if I graduated—my grades had slipped so much since the distraction of the baby, plus I hadn't applied to colleges, so I thought it'd be better to just sit the rest of the semester out. Though I hadn't told Stella or Emmy, I figured I would have to do a do-over, especially since I'd be missing so many days while I stayed in California. I was hoping that if I asked the administration to let me repeat my senior year, I might even have a chance of nailing Spanish the second time around.

"I'm not okay with this," Stella said. "I want you back." Another deep breath. "You've already missed a doctor's appointment, plus you've got school. You've got to be running out of money, and I'm not sending you any, because I want you home. I want you where I can see you. Home," she said again.

But home wasn't really a word that meant much to me, and I imagined a foreign space, a house we hadn't moved to yet, or another hotel. I thought of the blue-shuttered home in her painting. "It just feels too soon," I said again.

And she said, "I miss you, Lemon," which I believed when her voice slowed down like that, and then it got quiet behind her.

"Is he okay?" she finally asked.

I remembered the joint burning in Ryan's hand the first time we met. A grown man costumed in a headdress with a bumblebee for a girlfriend on New Year's Eve. "He works at the Fillmore and the Warfield," I said, hoping I got the names right.

"Of course he does." Her voice was sluggish, deflated. "Do what you want, Lemon, but I won't send you money. I won't write letters to the school. If you think you're so grown-up, you can take care of the details on your own."

Which seemed fair enough. I looked at the stained floor and dug my toe into the carpet. "It won't be long. Another week, maybe two," I lied.

"Find a doctor at least. You'll need another ultrasound eventually. You'll be able to find out the baby's sex next time if you want." It still surprised me that Stella was tracking the baby, and it made me miss her even if she hadn't said exactly what I wanted.

She didn't say, *This will turn out for the best. I believe in you.* She never said, *I understand.*

"It won't be long," I repeated, thinking if I said it enough times one of us might begin to believe it. "I'll call again soon," I told her right before she said she loved me.

Afterward, I read for a while, dozing in and out of sleep, but then the couple in the room next to mine started up again, the woman groaning and the man crying out in staggered rhythms. I didn't want to hear their thumping and clawing on the other side of the wall—it sounded lonely and desperate—so I took a shower and decided to walk to the purple house even though I'd already missed dinner. I arrived around seven, and when Cassie opened the door she just looked at me and shrugged.

"We already ate," she said, which made me feel like crap and wasn't exactly an invitation to come inside, but I followed her up the stairs anyway and into the living room again, where the air smelled like burgers and hash browns.

Ryan and Cassie were both on the couch, so I sat in the recliner across from them and apologized for missing dinner. I said something lame about it having been a really long day, and Ryan took one look at me and asked, "So are you a troublemaker? A delinquent?" which seemed like a pretty hypocritical question coming from a guy who had been at the same New Year's party as me the night before.

Cassie said, "Ryan, don't," but I couldn't let it slide.

"I'm not confident enough to be a troublemaker," I told him. I wasn't bold enough to earn the label, even if I did look like one to Ryan and Cassie as I sat across from them.

"Does Stella know you're here?" he asked, and I nodded. "So you're sixteen and knocked up, and you came to San Francisco with some friend on the 'hound?" His voice was flat, cold. "Shouldn't you be in school or something?"

I nodded and said, "I turned seventeen in September," and he looked at the floor, embarrassed, maybe, that he'd gotten the math wrong. And then I added, "My friend left today. Emmy went back east this morning."

Cassie sighed and leaned forward, perching her elbows on her knees, and Ryan said, "Holy shit."

I tried to think of something to say that would make my situation sound less desperate than it was. "Her dad is on his way home from Afghanistan because he got his leg blown off.

It's okay, though. I don't have to leave yet as long as I can pay for the hotel," I told them. I eyed the blue and green striped fish swimming in its bowl on the bookshelf next to me.

Ryan said "Jesus Christ" that time and slumped into the couch, and I figured he wished he had that joint again, but he reached over and put his hand on Cassie's leg instead, leaned his head back against the wall, and looked up at the ceiling.

Cassie said, "Well," and I thought she was going to say something important like, *Well, we're glad you're still here,* or maybe even something not that important like, *Well, we've got leftover burgers if you want them,* but she didn't say anything at all for a while as I listened to the lightbulb buzzing in the fixture in the hallway. It was horrible really, that kind of silence sitting on top of us like that, crushing the space separating them from me.

"Well, you can't stay in that hotel alone," Cassie finally said, and I was thankful she thought to say something mildly adult-like, since all I was getting from Ryan was a bunch of cuss words. "She can't stay in the Mission alone, Ryan."

His eyes had been closed for a while, and I was worried he might have nodded off, but then he said "Jesus" again.

I thought they might offer to pay for a nicer hotel with thicker walls so I wouldn't have to listen to all that sex next door, but Cassie said something about an air mattress and that I should save my money for groceries. "You're only here for a little longer, right?" she asked, and I nodded like I had a plan. "So, fine then. That's fine." She looked at me but moved her hand on top of Ryan's where it rested on her leg.

Ryan didn't say anything until I got up to leave, when he shook his head and offered, "Come by tomorrow afternoon. We'll get this sorted out."

I let myself out, and when I was back on the street I looked at the purple house and tried to imagine what it would feel like to wake there in the morning, to call it home, but I couldn't. Of all the places I had moved, I'd never expected to move in with him.

I turned six the year my mother packed us up for the first time and announced that we were moving from the only home I'd ever known. I had spent my entire life in my grandmother's house, and I didn't understand what moving meant. I thought we were going on a trip. I thought we were taking a vacation, maybe because that's what she told me—I don't remember how Stella explained it the first time she moved us. I just remember my grandmother crying as my mother sat on the floor labeling cardboard boxes. SUMMER CLOTHES. PHOTOS. ELECTRONICS. LEMON'S TOYS. We left at night, and it was hot in the car, the trunk tied down with black rope and the windows wide open as we backed out of the driveway. I could smell my mother's shampoo from the backseat when the wind moved into the car, the heat of summertime mixing its humidity with the drugstore scent of garden flowers. She was crying a little, too, I saw it in the side-view mirror when I leaned my head out to wave good-bye to Nan, and when I pulled back in and buckled up like she told me to, Stella reached behind her seat and held my hand.

"We're going to live in a big, beautiful castle," she said, "and I'm going to have a big, beautiful job." She wiped her tears off her face with the back of her wrist and told me about the coin-operated carousel out front of the grocery store we'd go to from then on. She said we would be fine. She said we would be happy. Just the two of us. "New York'll be the start of wonderful things for us, me and you, Lemon," she said, and

I believed her because I trusted her with the kind of blindness only children have.

Back in the hotel room the couple next door were quiet, and I began taking my clothes from the dresser and folding them into neat stacks that would fit easily into my backpack. I thought of how much I loved Stella back then, before the woman in the photo in the shoe and the woman who was my mother did not seem like such different people. She was probably scared when we drove away that night. It was the first time she'd be responsible for me alone, having left my grandmother in the driveway, but mostly I remembered her being happy, the way she drove with one hand and rubbed my leg in the backseat with the other until I fell asleep. She laughed a lot that trip, sang along with songs on the radio, and told me stories from when she was a kid. She was still young then, and I remembered thinking, as a six-year-old, that she would be my greatest friend, my partner. Maybe all children feel like that when they're little, when they don't know better yet. I remembered the distinct comfort of knowing that she loved me, that she had chosen to take me with her, and that I belonged to her. That first move was the only move I remembered making with a sense of security and excitement. With trust. Maybe because it was back before I understood what moving meant. It was before Stella had gotten beat down and sucked up by the job of being a mother, back when she thought raising me might be an easy and adventurous thing. I folded my sweatshirt, the one with the kangaroo pockets, and pressed it into the backpack before cinching the top closed. And I realized that the next day I would move into the first place I chose to live without Stella: my father's home.

The following afternoon I checked out of the hotel and met Aiden at a taquería in the Mission before he had to go to work. We ordered at the counter from a big-boned woman who spoke broken English, and then sat down at the table. I had my backpack with me, so he asked, "You running away again?" with a smile.

I told him about Cassie and Ryan's offer. "I guess I'm moving in with them after lunch," I said, and realized how completely ridiculous it sounded.

"Does your mom know?" Aiden asked.

The woman brought us our foil-wrapped burritos in yellow plastic baskets, and the food smelled so good I almost hated to eat it.

"She knows I came to look for him," I said, which didn't really answer his question. "She gave me his address."

"So they're friends."

"She knew him when she lived here back when she was young. But now he's just another guy she used to sleep with." I unwrapped my burrito and used the plastic knife to slice into the tortilla. Red salsa burst from the skin, and the smell of chicken and cheese rose to my face in the steam. "He's just like the rest of them, all the men she's screwed around with."

"Except he gave her you," Aiden said.

"Except for that, I guess. But she moved us to Pennsylvania before I was born. He never met me before this," I told him.

"I can't figure it out: Which one is the bad guy?" he asked. "Your mom or your dad?"

I shook my head because that's why I was there: to decide and finally have a place to put the blame. "I hate that I never knew him," I said, "which is her fault for making us leave."

I forked a piece of chicken into the tiny plastic cup of sour cream we ordered on the side. "But he didn't follow us, which is his fault for being selfish."

"Burritos aren't for utensils," Aiden said and stabbed at my fork with his, flirting.

"I don't actually want to like him, you know?" I said. "Ryan's supposed to be this loser who wouldn't have been good for us. He's supposed to—" I stopped and tried to work it out. "Meeting him is supposed to prove that Stella and I were better off without him, that we didn't need him. That my mom and I turned out just fine."

"Just like you don't need the father of your baby?"

I nodded. "Ryan's supposed to show me I'm going to be okay without the dad, without Johnny Drinko," I said.

Aiden lifted an eyebrow, picked up his burrito, and peeled the top half of the foil off in one long strip. He took a monstrous bite but stopped midchew to ask, "Why don't you just show yourself you're going to be okay? Why do you need your dad to prove it?"

But I didn't have an answer. At the counter a guy with a buzz cut ordered for himself and a waify girl who stood with her arm slung around his waist. He bent over and kissed her while he waited to sign the receipt.

"Okay," I said, and took a sip of my Sprite, "your turn. What's the story with your family?"

"It's boring, really," he said. "Dad's a doctor in Tiburon. Mom's a painter who teaches workshops. Only child. Well, there was one after me, but he didn't make it, and they never tried again." When he finished his food he crumpled the leftover foil in his fist. "Most of her paintings are sad and angry landscapes, lots of blues and browns. My dad is half-retired.

He only sees patients in his office and doesn't take calls anymore. He spends a lot of time at the racetrack." He reached for the soda we were sharing. "Boring and functional. We're normal—if normal exists."

But normal was exactly what you grew up with until you were old enough to recognize that nothing was actually normal. My normal had been suitcases and road trips, new towns and fresh starts. It had been my definition of ordinary.

"How long are you planning on staying?" he asked, changing the subject from him to me. "The band leaves tomorrow for a quick tour up north."

I thought it was his way of telling me he was leaving town. He would abandon me in the city just as I moved in with Ryan. First Emmy, now him. I felt all those beans and cheese and rice hit the bottom of my stomach and settle there like concrete.

"If I can figure out how to finance it, I'd like to stay for a month or so," I told him, realizing it as I said it out loud. "The baby isn't due until July, so I have plenty of time."

"You should get a doctor then, right?" he said, which I thought was sweet, and I told him I planned to find one as soon as I got settled. "Want to walk me to work?" he eventually asked.

Outside, the air was cold and the city was loud as we walked by flea markets and stands selling seaweed and dumplings and knockoff designer handbags. Aiden carried my backpack as we navigated through the crowd.

"What about school?" he asked, and I told him I was a senior, and that I should have been graduating that spring.

"I'll have to make up the semester if I stay here, but it doesn't really matter. I wouldn't be going to college next year anyway. Not with the baby."

We crossed through an intersection, and Aiden moved in closer to hear me over the sounds of the street. "I think kids in America go to college too young," he said. "I've got friends who went right after high school, not because they were ready but because that's what they thought they were supposed to do. But they got there and screwed the whole thing up," he said. "In Europe it's called a gap year: the time between high school and college when you figure out what you want. I like that," he said, and he pulled a cigarette out of his pack and held it up to me. "Is this okay?" he asked, and he lit it with a red lighter after I nodded.

"Is that what you're doing, a gap year?" I asked even though I knew most kids graduate when they're eighteen, and Aiden was twenty-one.

"I left Tiburon and moved to the city after high school." He smoked with one hand and used the other to nudge me around the corner when we turned onto Valencia Street. "I took a couple of classes but never committed. I don't know what I want to study, so for now I'm happy just to work. I really like writing music reviews and managing the band. The pizza gig's not that bad either. Good leftovers," he said. "It's nice just to be on my own, to give myself some time to figure out what I want." He took a slow drag and blew the smoke toward the street. "I don't know why people are in such a hurry," he said, and I wasn't sure if he meant the crowds moving by us on the sidewalk or the kids who went to college right away. "You should finish high school, though. When you can, you should go back. It'd be a rip-off not to. You deserve to finish," he said. "You're so young after all, still just a minor," he teased. "You've got lots of time to decide about college, but everyone needs a high school degree."

We were about a block from the pizza shop by then, and I recognized the Victorians like Ryan's and the cafés and markets of the neighborhood.

"The band leaves tomorrow for a quick tour up north," he repeated. "The keyboardist works for his uncle at a bookstore down on Twentieth, and I usually cover his shifts if I don't go on tour, but I thought maybe you could do it. Since you need the money."

"Are you going too?" I asked.

He shook his head. "Can't take off from work," he said. We were in front of the pizza place by then, and he gestured to the door. "The boss just fired a cook, so he needs the help." Then he explained that since the owner of the bookstore was the keyboardist's relative, he didn't care who worked the shifts as long as someone covered them. "If you can work a register and the numbers even out at the end of the day, he couldn't give a shit," he said. "The boss pays my friend, and my friend'll pay me, and I'll give the money to you. I can even pay you up front if you're interested," he said, and I told him that I was.

It was time for him to leave me, and I hoped he might kiss me right there on the sidewalk, the pizza shop on one side of us and Ryan's house on the other. I wanted him to close those green eyes and put his hand behind my back, pull me to him so our faces merged and our mouths intersected. I wanted to taste him, to smell his skin mixed with mine as he kissed me. But he didn't.

Instead he slid the backpack off and said, "Hang in there," and looked at the purple house across from us. "I'm here if you need me," he said, and he tilted his head down so that our foreheads met, his eyelashes brushing mine. "I'm right here," he said again, and I believed him.

BOOK THREE
Roots and Wings

The world will freely offer itself to you. To be
unmasked, it has no choice. It will roll
in ecstasy at your feet.
—Franz Kafka

CHAPTER SIXTEEN

CASSIE ANSWERED WHEN I KNOCKED, and she was wrapped in a towel, her long legs disappearing beneath a strip of cream-colored fabric that barely covered anything. Her face was dewy, her cheekbones flushed with heat, and her afro was wet and matted to her head.

"I figured it was you," she said, and then, "I had to shower, and Ryan's gone to work." She backed away and made room for me inside. "I don't usually answer the door half-naked. Just for the record."

I followed her up the stairs and kept my eyes on the grimy carpet as we moved to the second floor, the stains littering each landing like birthmarks, or scars of nights from the years they had lived there. She left me in the living room so she could get some clothes on, and I put my backpack on the couch and looked through the bookshelves while I waited for her to return. I ran my hand along the spines of hardbacks written by people I had never heard of: Walker Percy, Henry Miller, Annie Proulx, D. H. Lawrence, Charles Bukowski. I tapped my fingernail on the fishbowl. It didn't seem right only having one fish there in the bowl moving aimlessly among plastic plants, and I wondered if he was lonely. Cassie came out of the bedroom then and stopped in the doorway, eyeing me by the books.

"I keep meaning to weed through them and get rid of the ones we don't need, but Ryan won't let me. He says he wants to keep them, even though he's read them all a million times."

I backed away from the shelf and looked at her, nodding as if I already knew about Ryan's love of books.

"You can borrow any you like. Most of them were here when I moved in." She shrugged. "Want a tour?"

She showed me their bedroom at the end of the hall, a small space with a bay window, a bed with sheets untucked, and a dresser painted forest green. I could feel the heat of her shower still hovering in the bathroom when we got there, and she pointed out an empty shelf in the medicine cabinet she'd cleaned off for my stuff.

"Towels," she said when she opened the closet in the corner. "Extra toilet paper and washcloths."

We passed by the living room and moved into the doorway next to it, a dining room with another bay window facing Valencia Street below us. I stood by the glass and wondered whether, if I looked hard enough, I could see Aiden through the window on the other side of the road, working behind the register.

"We thought you could sleep here," Cassie said, and she straightened a photo hanging slanted on the wall, a black-and-white shot of a crowded street market. "We use this room the least. It always felt too big to me."

I watched two kids wearing leather and spikes standing on the street below us as a woman walked past them, talking on her cell phone. On the other side of Valencia, a man in a wheelchair pushed his way by a heavy-booted hipster walking down the pavement, his head tucked beneath a beanie.

Cassie perched in the doorway behind me, and when I turned around she asked, "You're in high school, right?"

I nodded.

"Do you like it?"

I liked seeing Emmy at the end of a crowded hallway, and bumping my way through the sea of students so I could spend the three-and-a-half minutes between classes with her talking about nothing, making her laugh. I liked the schedule of being in school, knowing what each day was going to look like even though I'd been just as ready as the next kid for winter break when it finally happened. I liked knowing I was supposed to be somewhere every day and that eventually someone would notice if I stopped showing up. And I liked Chloe Ford, the books she picked for us, the debates she instigated, and the way she could convince me I had something worthwhile to say even when I didn't think I did.

"I like some of it," I told Cassie. "I took wood shop in the fall, and I liked that. I made a spice rack. I wanted to take it again next semester so I could make a bookshelf, but you're not allowed to take it twice."

"That's a dumb rule," she said, and I agreed.

"Ryan made me a step stool once." She smiled and looked at the floor. "Didn't make a lot of sense, since I'm just about as tall as he is, but it was sweet. Watching him nail the pieces together, helping him measure the wood. It broke last summer when a friend of ours borrowed it to build his Burning Man float." She shrugged and shifted her weight to one leg. "Look, I know this is weird, for me and Ryan too, but it's probably good you spend some time together. I mean, you're family, right?" she said, and I wondered if I was supposed to answer, but before I had a chance she added, "I never even knew. He doesn't talk much about her, about your mom." She touched the edge of the picture frame again, adjusting. "And he never mentioned you."

I turned my back to her. "She never talks much about him either." And then I waited until I heard her move down the hall to the bathroom before I turned around again, the tears like a liquid fog filling my vision. The house was cold, and I suddenly missed my home in West Virginia, the antique desk in my bedroom that Stella and I found at a flea market, and the smell of my mother's lotions and perfumes in the bathroom. I missed my grandmother's red and gold quilt that we kept on the couch for winter nights—the fabric now thin and stained from all the moves.

Ryan's dining room wall was lined with wooden shelves, and I eyed the stacks of CDs, movies, and magazines, and the spines of more books I had never heard of. A glass vase sat empty on the mantel with a shoebox full of sheet music resting next to it. There was a long table pushed against the wall in the corner, and under it I saw the air mattress folded and deflated with a pile of blankets and a pillow stacked on top. I went to the kitchen and sat at the little wood table, flipped through a copy of *Rolling Stone* and read an article on Terence Blanchard that'd been dog-eared and circled. The interview said he was a trumpet player who wrote music for

Spike Lee, that he'd studied with Ellis Marsalis at the New Orleans Center for Creative Arts. "Ellis Marsalis" was circled in red ink. The photo of Blanchard had been shot on a crowded stage of black musicians, his cheeks puffed up with air as he played the horn.

I wondered if these were the kind of men Cassie dated before Ryan, black men with beautiful lips, long hands, and an appreciation for art and music. I couldn't imagine what Ryan, the stringy stoner with heavy eyes, could possibly give Cassie, and I wondered what she might have seen in him to love. A man who kept his own kid a secret. A father who didn't know his daughter's birthday. A boy who hadn't figured out how to grow up. Outside, tires squealed, someone yelled in Spanish, and I listened to the sounds of the city leaking through the walls as I pulled my cardigan around me and checked to make sure the window by the fridge was shut. The fire escape looked rusted, unstable, and endless as it disappeared above the windowsill.

"Ryan's in charge of setup and prepping the bar tonight," Cassie said from the doorway. She had the red lips on again, and the red leather boots, but this time she wore them over black leggings and a tight gray sweater dress that hugged her hip bones.

She was the most beautiful woman I'd ever seen up close.

"He'll be home early, but I'm closing. Help yourself to whatever's there." She nodded to the refrigerator. "Oh, and this." She handed over a key and a business card. "For the front door, and the name of a doctor for the baby. She's good—I've been using her for years," she said before she turned and disappeared down the hall. Once I heard her lock the door behind her, I sat down. The card listed the address and number for Lynn Harrison, MD, Gynecology.

I unpacked my backpack in the dining room and stacked my clothes in piles on the table before I took a shower. The towels smelled like mildew, and the shampoo was a generic brand of a summer smell I figured Cassie picked out. I ran the bar of white soap over my body even though it was dented and littered with tiny hairs, and I tried to relax, but the water pressure was weak and cool. I was an intruder trying to piece together a father from the disposable razor on the ledge of the sink and the pint glass full of pocket change on a table in the hallway. All the details of his house—the photos and the magazines and the powdered lemonade in the pantry—none of it made me feel like I knew Ryan any better. He could be anyone. Anyone. And I figured I would leave knowing just as little as when I got there.

I missed Emmy, and the way she always tried to make me laugh when she knew I was sad. I missed the four-leaf-clover necklace, the way it made me feel better when I saw it resting on her skin.

It was still cold when I went back to the living room and sat on the floor, thinking maybe it would've been easier if I'd left the past alone, left it behind like Stella always did. She told me once that looking back got you nowhere and that I'd spend my life tripping over shadows if I never moved away from all my questions.

"Forward movement is the only true movement, baby," she said once with conviction. "Haven't you learned anything?"

But she was tired and sad when she said it, and I was only thirteen, so I never did believe her. Not until that night, when I began to wonder if meeting Ryan would change anything at all. I would leave San Francisco still pregnant, and he would stay in California. A nonfather. An absent parent. And the baby would never have a dad, just the same as me.

It was dark by the time I left the house for dinner, but the Mission was filled with cars and restaurants and art kids moving through the streets. I was tired and maybe a little lonely, but I wouldn't let myself look in the pizza shop for Aiden and decided to find the bookstore where I would start working the following week. I headed toward Twentieth Street, but the neighborhood was darker than I remembered from when I'd explored it with Emmy, so I lost my nerve and ended up sticking close to the house and ducking into a Mexican place for dinner. I'd read that beans were good for the baby, full of folate and iron needed for development, and I figured I probably hadn't been eating what I should have.

I'd never eaten in a restaurant alone, so I asked for a table near the window and rushed my order, picking the first thing I saw that looked good. There were Christmas decorations on the walls, and a man in a small-brimmed cowboy hat wandered through the rows of tables playing music. Razor-tipped boots, a clean black-and-white suit, and dark eyes. My waitress was a curvy woman, and when she put my food on the table she smiled.

Next to me a family of four spoke Spanish, the syllables flicking off their tongues between noisy laughter. The son pulled a video game from his coat pocket, but the father snatched it from the boy's hands and gave it to the woman, who put the game in her purse while the little girl rolled her eyes. The son sulked until his food came, and the father drank tequila over ice. Halfway through dinner the mother had to clean salsa from the little girl's dress where her burrito had leaked onto her lap. I watched them as I ate, but when the father caught me staring, I looked away.

When I got back to the house, Ryan was asleep on the couch, the quilt thrown down by his feet and a book cracked open across his chest. There was music coming from the bedroom, reggae that time, but Cassie wasn't there, so I sat in the recliner in the living room and watched him. I looked for things in me that were his and realized Stella was right about the eyebrows—his were full and bushy just like mine. I wondered if Stella had seen him every time she looked at me, if she still missed him or if she'd let him go by the time I'd grown his traits. I figured all that moving, the running to and running from, always had something to do with him.

Eventually I leaned over and took *Less Than Zero* from his chest. The novel smelled like water and sawdust when I flipped the cover open, and then I turned the page and saw the inscription scrawled in pencil. My mother's messy cursive read, "Happy Birthday, Ryan. Maybe LA next? For now and everything after, ambiguous and infinite, absolute . . ." and next to it the year was neatly printed in a different handwriting: 1991. I imagined Ryan adding the date afterward, wanting to place them somewhere in time. I put the book back and went to the shelf, pulled *The Rum Diary* down, and found her words scrawled on the first page. Upper right-hand corner, my mother claiming it with her writing: "For Ryan, just because I love you. Add San Juan to the list . . ." The next three I checked were all marked by her with similar inscriptions. *Dharma Bums* was there too, one of my favorites. "Matterhorn Peak? I'll go if you go . . ." Stella's signature imagining all the places she wanted him to take her, the trips she hoped to make. And I realized I'd been wrong: He hadn't erased her by then. My mother was still in every room. All the books were gifts from Stella, pieces of her lined up on wooden shelves, and he'd read every one of them. He hadn't let her leave him so easily after all.

CHAPTER SEVENTEEN

WHEN I WOKE IN THE MORNING, Ryan was still sleeping on the couch, and Cassie was in the kitchen making coffee. She filled a mug, sat at the table, scanned the *San Francisco Chronicle*, and settled on an article about a peace rally scheduled for later that week. I hovered and read over her shoulder, and thought of Emmy's dad and of Nelson and Bobby Elder's family. The article listed the streets in town that would be closed and the alternate bus routes to use on the day of the protest. I had never been in a place that actually had peace rallies, and it was pretty remarkable to see how organized and calm the city was about the whole thing. I moved to the fridge, got a glass of milk, and thanked Cassie for the doctor's number.

She closed the paper. "Did you make an appointment?"

"I left a message yesterday," I said, and took a banana from the counter and held it up, asking permission.

She nodded, so I tore open the bruised yellow skin and took a bite.

"How do you feel?" she asked.

"Full," I said automatically. "Like a shoe a size too small for the foot that's wearing it."

She smiled. "I like that. You're funny," and then she got up and went to rinse out her coffee mug as I sat down at the table. "I was pregnant once," she said when the water was off again, and she turned to me and leaned her back against the sink. "I lost it, though. Didn't last the first trimester." She was looking past me then, over my shoulder and out the window, maybe at the fire escape designated for emergencies only. "I always figured Ryan could make a beautiful baby," she said just before her face shifted, the muscles flat and tight as her eyes returned to me. "I didn't know he already had."

I imagined her colors mixed with his, a flawless cinnamon child, smooth skin, dark eyes, and a tiny perfect nose.

"I've got a photography class all day, but Ryan'll be around." She picked up the paper again and folded it. "It's Sunday so he'll be heading to the Haight. You should go along."

I waited in the kitchen until I heard her shut the front door, and then I found Ryan in the living room, *Less Than Zero* in his hands. "What's his name?" I asked as I leaned against the door frame and looked at the fish swimming circles in his bowl.

Ryan's hair was parted down the middle and hung messily around his face, framing the creases in his forehead. "Blue Heaven, for a place in Key West, a bar I went to once."

He was thin shouldered and thin waisted, all sharp edges and ninety-degree angles stooped on the couch. My height was his, but my curves were Stella's.

"Sleep okay?" he asked as he traded the book for a glass of water on the table.

I nodded and searched for similarities between him and the other men Stella had been with. He seemed careless and casual with his long, knotted hair and his face tanned and stubbled. Denny had been all tattoos and mustache, and Rocco was hair product and cheap business suits, a gold chain hanging from his neck. Ryan looked more like Simon than any of the others.

"I kind of got a job," I said. "A bookstore. A few shifts for a few weeks," I told him because I wanted him to know I'd be staying for a while. I couldn't leave until he gave me something to convince me we'd been better off without him. Or even something to convince me we hadn't.

"You didn't have to do that. We can pay for what you need," he said. "It's no big deal."

I thanked him but said I was glad to have something to keep me busy while I hung around. I looked at him and he looked at the floor, my mind coming up empty when I tried to think of something else to say.

"I play music on Haight Street on Sundays," he said eventually. "You can come along," he offered, "if you don't have plans." He said he had a trumpet and he'd been playing every weekend for as long as he could remember. "I do it on the street so Cassie doesn't have to listen," and then he smiled.

"She's really beautiful," I told him.

He said they met down at the bus stop on Fillmore back when he was twenty-eight, and I nodded like I knew him then. "She'd just lost her little brother, a hit-and-run in Bakersfield," he told me, and I tried to imagine her when she was young and suffering through grief. "She was pretty beat up about it when I met her, and had fled to San Francisco to distract herself."

Just like Stella, I thought, and I wondered what Ryan had fled from, if he had done the same. I wondered if he had been Cassie's rescuer or the other way around.

"We take good care of each other," he said. "I still can't believe she puts up with me. I'm lucky to have her as my partner in crime," and I nodded as if I understood what it was like, to be in a relationship that made life easier to endure.

We agreed to leave around eleven for Haight Street, and then I asked if it was okay to use the phone to call my friend in West Virginia.

"I've got my own cell, but the battery's dead," I told him.

"Mi casa es su casa," he said.

The cord on the kitchen phone was long enough to stretch into the dining room, where I sat on the air mattress and punched the number for Emmy's. I had found the toy car from Jonah the day before when I unpacked, and I rolled it across the blond floorboards between my legs while I waited for Emmy's voice to break the distance. She picked up on the third ring, and her breath was quick and hurried like she'd just come in from being somewhere else.

"Hey there," I said, and then she said, "Lemon Raine, my personal superhero," which meant she was in a good mood, that maybe she'd already forgiven me for the one-way bus ticket. She told me she'd just gotten in from Dylan's—he was helping her prep for a chemistry test—and it was the perfect time for me to call.

I asked how she was doing.

"Well, I'm not lying facedown in the bathtub, if that's what you mean. I'm not sticking my head in the oven," she said, and I imagined her in her bedroom, sitting on the floor, the tan carpet stretched around her like a field of sand. "Give me some good news. Are you banging the pizza boy yet?" she asked.

"Jesus, Emmy, no. I just met the guy." I paused and tried to figure out the best way to tell her how much he was starting to mean to me without sounding totally squishy and lame. "It's been good to have him around. It's like he actually enjoys keeping me company. He's pretty incredible, really," I told her.

"Lucky Lemon," she said. "You know, I can actually hear you smiling," and then she added, "Dylan and I can't keep our hands off each other now. He quit smoking pot and now he thinks he loves me. He's gone all straight edge, but it's really kind of sweet," she said. "I think he felt shafted when we didn't invite him to California. He missed us a ton while we were gone," and the way she said "we" made me realize that aside from being Emmy's boyfriend, Dylan was a good friend to me too. Someone who'd be there waiting when I decided to go back.

I told her about moving into the eggplant-colored house and about the temp job at the bookstore.

"Tell me it's not a chain," she said.

"I'm not that desperate for money. Yet. Aiden set it up, so I'm guessing it's an indie that sells books and novels by amazing authors most people have heard of."

"That's my girl," she said.

I didn't mention Ryan's books, since I wasn't sure yet how I felt about knowing he had kept them all like that, about the discovery that my mother had imagined traveling with him, all the places she had wanted to go. It seemed to be another thing I'd stolen from her, the possibility of touring the world with Ryan, of being independent and free, and that made me feel guilty somehow. Every book she bought for him was her way of planning their future together, of picking new places for them to go to. But then she got pregnant and just walked away.

I told Emmy I found out Ryan played the trumpet, which seemed a little lame since I'd imagined him a drummer.

"So he's full of surprises. You think he's a loser just like Stella told you?" she asked.

I said I hadn't decided yet. "I'm not sure what'll be worse, really. Liking him or not. If he turns out to be wonderful, I'll never forgive my mother," I said. "And if he's a loser . . ." I tried to find the words, but Emmy finished for me.

"It'll break your heart," she said, and I nodded even though she couldn't see me. Eventually I asked about her dad, who'd arrived at Walter Reed.

"My mom's in D.C.," she told me. "Dad's had one surgery so far, but he needs one more. They say he'll be there for another month or so, and then he'll get a leg. A plastic one, I guess." She stopped and I waited, listened to her breathing. "After that it'll be all outpatient, learning to walk again and stuff."

I could hear Ryan in the kitchen, on the other side of the wall, as he opened a cabinet and put a dish on the counter. I pushed Jonah's car away from me and watched it bounce off the molding and flip over on its side.

"Mom and I saw Stella walking the other day," Emmy said, shifting the subject.

"Walking where?" I asked, and I imagined her car broken down on the side of the road, my mother stomping through snowbanks on her way home with grocery bags or a new set of paint from the art store.

"No, just walking," Emmy said. "Like Forrest Gump or something. Walking just to walk."

"I don't know what that means," I told her.

"I'm serious. We pulled over and asked if she needed a ride, but she said something about getting fresh air, about exercising. I swear to God, Lemon, your mother was wearing tennis shoes."

I tried to imagine it, but it was hard. I'd never seen Stella in tennis shoes before, and I had definitely never seen her voluntarily break a sweat, let alone exercise in the middle of the winter.

"She also said she misses you like crazy, Lemon." There was a long pause before Emmy told me she had to get going, which I hated, but then she added, "I miss you too, just like family." And when I couldn't say anything because I almost started crying, she said, "Make sure you come back eventually. I just might slit my wrist if I have to make new friends," which made me laugh. I found my voice and told her I'd call again soon.

We left the house at eleven and found two seats in the back of the bus. Ryan sat in front of me with his black trumpet case propped up next to him and said he liked to play the horn for extra money, liked to have somewhere to be on Sundays.

"It keeps me out of trouble on Saturday nights." He smiled. "Can't be up playing music in the morning if I don't keep tabs on myself the night before." We moved north away from the Mission, and he sat sideways, leaning against the window with his arm lying across the headrest between us.

Eventually, I leaned forward and asked, "Where did you grow up?" It was something I should've known.

He shrugged as if he couldn't remember and looked at the exit door on the other side of the aisle. At the next stop, a hippie in a patchwork skirt slid in without paying. She flipped the middle finger to a man on the curb with a grocery cart before the door shut and we pulled away.

"Mother pisser," she said loudly.

I looked down at a chewed-up piece of gum wedged into a crevice on the floor.

"Montana," he said finally. "You've got no grandparents left on my side, but that's where they used to live."

I'd never thought of grandparents or of being related to people related to Ryan. "What'd they used to do?" I asked as I imagined cattle and cowboys, rows of cornfields, and tomatoes the size of softballs.

"My dad was a truck driver, worked seven days on and seven days off when I was growing up," he said. "My mom was gone by the time I turned fifteen, got tired of his schedule. I didn't blame her, though." He dug his fingernail into a crack in the pleather headrest. "He was an asshole, really. Nothing much to speak of."

The bus stopped again, and a large group of Latino kids were waiting on the corner: boys in black jeans and baseball caps, slick skin and dark eyes.

It was obvious the seats would be full, so Ryan got up and moved in next to me, placing the trumpet in his lap. "This okay?" he asked, and I nodded.

I recognized the moment, the closeness of our bodies, my father's next to mine. His shirt sleeve brushed against me, and he smelled like sweat and the soap from the shower, the white dented bar I used the day before, and I wondered if we smelled the same then.

"I doubt they have anything like this in West Virginia," he said when we turned onto Haight Street. "We'll have to walk from here, unless you want to transfer. It's kind of a trek, but it'll be a good way for you to check out the area."

We got out at the corner of Haight and Fillmore and headed past Thai restaurants and record shops and pipe stores. We trudged up a hill after we crossed Divisadero and made our way past a green and empty park. Then the neighborhood changed, and the sidewalks smelled like pot and were full of stoners and rastas, Emo kids and artists with paintings set up on street corners, begging for change. The buildings were bright pink and purple, a kaleidoscope of colored storefronts squatting next to one another between bars and shoe shops, head shops and tattoo parlors that made me think of Johnny Drinko. Tie-dyes hung in the windows, and the traffic of tourists and local headies clogged the sidewalk. A group of skinny kids huddled in a doorway, selling glass bowls and hemp necklaces they'd laid out on a blanket, and a boy in a wheelchair sat next to Ben & Jerry's with a sign that read THIRSTY. CHANGE FOR BOOZE. Eventually we arrived at Amoeba Music, a place I remembered reading about in the travel book, and I said so when we got there.

"Let's go in," Ryan offered. "I always like to wander in here before I play." He smiled. "Inspiration."

We checked my bag and his trumpet at the door and moved past metal detectors into the main room of the store, where skaters and ravers and hippies meandered up and down the aisles. Amoeba was an endless space filled with rows of CDs and movies and records and tapes, and the walls were plastered with posters, the floors covered by stacks of music and films. It was gritty and crowded and hot inside, and I imagined me and Dylan and Emmy hanging out there every weekend if we lived in the city, standing in the aisle sampling albums through headphones hooked to display shelves, discovering new bands. A group of angsty Goth kids had staked out a corner and were sitting on the cracked concrete floor digging through a plastic bin of CDs, and a few rows down, toward the back of the store, I caught a lanky hipster giving another boy a wad of cash in exchange for a bag of weed.

Ryan came up behind me and nodded to a small stage set up in the side nook of the main room. "Stella and I saw some great music here," he said, and I listened to her name hang inside his mouth. It was strange to hear him say the word so casually, as if he spoke it often.

I tried to imagine Ryan and Stella in the store listening to the music of small bands from the nineties, my mother with long hair and Ryan back when he was younger. Tighter pants, probably, fewer wrinkles carved around his eyes.

Afterward, we crossed the street and stood in front of a grocery store, Cal-Mart, with the parking lot behind us. "It's a direct route to the beach from here," and he nodded in the direction of the Golden Gate Park entrance. He put his case on the sidewalk and snapped it open.

A stack of music sheets lay on top of the horn, and I remembered the box on the mantel and the article marked in *Rolling Stone*. He left the case open and put three dollar bills inside to start it off. I sat on the curb while he wiped down the instrument with an old T-shirt and looked over some songs in the pile of papers. A damp fog had rolled in, and I buried my head in my sweatshirt and looked down at my Converse shoes and then over at his: ratty Pumas, the white stripe brown with mud or booze. It made me realize his night shifts could have been exhausting, as he shuttled band equipment and served beers from behind the bar. I'd never been to a real music venue, but I imagined it was hard work, standing on your feet all night hustling for tips.

"Was it a rough night working the show?" I asked as he organized himself and set the sheet music back in the case.

"You know it," he said, and he ran his hand through his hair, untangling the knots before he pulled it back into a low ponytail.

"But you like it?" I asked. "Working there?"

His response was automatic. "There's nowhere I'd rather work than a place that supports musicians," he said. "It's hard work, but I love the energy of a good show, the way the crowd moves like one big shadow when a band rocks a perfect song, the kind of song you get lost in. When it's hot like that and you know everyone in the room is in the same place, everyone digging the beats and the lyrics and the motion like there's nothing else that matters," he said, his cheeks getting red as he talked, "well, it makes the work worth it, you know?" He smiled, and I noticed the dimple in his left cheek. "I think that's the key, finding a job that's based around the one thing you love the most." He shrugged. "Plus, meeting rock stars is always pretty cool. But what the hell do I know?"

I saw him differently then, working hard so he could pay the rent and work in a place surrounded by people who cared about the same things he did—music and art, I guessed. He was just like the way I imagined Dylan would be, the kind of man who would never hold a nine-to-five and never wear a suit to work, and I realized that didn't make him a loser or a slacker, that maybe it just meant he believed in something more than a big paycheck.

In front of us people wandered down Haight Street, and he settled his legs into a musician's stance and began playing. He started with a slow song that sounded lonely, but then it shifted gears halfway through, and the notes moved like the rain clouds rolling in as one sound toppled over another like wind whipping down the sidewalk. Ryan played with his eyes closed, and I was thankful he couldn't see me staring. The tempo kept increasing, and I could feel his heat above me as he blew into the horn, his cheeks tight and round, his face flushed and deliberate. The music ran in circles, the sounds quick and rushed, punching out into the street, and I watched as he tried to keep up with it, his fingers working hard, as if he couldn't stop them. I could tell he was alone then, that when he played he shut everything else out. If I had walked away, he might not have even noticed, that's how important the music was to him—engulfing and absolute. It was written all over his body, the way he swayed, and the way he never opened his eyes. I wanted to know what he was holding in and what he was shutting out, the emotions weaving through him like water, but then the song slowed down, and I knew it'd end soon when the notes started getting long and mellow and his shoulders loosened up. The last of it was tired and sad again, and when it finally ended I could tell he cared more about that music than I cared about anything, and that bringing me to see him play had been his version of a gift.

I hadn't noticed when it started, but a crowd had gathered on the sidewalk, a small group of hippie kids and the boy in the wheelchair, a crunchy woman with a chocolate lab and a man in a corduroy jacket with leather elbow patches. When

Ryan started the next song, a few of them began dancing, and a teenaged boy emerged with a small drum. He sat on the curb with me, and when my father nodded to him, he began tapping the beat of Ryan's tempo. The woman with the dog was twirling in circles, and two kids in zip-up sweatshirts were clapping with the drum. I don't know when I stood up, but I was on my feet by the third song or so, swaying a little and nodding my head as Ryan kept us moving. He must have felt all that motion, because eventually he opened his eyes, his stare finding me as I smiled and nodded with the music. His lips were wrapped around the horn, but I could tell he was smiling back, his dark eyes meeting mine before he closed them again.

The group clapped a little when Ryan took a break from playing, some of them tossed money in the case, and a woman with pale skin and black hair stashed a pint of Jack Daniels at his feet with a nod. He sucked on the liquor in between songs, until it got too dark for him to see his fingers on the horn. In the end we counted forty-three dollars and packed up all his stuff. Ryan asked if I was hungry when we walked back toward the bus stop, but I figured he was kind of drunk, so I lied and said no, thinking he just wanted to head home.

"I usually work Sundays, but I took tonight off," he said when we were back on the bus. It wasn't very crowded, but he shared my seat that time and leaned against the window. "I don't usually drink when I play, but since I don't have to work . . . ," he said, and I could tell he was embarrassed. "Plus, you make me nervous." He looked out the window, where we watched a kid on the sidewalk bend down to pick up some change. "I don't know why I said that."

"My friend Emmy and I take bottles from Stella sometimes,"

I told him, trying to even out the score. "Vodka. Well, before the baby," I said, and he nodded.

Across the aisle a man began talking to himself. Ryan was slumped in his seat with the horn case on his lap, and I wondered what he was thinking as he looked at the night crowd passing by us. But he didn't say anything until three or four stops later.

"It was like a greenhouse back then, me and Stella. All the people we ran with were transplants, kids who moved to the city to grow into more important versions of themselves."

I held my breath, knowing he was trying to tell me something significant. He took another pull from the bottle and squinted just like Emmy when she took too big a gulp.

"But the city was an obligation. It pushed itself on you and changed you into someone new, whether you wanted it or not. Stella was different when she left," he said, his voice slowing down as he looked at me.

I nodded like I understood.

"We thought we were becoming better people, and building something important, when really we were just bonding over broken pieces, running from our pasts. Carter turned out okay after rehab. Tessa disappeared and went back home, I think, maybe went to college. But with Stella it was different." He looked into his lap. "I thought it was her dad catching up with her, you know? The grief finally hitting home, wedging itself between us. But then she moved away before I got the chance to fix it."

I wanted to touch him then, to put my hand on his arm, but I didn't.

"Your mother was always good at running," he said. "I thought it was a phase, the fighting and the secrets. I thought we were still just getting started, and laying a foundation," he said, and looked away.

I did the math and realized he couldn't have known her for very long before the pregnancy. My mother lived in San Francisco for less than two years, a time frame that seemed too fast when I looked over at Ryan, still longing for answers.

In front of us someone yanked the cord on the bus, and we pulled over to the curb at the next stop. "Please exit through the rear doors," the recording said, a woman's voice.

Ryan didn't say anything more after that, not until we got off the bus in the Mission and headed back to the house. I thought about the photos of my mother in the shoes, the Stella that existed before I came along and she had to move to Pennsylvania. I'd imagined her happy before the pregnancy, before she moved us in with my grandmother and a little happy still before she moved us out again. For me she fell apart when she had to support me on her own, a child she never asked for. But it wasn't that clean or simple, because before she became a mother she was a girlfriend who wasn't sure what she wanted. She was a daughter who'd lost her father. All that movement and sadness was too big to blame on me, and I realized my perception of Stella had been fragmented. And maybe he knew he was doing it or maybe he didn't, but that's what Ryan gave me that night, the understanding that my mother was more than I had recognized, and that I was not to blame for all the sadness I had seen in her while I was growing up. She had been self-contained, sealed shut, and Ryan was helping me split her open. All the way from California, I was learning who she was.

"Does she take good care of you?" he asked as we walked through the streets in the Mission past the bacon-wrapped-hot-dog vendors and the homeless man with dreadlocks. "I mean, I can tell that *you* take care of you, but is she good to you at least?"

And the answer was immediate: "Yes," I told him. Because I knew that as much as she moved around, she would always take me with her if I wanted to go. That as bad as things had been at times, she never made me feel I was alone. And I also knew that she was back home waiting for me to show up. Because that's what good mothers do. They let you go. They wait. And then they take you back.

CHAPTER EIGHTEEN

I CALLED STELLA A FEW DAYS LATER: THE evening after I'd had my first doctor's appointment in San Francisco, and the day before I was scheduled to work my first shift at the bookstore.

She answered with, "Say you're on the road. Say you're almost home." She sounded tired.

"I'm not on the road," I said.

I heard her sigh and mumble "Jesus Christ," but I wanted to tell her the truth.

"I'm at Ryan's," I said and explained I couldn't afford the hotel once Emmy left for West Virginia. "I'm staying here until I'm ready to come back."

I was worried she'd be angry, but mostly she just sounded sad. "It just doesn't feel right having you so far away," she said, and I could tell she was in a muted mood, one of the ones that arrived on off days when she was feeling lonely.

I tried to distract her and talked about the doctor's appointment I'd had the day before and about taking the Muni to the hospital in the morning, the electric bus hooked to wires strewn throughout the city. I told her that the doctor had reviewed my files faxed from West Virginia and the nurse had weighed me in at one hundred thirty pounds.

"Is that good?" Stella asked, and behind her I heard Pace barking.

"I've gained six pounds. It sure doesn't feel good, but yeah, it's average I guess."

I told her about the heartburn and the Zantac prescription and the blood work, but I didn't tell her about all the fainting, and she didn't ask how I'd found a doctor, which I was glad for. I figured knowing I was living with Ryan was hard enough—she didn't need to know about the girlfriend with perfect chocolate skin and a kick-ass wardrobe.

"School started Tuesday," she said, but I ignored her and asked if Simon was around and how things were going with them.

"The North Face hired him for another product shoot, so he's working a lot," and then she yelled at Pace to shut the hell up, her voice flipping to anger when the barking wouldn't stop. "I miss having him around. I miss knowing where he is," she said.

I asked if she'd told him that, and I could almost hear her shrug.

"He knows how much I care about him. And the work stuff is a good thing. It'll pass," she said, which struck me as an unusually grown-up perspective for Stella to have when a man wasn't paying enough attention to her. "I just wish I got to see him more often," she said.

"Emmy said you're exercising," I told her.

"I'm thirty-six years old, Lemon. It's time for some personal maintenance." She sighed. "There's nothing hot about a beer gut, no matter how you slice it."

"I didn't know you knew how to exercise," I said, trying to lighten things.

"Don't be smart. Aging, unfortunately, is not an option, it's a guarantee. I figured it was time I tried to make it as smooth a process as possible. Plus, I'm about to be a grandmother—I've got to get my shit together. You have no idea how much energy it takes to keep up with a kid."

It was bizarre to think of Stella as a grandmother, but that was exactly what I was about to make her, and I realized we were both preparing for new roles.

"I'm not okay with this," she told me, and I wasn't sure if she was still talking about her getting older or about me living with Ryan, but then she said, "I don't know why I let you go in the first place. I don't even know why you left."

But she wasn't talking loud enough, her voice was diluted, and I couldn't tell what she said after that, the words lost between the telephones. I almost told her I went to California to find my father, but that wasn't really true. He was never lost, since I always figured he was in San Francisco, where she deserted him. And then I almost said I left to find a new home, but that wasn't true either, because by then I'd realized Stella was home. That her being there, wherever "there" was, made it my home. Maybe I'd left to find her, to find out who she'd been before she became my mother. And I'd left to find me, to figure out what kind of person I hoped to become.

But I didn't say any of that. "I met a boy," I said instead, and then I told her about Aiden and about working for a few weeks in a bookstore so I could afford the bus ticket back, which I hoped she'd like the sound of.

"We talk every day until then," she decided. "From now on you check in every morning. That's what the cell is for."

I sat on the air mattress with the ridiculous shiny blue phone to my ear and thought of how much she was worrying and how she needed to know I was safe even though she was angry, how she probably felt so far away, such lack of control. So I told her I would call every day before I went to work, which seemed to settle her.

"Is he taking care of you?" she asked, and I thought of how I hadn't paid for any groceries, and how every night since I'd gotten there Ryan had left me bus money on the kitchen table before he left for work.

"He's not that bad of a guy," I said even though I knew she wanted something else.

"I never said he was."

But I wouldn't let her get away with that. "Yes, you kind of did."

I listened to her breathing, the dog quiet then. "I didn't leave because he was a bad guy," she said, her stories getting muddled as I thought of all the things she'd told me through the years. "I was a kid. And he was not a father."

I realized Ryan was probably just a little older than Aiden when she moved us in with my grandmother.

"We hardly knew each other. I was just a kid," she said again, tired and slow.

It was almost nine thirty there, her voice separated from

mine by three time zones' worth of space, and I wondered why she was home and not out drinking with her girlfriends.

"I left for me. For me and you, and for what I thought was best then," she said. "I didn't leave because of him."

It seemed to be the most honest thing she'd told me about their past.

"I miss you," I said.

And I did.

I called her almost every morning from then on. She talked about her painting class, and I talked about my job and about living in the city. I told her about the bacon-wrapped hot dogs, which I'd finally tried with Aiden, and she told me about the views of the Blue Ridge Mountains when she and Simon went snowshoeing. I asked her to paint it, and she asked me to buy a disposable camera and document my time in San Francisco.

"Nothing looks exactly as it does the first time you see it," she said.

She also asked me to come home. Almost every morning we talked she told me it was time, and I told her I wasn't ready.

The bookstore was a mellow job, and I spent the rest of the week alphabetizing novels and ringing up customers for eight-fifty an hour, working for a guy named Miller, the keyboard-ist's uncle, who Aiden introduced me to on my first day at the shop. The training was nonexistent.

"You know how to run a register?" Miller asked, and I nodded. He looked me over long and hard. "You an honest kid?" I said I was, and then Aiden said I was, then Miller said, "That's fine, then, she'll do," and he disappeared into his office, shutting the door behind him.

"Welcome to the working world," Aiden said.

"Looks good to me," I told him, and then I took out the disposable camera I'd recently bought and snapped a photo of the bumper sticker plastered in the center of Miller's office door: YOU'RE EITHER ON THE BUS OR OFF THE BUS.

Aiden showed me what to do, and I never saw much of Miller after that. It worked just like Aiden said: He paid me, and I assumed the keyboardist paid him.

I liked the routine of stocking shelves, the smell of the books, and the customers who came in with long lists of authors and poets I had never heard of. I picked novels and read them in the back during my breaks, books about musicians and short stories about families in the Midwest living on ranches, trying to survive the storms of the landscape. I read Tom Wolfe because Aiden said that's where Miller's bumper sticker quote came from, and I read Kurt Vonnegut because Ryan mentioned liking his books back when he was my age. I also read Flannery O'Connor, since Emmy told me Ms. Ford had assigned them her collection of short stories for class. The job grounded me and gave me a schedule and a place to be each day, and it felt good to engage with the city in that way. I usually met Aiden for dinner after work, and we ate Cuban meals or shared tapas, split leftover pizzas at the shop, or tried different taquerías in the Mission, a place I became more impressed with the longer I stayed there. The days moved quickly, and I rarely saw Cassie or Ryan, since I left for work in the morning and they worked the venues at night.

"You have everything you need?" Ryan asked when we

passed in the hallway. "You eating okay?" he'd say. "Getting enough sleep?"

And nothing felt all that significant until the following week, when I woke to the sound of my cell phone ringing in the kitchen, where I'd left it the night before to charge. I was off the air mattress quickly and picked up on the fourth ring, wondering if I was the only person home.

"Lemon," she said, "it's Doctor Harrison." My heart dropped to my stomach as I moved to the chair at the table and sat down.

Ryan came into the kitchen, nodded groggily, and began searching through the cabinets.

She said she knew that one of the nurses had already called the week before, "but I wanted to follow up and make sure you didn't have any questions."

"I haven't heard from anyone," I told her, and she mumbled, "Oh, God," and then, "I'm sorry you weren't contacted sooner."

Ryan pulled a box of Honey Nut Cheerios out of the cupboard, and I watched him as he stood in his boxers with his long hair tangled, his face still marked by the crease of his pillow. He turned his back to me, and I eyed the lines of muscles toned and tight, noticed a small scar below his right shoulder blade. It was the first time I'd seen him stripped like that.

"You're anemic. Your iron count's too low," Dr. Harrison said, and I thought of all the dizziness, and of fainting at the concert and at the house that first night. It seemed so long ago. "You should be taking supplements, and you've got to pay attention to your diet."

I vaguely considered looking for a pen and pad of paper to take notes on, but she spoke too quickly, and I missed some of the details.

"Hey, Ryan," I said after I hung up. He turned from the counter and tugged at the top of his boxers. "Where's the closest drugstore?"

We sat across from each other while he ate his cereal, and I told him about being anemic, about having to pick up the pills that afternoon and needing to eat more fiber and iron.

"Was she worried?" he asked. "Should you call Stella or something?" he offered.

"I call her every morning before I leave for work," I confessed. "I use my own cell," I said, so he didn't think I'd been racking up his phone bill.

He nodded, and I thought he might be pissed, but he was thinking of something else by then, his forehead wrinkled and his eyes far away. "I missed all that, you know?" he said. "With Stella I never knew if she was sick, if the pregnancy was normal."

I looked at the leftover O's, bloated and soggy in the bowl of milk. "She could have called you," I said even though I kind of thought it should have worked the other way around. He could have called her too, and I decided that, somehow, both of them had failed. The blame didn't belong to just one of them, it was shared.

He shook his head. "It works both ways," he said. "I know that now."

Stella said she'd called him in the beginning, but I wanted to ask how often and why the phone calls stopped, who'd been the one to cut the ties. She was always good at leaving out info she didn't want to deal with, and I wondered if she'd ever gotten in touch with him during the years we moved around, or if he'd ever asked for updates. But instead I said, "Did you miss her? When she left?"

He pushed the bowl away from him. "She was already gone before she left, you know? It wasn't good, things between us. Those last months were wasted time."

I heard Cassie padding down the hallway. She shut the door to the bathroom and turned on the sink.

"I don't know what she told you," he said, and I realized he had no idea how little Stella spoke of him or how strong willed she'd been about keeping him a secret. The information Stella gave me was knotted and tangled and as hard to follow as a ball of fishing line in a neglected tackle box, a kink of nylon wire with no beginning and no end. His story was a pile of hooks and weights locked to one another randomly.

"I never cheated on Stella," he told me, though I hadn't asked. "Not once. It was months after she left before I thought about women again." He looked down, and I followed his eyes. His chest was thin and tanned, his stomach lined with muscle and patches of dark hair.

"Cassie and I came a lot later. And we've got our own problems too, but with Stella—" He stopped, picking words. "I never knew a woman could make you feel so bad. Watching her walk away was like . . ." But he couldn't seem to find the words.

"My grandmother used to say Stella was always like that," I told him. "That she did whatever she wanted—strong willed and determined. Stella thinks I'm the same, that I inherited that from her, and she worries my stubbornness will get me into trouble. When I told her I was leaving, I think she saw herself in me," I said. "But I'm not sure I want them, those traits of hers in me."

Ryan ran his fingers along the edge of the table, his words

slow when he finally said, "The thing about inheritance is that it has nothing to do with choice. It's like fear. You don't always get to pick it for yourself."

Like fear. Or motherhood, maybe.

CHAPTER NINETEEN

AIDEN TOOK ME TO DINNER THAT NIGHT at a Vietnamese restaurant on Sixteenth Street, and even though I'd never eaten Vietnamese food before, I tried to pretend I liked the flavors as I nudged a bundle of tangled yellow noodles around my dish. A pile of green leaves lay buried beneath a mound of red chunky sauce.

"Bánh bao," Aiden said, and he lifted a pocket of food off his plate and put it onto mine. "Steamed dumplings stuffed with vegetables and ground pork."

I tore into the soft casing with my fork and watched the meaty brown sludge fall out of its skin, wondering if Aiden would still like me if I ended up yacking at the table, if it would ruin my chance of him ever kissing me. We spent most of dinner talking about how much I liked working at the bookstore and about how things were going for the band, which had left Seattle and was playing a gig in Portland that night. Eventually I told him about *Less Than Zero* and my mother's inscription to Ryan, about the books in the house being gifts from Stella to him.

"You know, I've never seen my mother with a book. Not once." I'd seen all kinds of things clutched in her hands: vodka cocktails, skinny menthol cigarettes, suitcases and duffel bags, car keys and road maps. But never a book. "It's weird I never thought of it before. As much as I like reading, she's never really encouraged it." My water glass was empty, so I reached over for a sip of Aiden's. "I can't imagine her shopping in a bookstore."

He took the dumpling back, noticing my half, deserted and uneaten. Somewhere in the restaurant a baby started to cry, and a telephone was ringing.

"So she bought them for your dad even though reading was never her thing?"

A waiter answered the phone by the cash register and began speaking in a language I didn't recognize.

"But she never bought books for me or for her," I told Aiden.

I'd seen my mother pack countless times in patterns that had become predictable by then. Our clothes went first, the skirts and sweaters that made her feel beautiful, and the outfits she'd use in the following town to land her next boyfriend. The photos came second, two framed shots of my grandparents and her, back when she was small: a child with big, startling eyes, a father who sold insurance, and a mother who typed medical transcripts for the local hospital. The picture album was always third on the list, the collection of images she kept from our life together, six cities censored down into thirty pages of photos slipped into slots of plastic cellophane. She'd pack the camera and the stereo after that, our small TV, then the microwave wrapped in the bathroom towels. Her makeup and her perfumes came next. But there were never books. She never brought one story with us when we moved away. My love of books was never shared between us; it was shared between me and Ryan. I wondered if that had bothered her all those years, seeing his habits in me even though I'd never met him.

After dinner we sat in Dolores Park, and I told Aiden about Ryan playing on Haight Street and how I thought Ryan loved music as much as I'd seen anyone love anything before. It was dark by then, and the park was mostly quiet, but the city view was lit up by cars and restaurants and all the people moving below us. In the distance I watched the Pyramid building piercing the skyline while I told Aiden I thought Ryan picked his job at the Warfield and the Fillmore just so he could work with musicians.

"I wish I had something like that," I said. "Something to latch on to, something I care so much about," I told him, "that it'd hurt to give it up."

For me reading was the one thing I could never imagine letting go of, the hours of exploring other people's lives through the rhythms and tempos of well-written stories. It was an internal reward, though, where making music for Ryan seemed to be his attempt at giving something away, of putting something into the world that felt important, and I wondered if that's how Stella felt about her painting. I'd never felt like that about anything, not really, and I told Aiden I wondered if that's what the baby would become. If that's what being a mother would give me.

"Something I love so much it hurts," I said, "something that makes me feel like I'm actually contributing in some way," and I wasn't even thinking of it, but that's when he finally kissed me.

His hand was on my knee, his palm grazing my leg, stopping when he squeezed my thigh and leaned in. His tongue was slow and careful inside my mouth as his other hand moved around my back, pulling me to him. His heart hammered against mine through our chests like bass notes of a song, warm and fast and close. It was clean and comforting, a soft bite on my bottom lip, and a rub of his nose against mine before he pulled away. It was everything that being with Johnny Drinko was not, and I knew it was what being with a boy was supposed to feel like when it was a good thing, something right. It felt essential and transformative, like sleep.

We didn't say much on the walk back to Ryan's, but just before he turned to cross the street where he'd left his Vespa after work, he said, "I've been waiting to do that since the first time I saw you."

The house was empty when I got back, and the stomach cramps kicked in just after I fed Blue Heaven and settled on the couch with Ryan's *Rolling Stone*. I wished I'd skipped all the unfamiliar food at the restaurant and had stuck to rice and vegetables at dinner, but then the pain shifted, becoming strong and sharp as it moved in sheets through my stomach. By the time I made it to the bathroom, the bleeding had started. The heat came in full, ripe bursts, blooming in my belly and flowering out across my body, stretching and engulfing me. I took deep breaths and listened to the room, a room crowded by the realization there was nothing I could do to fix this. There

was noise between my ears like a radio caught between sta-
tions, the crackling like fizz or soda bubbles growing louder
as I unwrapped myself until I was nothing but a collection
of nerves, fibers, cells. Water and air. A stagnant space in the
bathroom of my father's home. My mind clenched tight and
caged itself in as the sound became white noise. And then it
was silent. By the time Ryan and Cassie found me on the floor,
I'd settled into the hollowed stillness of sadness.

Phone calls were made. First by Cassie while Ryan helped
me to the bed, and then by Ryan while Cassie helped me into
the taxi. And I sat above the ache of grief and below the fog of
shock, in between, with one word racing through my mind as
we moved through the city to the hospital. StellaStellaStella.

Tests were done, a haze of movement and machines and
voices once I was admitted. I was given pills—"Swallow. Take
a deep breath"—and all the while I was floating away, down
the hall into the parking lot, pushing out of the city and back
over the bridge.

Someone said my mother was taking a plane.

Someone said the baby was gone.

I wanted to know where. "Gone where?" I asked.

"A loss," someone said. "A miscarriage. He's gone."

A boy. *He.* He's gone.

I wondered exactly where he had gone to and had the vague
recognition I'd never seen a cemetery in the city. I wanted to
know where all the bodies went.

Maybe I slept, or maybe the fast-forward movement of
time erupted at full speed, and then Stella suddenly appeared
with her hair loose and hanging, the face of my mother looking down at me: a face of fear and love and memory and hope

and sadness, the face of all the strings that tied me to her. Stella was there the night I lost the baby I never expected to miss as much as I did once he was gone.

I would like to say I don't remember any of it, but that's not true: I remember being cold under the thin hospital gown and blankets. I never stopped being cold. I remember the sound of strangers' voices reading numbers from machines hooked into blue bruises on my arms. I was given medicine, and I was told to wait, it would pass. Pass. I remember Dr. Harrison's breath smelled like coffee and cinnamon, bitter but sweet. I wish I'd found a way to block the feeling of something part-mine and part-not-mine slipping away from me. But I remember the sound of losing the baby and the bright and brilliant ache as my body let go of something that never really fit there in the first place. A baby that wasn't made from all the things children should be made from: love and hope and faith. A baby that happened by accident with a man who scarred skin for a living, the colors of the ink a permanent camouflage. No one would look at me, their eyes stuck to the floor and the machines as I shuttled myself between the hospital bed and the bathroom, their eyes on their hands and their lab coats and their files of paper. Except Stella, whose eyes never left mine.

Afterward I slept, and when I woke she was there just like I knew she would be, sitting in a chair next to the window. It was early morning, and the sun had painted the sky behind her the muted pastel colors of things soft.

"You're okay," she said. And then she repeated it twice.

I looked over her shoulder and wondered if she was right.

"When you were a baby, you hated to sleep," she started. "You'd scream to keep yourself awake, to fight being tired. I half expected your grandmother to kick us out," she said, and then she moved to the bed, sat on the edge, and looked down at me. "Eventually I realized you would sleep in loud places. Restaurants, concerts and clubs, the food court at the mall. I thought it meant you were unshakable. That you needed movement, and that you were born with endurance. I thought it meant I could take you with me wherever I wanted to go and you'd always be able to keep up."

The hospital room was tiled white, the walls around us painted a fresh cream color that made her blue eyes bright, and I thought of ocean waves in summertime heat. She'd cut back on all the boozing since I'd left, and her skin was clear and cool. She looked more beautiful that day than I'd ever seen her look, even under all that sadness.

"I know now that really it meant you longed for assurance, that even as you slept you needed verification the world continued around you. You needed the sounds of voices to prove you were safe." She ran her hand down my arm and circled her fingers around my wrist, covering my hospital bracelet. "But I didn't know how to be a mother, and it took me a long time to realize children need assurance just as much as they need independence."

Outside, a bus went by, strung into the system of wires that stretched across the city. In the cold the cables sounded dry. Like bones or sand.

"I know it's been hard on you," she said, "the way I never put down any roots for us." I looked at her fingers and at the ID bracelet peeking out from underneath, the one bracelet where there should have been two. One for me, and one for the baby, too. "The thing about roots, though, is they tie you down, and I never wanted that for you. I wanted you to feel that you were never bound, that you were limitless, free to change and grow," she said, and she looked around the room as if everything important in the world was shut inside that tiny space. "I never found a place good enough for you. I always wanted something better than where we were, so when things got bad, I would make us leave."

And I tried so hard to believe her, to let her excuse for all that movement make sense, but it didn't really matter if I believed, because after all that time she was finally tearing down the walls and trying to explain why things had been the way they'd been. And that mattered more than the truth.

"You probably think this is for the best, that I didn't become a mom. That it's better this way," I said.

She squeezed my wrist hard then, and I could feel the edge of the bracelet cutting into my skin.

"Nothing was better for me than you," she said. "I finally understood what people meant when they talked about the rewards of responsibility, about perspective and purpose." Her eyes were stripped and wide when she said it. "And the same thing will happen to you when it's your turn. You'll see. It won't be easy, but it'll be worth it."

I loved her too much then, for showing me all that honesty and finally giving me something I could hold on to.

"Emmy sent you something," she said. "I ran into her at the gas station on my way out of town, and when I told her what happened, she gave me this." Stella pulled out a picture from her purse, the photo Emmy took on the trip out to San Francisco: my image pushed up against the bus window with a WELCOME TO CALIFORNIA road sign blurred behind me. I looked happy, a little nervous too, but ready for all the things in front of me. It was the first time I realized I could look beautiful like that.

"You will feel this good again, Lemon," Stella said, but I turned my face away from the picture.

"I feel like a jack-in-the-box. Like my parts are all sprung out and busted," I told her.

She took my chin and turned my face back to the photo. "You *will* feel this good again," she repeated, and I finally let the tears come.

"How can you be sure?" I asked.

"Because you're mine. You know by now the most important thing is to fight for something better than what you have."

And that was her way, that was the reason for all the running. Stella had always wanted something more and had believed we deserved better.

She told me Simon had wanted to come with her, but she'd decided it was best he stayed in West Virginia. "He asked me to tell you that he'll be there when you get back, though, waiting to help take care of you again," she said. "He really cares about us, Lemon." She smiled and shook her head. "God knows how he has the patience for it."

There was a knock on the door, and then Ryan moved into the room, shuffling his feet and chewing on his bottom lip.

"Hey, kid," he said. He had a duffel, and he dropped it on the floor and told me, "I brought some of your things. Stella said to bring clothes. Your toothbrush and stuff."

And then he looked to Stella. "You," he said.

She nodded.

They had spoken by then, on the phone I guessed, a quick call to Stella from his cell when we first left for the hospital, and I tried to imagine him giving her the news, telling her to get a flight.

I'm here, he probably said. Or maybe, *I'm here, but you should be too.*

I watched them watching each other and tried to imagine the thoughts passing back and forth. They were older—it was over seventeen years since they'd last been together—but there was something familiar between them. It was in the way he smiled when she told him to sit down, or maybe the way the room sounded with their voices filling up all that space. Small talk about her flight, questions about my recovery. The cadences of their conversation bouncing off the wall sounded like a memory or like a puzzle putting itself together.

And I guess she could sense the ties between us, because she thanked Ryan for taking such good care of me those last weeks. "It's good that she came here," Stella said. "I'm glad for it."

The three of us sat in that hospital room for an hour or so, and they talked about his job and about the house in West Virginia, her hikes along the Blue Ridge Parkway and his occasional gigs at a neighborhood bar. Stella said she'd finished her first art class and had enrolled in the advanced course for the spring. Ryan told her he'd been writing some of his own music and had gotten interest from a producer he met through the Fillmore. He said he'd been improving.

"One step at a time," he said.

Ryan offered to let Stella stay at the house, but she told him she'd found a hotel near the hospital, that she'd stay the night there and be back when they released me in the morning.

They didn't talk about the past, and they didn't talk about Cassie or Simon.

Eventually Ryan had to get going, needed to stop by the house before his shift that night, but he said he'd swing by in the morning and then, to her, "It's good to see you, Stella. I'm glad you're here." He squeezed me on the shoulder and put the back of his hand against my cheek, leaving it there when he told me, "It makes me sick you had to go through this."

Afterward I asked if she was okay.

"It's funny, the roles we play, the way we have to give up the old ones before we have room for the new ones. The first-love stuff never goes away in here," she said, pointing to her head. "It makes you who you are. But in here," putting her hand on her chest, "time lets that grow and change. You'll see."

"He kept all the books you gave him," I told her. "All the novels with the inscriptions. How come you didn't take any with you when you left?"

She shrugged. "They were his, not mine. You know reading's not my thing. And when I left I wanted to give him something to mark our time together. It seemed important to leave part of me behind with him. The inscriptions . . . I wanted him to know I had meant them, even if I did leave in the end." She looked at the floor. "The books were always his, not mine," she repeated.

I wanted to tell her he didn't need a room full of books to remind him of their life together, but I didn't. I figured she knew that by then.

She let me sleep for a while, and she watched bad television and picked at the pasta and cookie the nurse brought on a tray for dinner, but eventually I just wanted to be alone.

"I'll be fine if you want to head to the hotel," I said. "It's okay. You can go. I'll see you in the morning."

"Okay." She nodded reluctantly. "But there's one more thing," she said, and she pulled her purse from the floor to her lap and began digging inside. She handed me a four-by-six painting just like the one I'd been using as a bookmark. It was a picture of a carnival setting, with blurry strokes framing a Ferris wheel painted prominently in the center. The ride was red and the background was yellow.

"Two colors," I said.

"Yellow for you, and red for me."

"But two?" I asked.

"It's been snowing a lot since you left," she told me. "And I started paying attention. People think snow is white, and it is, obviously. But when the light changes and the sky is clear, it can be blue, too." She smiled. "A brilliant blue. Nothing is really just one color. There are filters and reflections, influences. I wanted to acknowledge that."

I looked closer and saw she'd actually used yellow on the ride and red in the background as well.

"You know why I named you Lemon?" she asked.

"The color that month, the paint."

"That yellow looked like hope to me," she said. She was on her feet then, bending over to kiss me on the forehead. "Don't you forget." And then she was gone.

CHAPTER TWENTY

IN THE MORNING STELLA SHOWED UP talking taxis and
flights, but by then I had decided I wasn't going back to West
Virginia.

We stood outside the hospital as I listened to her tell me
Simon had been trying to track down the cheapest rates for
direct flights into D.C., where he was pitching his photos that
week. "He's got a meeting this afternoon with a gallery owner,
but he drove up and will be finished with work stuff tonight.
You need to pack your things," she said. "We'll go to Ryan's
to get your stuff. You can stay with me at the hotel, and then
we'll leave tomorrow."

"But I'm not ready," I said.

She shifted her purse from the right shoulder to the left
and reached out to nudge me off the sidewalk and onto a
small patch of grass where visitors and patients mulled around

scattered benches smoking cigarettes and exchanging news. Deaths and babies, I guessed, diagnoses and tests results. In front of us lunchtime traffic clogged the street.

"I know this is hard, Lemon, but it'll be easier if you're at home. You need time to adjust to what's happened," she said, but I was shaking my head.

"What does that even mean? You have no idea what's happened since I've been here," I said, which wasn't really fair, but I was angry she'd made so many assumptions. I would stay with her. We would leave tomorrow. My road-trip stunt was over, and it was time to go back east. I took a deep breath and reminded myself the conversation would go much better if I remained calm. "It's too soon, and I know you'd understand that if you just tried. You remember. This city is too big to leave so quickly."

"Lemon," she said.

"Stella," I said back. By then I knew there were things that could be changed and things that could not. My mother's job as a decision maker for me was not a permanent role, and I was ready to take over. "A horrendous thing has happened, and I don't even know what it means yet," I said. I'd spent the night thinking about all the things I'd left behind and all the things I missed from back east, and then I thought about how inspired I felt in San Francisco, with Ryan and Cassie and Aiden, how good it felt to be in a place with so many opportunities. I couldn't be certain if the new energy I'd been feeling those last weeks came from the exposure to all those books, from the gritty street scene and from listening to Ryan's music, or if it had come from the baby, and finally being able to make my own decisions. Either way, I'd realized how important it was to not walk away too soon. I couldn't desert the opportunity to spend more time with my father.

Stella was talking about school and Simon then, about the people in West Virginia who loved me, and how I'd feel better once I got home, but I stopped her.

"What if," I began, but Stella was shaking her head and a car was honking a horn, and behind us an ambulance siren was screaming in the ER parking lot. So I waited. And then when it was quiet again I said, "What if West Virginia isn't home anymore?"

Losing the baby made me realize how important it was for me to cultivate my relationship with Ryan, to give him a chance. "He's my father," I said. "And I like it here. I have a job. And a boyfriend," using the word for the first time.

"You're grieving," she said, and I told her that was exactly why I wanted to stay.

"I want more time. I just don't think West Virginia is where I belong right now."

She sulked for a while, and then, finally, she said, "If you stay, I stay. Ten days. That's it, though."

"Six weeks," I said. "I need at least a month," but she was shaking her head.

"Are you crazy? No way. Two weeks, tops. You're still a minor. I get to decide."

But two weeks didn't sound nearly long enough. "Four?" I asked, and then I added, "Please, Stella. I need to do this. *Please*."

"Three, Lemon. That's it. Take some time, get some closure, but then we leave. You have to go back and finish school. You're just a kid," she said, which I didn't agree with, but I settled for three weeks and figured I'd try to talk her into longer when the time came.

Instead of the hotel by the hospital, we found a long-term, low-budget efficiency housing unit which seemed like a fancy way of saying a hostel for adults, and we moved in that evening. I mostly just slept the first few days. We ordered take-out Chinese and pizza delivery, watched made-for-TV movies, and even sprung for tickets to a comedy club one night, but the area wasn't nearly as gritty or interesting as the Mission. I missed the taquerías and the bacon-wrapped hot dogs, I missed knowing Aiden was across the street tossing pizza dough, and I missed the air mattress even though I knew I should be staying with my mom. But I was going crazy thinking about the baby and the things I could have done differently. I catalogued my eating habits during the pregnancy, tried to count up all the cups of coffee I'd drunk, and even numbered the afternoons I'd spent in the truck with Emmy breathing in her secondhand cigarette smoke. I wondered about the anemia and blamed myself for not doing something earlier, for not telling the doctor about all the fainting. Maybe I could have fixed it, if I'd eaten better food and gotten more sleep, if I'd been more careful. The doctors said there were a million reasons miscarriages happened and none of them had anything to do with anything I could have changed, but I couldn't help but wonder. Some nights I locked myself in the bathroom and cried in the tub, certain I could have stopped it from happening if I had tried harder, but Stella never had much of a tolerance for self-pity.

"You're becoming a Lifetime movie in there," she'd say from the other side of the door. "Come on, baby, come out. You need some fresh air. Some food, maybe."

There was a small café on Van Ness that we liked to go to in the mornings, and about two weeks after I'd left the hospital, she finally put her foot down. "We're here because of you. You remember that conversation, right?" she asked. "You love your job. And you have a boyfriend. You can't leave the city until you spend more time with your father," she said. She blew on her coffee, waiting for it to cool while I stirred raw sugar into my latte. "But it's been nine days, Lemon."

"You're counting?"

"Look, I know that's not long for such a terrible loss," she said carefully, "but you're not working. You're not spending time with the boy. And five-minute phone calls to Ryan don't count as father-daughter bonding. I love you, Lemon, but there's only so long we can sit in that hotel room. Movement," she said. "That's why we're still here. Do. Some. Thing. Three weeks, remember? Use the time you have left."

I moved back into Ryan and Cassie's house that afternoon. Stella and I had been sharing a bed at the hotel, and between the heavy walker renting the room above us and Stella's night-owl habits, I hadn't been sleeping well, so she agreed to let me go back. There was more space at Ryan's, and the house was close to the bookstore, and close to Aiden. Stella took the bus over with me and stood on the sidewalk watching as Ryan hauled my backpack up the steps. At the front door he turned and invited her in.

"I can make coffee. You can poke around," he said, but I knew she wanted to leave her image of the house inside her head just as she remembered it from seventeen years earlier.

"I gotta get back and straighten up," she told him. "You wouldn't believe how quickly Lemon converted our room into a junk dump. Takeout cartons, magazines, and trash all over the place," she said. "Thanks, though."

I told Ryan I'd be in in a second, and then I went back

down to her on the sidewalk. "You sure you're okay with this?"

"I'm fine," she said. "Please. A little time alone will do me good. You need to sort some things out, and sitting in the hotel room wallowing isn't going to cut it." She leaned in and pressed our foreheads together, locking her eyes with mine. Her breath smelled like coffee and the lavender scones from the café. "As long as you know this residence isn't permanent."

"This residence isn't permanent," I told her.

"Agreed." She leaned back and adjusted her coat, ran her hand through her hair, and pulled her sunglasses out of her pocket. "Simon's shipping some sketch pads and drawing pencils. It'll be good to get some of the old haunts down on paper." She adjusted her purse and reached out, ran the back of her hand over my cheek. "Don't be a stranger," she said, and then she turned and headed down Valencia Street.

I called Aiden that afternoon and told him I was ready to take the bookstore shifts back since he'd asked another friend to cover them when I went to the hospital.

"To be honest, Miller didn't even notice my buddy had picked them up," he said.

"Can I see you?" I asked, talking into my blue cell as I sat on the air mattress back at Ryan's.

"Anytime you want. You name it."

"I want a few days of downtime with Cassie and Ryan. How about this weekend?" I asked. "You can pick me up on your cute baby blue scooter."

"You mean my masculine motorcycle? You got it."

"Does a Vespa really qualify as a motorcycle? It's a sport-bike, right? A cruiser?"

"Ouch," he said.

"I'm kidding," I said back.

"I've missed you," he said.

That Friday, David Byrne played at the Fillmore, and Ryan came in late from work, two or so in the morning, when he found me pacing the dining room, wearing grooves into the floor as I tried to quiet my thoughts. Cassie had gone to bed after three rounds of Scrabble and Steven Sebring's documentary of Patti Smith on PBS.

"You all right?" he asked. He was in the hooded sweatshirt and the jeans he wore to work, and I could smell the sweat on him from the doorway where he stood.

"I don't really know what I'm doing," I said. I was sweating a little, and maybe crying, too. The sadness came at me like the morning sickness had, unexpected and unwavering. "I feel like I'm biding time," I said, "like I'm running in place." I stopped as he moved into the room.

He told me to sit down, and he took Jay McInerney's *Bright Lights, Big City* off my chair—Aiden's recommendation that time. "You're just like me," he said. "I usually read three at a time. Stella used to say I'd read one for each mood," he told me, shaking his head but smiling. He pulled out another dining room chair, and we sat across from each other. "Here." He tugged my feet into his lap.

I leaned my head back and felt my calf muscles stretch from my body to his, connecting us. The ceiling was white and edged with crown molding, the nooks and crannies strewn with cobwebs. I closed my eyes and felt his palms fit into the curves of my arches, as he threaded his fingers through my toes. He pulled the balls of my feet toward him, stretching my muscles.

"I'm just restless," I said, and I wiped my eyes on my

shirtsleeve. "It's not really that bad, I'm just . . ." But I wasn't sure how to finish the sentence.

"Grieving," he said. "And trying to get your bearings, trying to figure things out." He asked if it felt good to be back working at the bookstore, and if I was still spending time with the boy on the Vespa.

I told him yes.

"He's a good kid?" he asked, and I nodded.

I realized Aiden had become the most important boy I'd ever been with, the first one who liked me in the way I wanted to be liked. With Aiden I didn't have to worry about being anyone other than who I was. Kind of how it felt when I was with Emmy.

"There's somewhere I want to take you," Ryan said. He used his thumb to knead the arch of my foot and work out all the knots. "A hike in Marin—the views of the city are amazing," he told me. "If you feel up to it, we'll go next week."

I took a deep breath and tried to memorize the size of his hand against my foot, the way his fingers felt on my skin. I wanted to take the moment and pack it somewhere safe, somewhere constant and reliable.

We stayed like that for a while, me with my feet in his lap, and I almost fell asleep sitting in that chair. It was suddenly more comfortable than the hotel bed or the air mattress, more comfortable than anywhere I'd been in a very long time.

In the morning I overheard them in the kitchen, rummaging through the cabinets and making coffee.

"I think we should offer her our room," Ryan said to Cassie before the shutting of a drawer, the clang of a spoon or a fork. "She's not comfortable," he said, "and she's not sleeping. I've got my kid crashing on the floor in there," he said.

"My daughter's going through a really rough time, and we've got her lying under a dining room table," but then someone started the blender or the coffee bean grinder, something loud and drowning, and the conversation was done by the time it turned off.

They never did offer to let me use their room, but it didn't matter so much since I knew he had tried.

CHAPTER TWENTY-ONE

THE NEXT NIGHT AFTER WORK, Aiden picked me up on his Vespa and took me out to the Sutro Baths, the algae-covered remains of six saltwater swimming pools overlooking the Pacific near the top of Ocean Beach. I pressed my chest against his back and wrapped my arms around his waist, noticing the closeness of our bodies as he steered the bike through the streets, the heat rising between us, even in the cold. We parked and left the scooter in the lot among VW buses, Harley-Davidson motorcycles, Zipcars and hybrids, and he took my hand and led me down the trail.

"The westernmost tip of San Francisco's coastline," Aiden announced when we settled onto the ground once we'd descended into the ruins. The grass was damp and cold, but that didn't seem to matter much when Aiden put his arm around me and said, "I've been missing you, you know," since we hadn't seen each other since before the hospital. "How you holding up?" he asked, and I shrugged.

"I feel deflated."

"It'll get better," he said, and then, after a pause, "You know what? I take that back. I mean, that's what everyone says, right? That's what we're supposed to tell you, but really it's just bullshit."

"If this is your version of a pep talk, you need some serious help," I told him, but I smiled for the first time since I'd left the hospital.

"I just mean that it'll be different now, I guess. That it won't be better or worse, just different, I bet."

It smelled like salt and mud, and I maneuvered myself to sit between his legs. I shut my eyes and pulled his arms around me, leaned my head back against his chest.

"I can't imagine anything will ever look the same," he said. "And that's not a good or a bad thing, you know? It's just life."

He almost made it sound simple, boiled down like that.

"Have you talked to Emmy?" he asked, and I nodded.

"A few days after I left the hospital," I told him, and I remembered sitting on the bathroom floor in the hotel while Stella watched TV on the other side of the wall in the bedroom. The tile was cool against my legs, and the cell phone was warm in my fist when I dialed Emmy's number. She already knew about the baby by then, but it was good to hear her voice and have the opportunity to put the loss into my own words.

"What'd she say?"

"She asked if this means we get to go to Senior Week at the beach," I told him.

"Of course she did."

We both laughed then. A group of boys walked past us toward the water, nudging one another and shuttling a bottle of liquor between them, rowdy and loud.

Aiden waited until they'd passed before asking, "What about your mom? How's she doing?"

"I think she's bored. She misses Simon and her painting classes. I think she's just biding her time until we leave."

Aiden pulled his pack of smokes out and asked if it was okay. When I nodded, he lit a cigarette. "It's hard to imagine you leaving. I hadn't really thought about it yet. I mean, I guess you'll have to eventually, but still. Part of me thinks you could stay forever if you want."

"Me too," I said. I hadn't told Aiden yet about the three-week deadline Stella had set, partly because I hoped that I could change it, and partly because I worried that I couldn't. I knew it wasn't fair, keeping Stella in San Francisco when she'd finally set up a life she actually liked and wanted back in West Virginia, but at the same time I felt like maybe it was my turn to pick where we lived for a while. She'd been doing it to me for seventeen years.

"It's like I can't see anything past you now," he said.

I shifted my body around to kiss him, soft at first, but then the heat started, the electric, wet warmth spreading over me as my lips parted, letting our tongues loop and weave around each other. One of his hands found its way to my face, and he tangled his fingers in my hair.

When we finally pulled apart and caught our breath I told him, "I don't think anything will feel the same back in West Virginia now."

Down by the edge of the cliffs, the boys were taking turns throwing rocks over the ledge as they stood in front of the pool that puddled on the ridge. One boy pointed out toward the water, and I followed his finger to the full moon hanging in the horizon.

"It's like I came here wanting to make someone responsible for breaking up my family, but now I can't blame either of them. No one was all right or all wrong," I said. "Before the trip I imagined all the bad memories might disappear if I found a place to put the blame, but then I realized it wasn't that easy."

I shut my eyes and tried to memorize his voice when he said, "The thing about family is the history, all those memories from your past. Ignoring them is impossible—it doesn't matter who you decide to blame." Aiden laced his fingers through mine. "When you leave, you're still going to take those memories with you. You've got even more of them now than when you came here, and there's no way to let that go."

"I just hoped that once I met Ryan I might've felt more rooted. I guess I wanted to be more than just Stella's daughter. I wanted a family bigger than that."

"But you have one," he said. "All the places you've been and the people you've met, the images and anecdotes you can't let go of—all those memories make your family. Those are the people and moments that shape and mark you. It's like fingerprints. You don't always see them right away, but they're there. We leave them on each other all the time."

I thought of San Francisco with my father and the memories of the city street views from the bay windows at his house, watching him play music on the sidewalk on Haight and the feeling of his hands on my feet in the living room. The books on the shelves with the inscriptions that mattered even though my parents' relationship hadn't lasted, the way the inscriptions were important just because they were there. The words between Ryan and me inevitably insufficient, the apology I was still waiting for. My history and my family—all of the memories of them—were permanent and endlessly linked together. The bus ride and the way the land had stretched out so far in front of me I couldn't see its end. The hotel with the tiny pink door where Emmy and I had stayed our first days in the city. The Vespa and the taste of unfamiliar spices in loud restaurants, the memory of Aiden finally pressing his mouth against mine for the first time. I'd been marked by all of it, and I couldn't be defined by just one thing or just one person. I was a compilation, a landscape of all the people and places that had moved through my life.

"And family doesn't have to be one certain thing," Aiden said. "It changes all the time."

Mine was Ryan and Emmy and Aiden, the way they made me feel like I was a better person than I believed I was. It was Cassie in her red boots and my grandmother from all those years ago, the home I shared with her, the first home I ever had. And always Stella, my mother, and the moments when I'd found her traits in me, all the towns we'd lived in, the friends we'd left behind. I realized family didn't have to be about the links of birth and blood. It was about an innate and immediate connection, too. Love, maybe.

The wind was picking up, so Aiden pulled me in tighter. He smelled like pizza dough and toothpaste.

"If you accept that, then you don't need someone to blame. All of it, the good and the bad stuff, made you who you are," he said.

We were quiet for a while, but then Aiden told me everything he could remember about the Sutro Baths.

"It used to be one of the largest indoor swimming areas in the world," Aiden said, which wasn't too hard to imagine as I eyed the valley of earth in front of us.

The boys were sitting by then, their bodies just shadows and shapes in front of the sky as they passed the bottle back and forth. Though the pools weren't filled with much water anymore, I could still see the remains, by the curves that had been scarred into the side of the cliff. Aiden said during high tide they would fill from the ocean, recycling water in an ongoing motion.

"It was too expensive to maintain, so it shut down. The building lasted for years, though, deserted and vacant until a fire in the sixties, when the whole thing went up in flames."

I eyed the red warning signs posted down near the ledge that separated the ocean from the water puddling in front of us. One of the boys threw the bottle over the edge, and I couldn't hear the splash, but I imagined the glass hitting the Pacific and slicing through the waves, getting sucked underneath the crests and troughs of the tide.

"Every few years someone dies here, gets swept away by some big wave that pulls them over," he said.

It was raining by then, drops of water falling relentlessly on us when we kissed again. His mouth was quicker and harder that time, and I felt the warmth between my legs as I led his hand there, the heat on my face as chills spread down my arms. Eventually we stood and headed up the hill. The water plucked our shoulders as we rode back on the Vespa, the raindrops snapping on our faces and the wind blowing through our skin.

Back in the house that night, Ryan was sleeping on the couch, so I took my book, Ryan's copy of Raymond Carver's *Where*

I'm Calling From that time, and settled next to him, by his feet. He never noticed me there as I read through the stories, taking a break only to cover him with the blanket when the room cooled down. I even managed to take a photo with the disposable camera, no flash, just the shadows and angles of my father sprawled out after a long night at work. Eventually I got restless and wandered to the kitchen for a glass of water.

I found a note from Cassie on the table, and I wasn't sure if it was for me or for Ryan, but it said she was closing and that she'd be out late. I tried to imagine how they worked and how much he must have loved her, and I figured that when they were together it felt as good as being with Aiden felt for me. Ryan and Cassie linked, like a braid of black and white.

I'd never been with a black boy before, but back in Virginia, Molly-Warner had hooked up with a senior named Marcus who hung out with us at the pool the summer before I left town. Marcus was a kid we knew from school, a boy who planned to go to Tech in the fall. He had black skin like nighttime and lips, dark and wide, that went on forever when he smiled at us in our lounge chairs. He and Molly-Warner made out a few times, and I always thought she liked him more than she let on, but she called it off after a couple of weeks. She was worried her parents might hear about it over at the factory. Marcus's mom worked there too, and Molly-Warner figured their parents wouldn't like it if they found out she and Marcus had gotten together.

It made me sad to think she hadn't been brave enough to date him anyway. I couldn't imagine Ryan caring about what other people thought when he was with Cassie. It seemed like he loved her too much to be bothered by the idea that some people may not like it.

I finished my glass of water and wandered down the hall-way past the concert posters from the Warfield and a black-and-white photo of Cassie and Ryan standing on the Golden Gate Bridge. And I didn't plan it, I didn't mean to be, but then I was in their bedroom, my fingers smoothing out their sheets, my face in their mirror hung above the bed. Cassie had her jewelry in a little wooden box on the dresser by the door, tiny earrings, a silver chain, and a chunky turquoise ring. Ryan and Cassie each had their own nightstand, Ryan's on the left with a glass of water and an autobiography of Miles Davis on it, and Cassie's on the right with a mug of milky tea, the bag bloated in the bottom and soaking in the leftover liquid. And then I saw a second dresser, Ryan's set behind the door, a tall green piece of furniture that matched the first, with half as many drawers as Cassie's. And then my hands were pulling at the knobs, rummaging through his socks and T-shirts and stacks of pants that smelled like stale beer from the venues and pot smoke from the Haight. I was on my knees digging through the bottom drawer, searching. Looking for Stella—letters I had hoped she'd written or photos of me as a kid I hoped she'd mailed. I wanted proof she hadn't kept me to herself all those years, needed evidence that she'd tried to share me with him. Maybe I was looking for a hiding spot like the shoes Stella kept those pictures in, for a place he might have buried us. I wanted to know if he had been the one to create all that distance between us and him, or if it had been the other way around. But there was nothing. Just a pair of corduroys, and a sweater full of creases from too much time folded into shape. And I realized then that knowing wouldn't have made a difference, that those years of separation couldn't be undone no matter whose fault it was. Like Stella'd always said, there was only forward movement—I had to put the past behind me.

And then Cassie was in the doorway. Cassie in her red boots and a black dress, her afro a perfect globe of hair sprouting above the gold eye shadow and the glossy lips. She was a little drunk. I knew as soon as she slumped against the door frame—I recognized the stance. She looked like my mother when she'd had too many glasses of vodka. She looked like Johnny Drinko searching for his balance when he pulled on his tennis shoes in the apartment that smelled like bread. She watched me put the sweater back, though I couldn't remember pulling it out, and she waited while I refolded the pair of pants and shut the drawer. My cheeks were red—I could feel it as I stumbled for words. It was worse than the awkwardness of meeting Ryan for the first time, worse even than the embarrassment I'd felt when I fainted at the concert. The shame of being caught like that was suffocating, and I couldn't shake the feeling of her watching me, of her eyes following my movements while I tried to dodge her gaze.

I can't be sure what I said then. *I'm sorry.* Or maybe not. I might have lied and said Ryan asked me to get him a sweater. He was cold. They should get their heat fixed. There should have been more blankets in the house. It was always cold and damp, the cracks in the brick walls leaking. It didn't really matter what I said, because she pulled me to my feet, her breath hot and boozy when she yanked me up by my elbows and leaned down, our faces almost touching.

"Ryan says you're brave," she slurred. Or, "Ryan wants you saved." I wasn't sure. Her tired eyes were bloodshot, a map of red lines mazing under smeared black eyeliner. "You look like her," she said. "It's your eyes." Or, "I'm not surprised." She let me go then, and I stumbled backward and had to catch my balance.

And maybe she just needed a little space between us, because once there was a foot or two of air separating our bodies, she reevaluated the scene. I wasn't crying, not yet, but I must have looked pretty shook up, because she moved in next to me and sat down on the bed.

"I'm sorry," she whispered. "God, what am I doing? You've been through so much already."

"I'm sorry too," I said back. For snooping in their bedroom, for showing up out of nowhere, for looking like my mother, and for reminding her that before she was there, there was someone else. There was Stella.

"It just took a long time," she said, "for us to get here. I don't know what I would do if he left," she said, and all that anger was gone, her voice tender and threatened.

Just because she was beautiful, just because he was hers then, it didn't make her immune. It didn't make her more safe or any different from the rest of us.

"He's everything to me now," she said, which I believed. "I can't imagine anything without him."

I realized she'd felt threatened those last weeks. As much as she wanted to help me, she also knew nothing would be the same once I entered their life, once she invited me into their home. And because of me, Stella was there too.

"Do you know how long you're staying?" she asked with her eyes to the floor and her hands pressed on the bed beside her, balancing. "It's okay. It doesn't really matter. We want you here." She paused. "But still."

I noticed a tear in her leggings and a black scuff on her right boot.

I didn't really know when I'd leave, how much longer I'd be able to convince Stella to let me stay, so I told her, "Until it's better," which didn't really answer anything, but she nodded like something had been made clear. And then she lay down on her side, red boots on the bedspread. And even though she was half-drunk and who knows what else, I still thought she was beautiful when she closed her eyes.

In the morning I called Emmy while Ryan and Cassie were still in bed.

"Lemon Drop," she said when she answered, "you literally just saved my life. I'm in the middle of my WVU application and I was just about to chug a bottle of Drano. Seriously. There's nothing as painful as college apps."

I laughed. "Are you sure you don't want to call me back?" I asked.

"You are officially the perfect reason to take a smoke break," she said, and then, "Give me two seconds," and I imagined her ditching the stacks of papers at the kitchen table and grabbing her coat from the hall closet.

The last time we talked I was still staying at the hotel with Stella, so I curled up on the couch and told Emmy about moving back in with Ryan.

"It feels good here, you know?" I said, and I heard a door close and the flick of a lighter on Emmy's end of the phone line. "It's like I can do whatever I want," I told her, knowing I wasn't getting the words right but hoping she would understand anyway. "I'm here for me, not for anyone else. It feels like the first time I've gotten to make my own decisions."

"So it's good?" she asked. "To be with your dad on a day-to-day basis?"

"Being with Ryan isn't perfect," I said. "He's sloppy and he's distant sometimes. He can be moody just like anybody can. I'm not saying I'm living in *Leave It to Beaver* land here, but still"—I paused and tried to work it out in my head—"knowing him, learning about his life before with Stella and seeing his life now with Cassie, I don't know. It makes me feel like I don't have to be so scared to try for the things I really want. That I can be more independent. I can work and date and make my own decisions, and even if they're wrong, it's not that big of a deal."

"God knows I'm all for the independent-person thing," Emmy said. "And I'm glad you've got a new perspective, I really am. But do you have to stand on your own all the way on the other side of the country? I mean, come on, I'm dying here." She stopped, and I listened to the inhale and exhale of her smoke. "Don't get me wrong. You shouldn't come back until you're ready. But"—another pause—"I miss you. These are the last months of school—spring fever and senioritis and cutting class. It doesn't feel right finishing up without you."

"But I wouldn't be in school anyway, Emmy," I reminded her. "Even if I was in town, they wouldn't let me back now. I've missed too many days," I said, which was true. "I'll have to repeat my senior year," I told her.

"What about Stella?" she said. "She's got a life here, Lemon. You can't forget that."

"And I've got a life *here* now," I told her. "I didn't ask her to stay. She can leave if she wants," I said even though I knew it wasn't the truth. If I stayed, Stella stayed. That's just how we worked.

"She's got a job, Lemon. And a real relationship," she said. "Don't be selfish." And I thought of Simon, how nice he'd always been to me and Stella. "You want that for her, don't you?" she asked, her voice picking up speed, rising. "You want your mother to have those things, right?"

I'd never fought with Emmy, not really, and I didn't want to start then, with me being too far away to fix it in person, so I tried to slow the conversation down.

"I want her to be happy," I said carefully. "But I want to be happy too. What if West Virginia isn't the place I'm supposed to be anymore?"

"Then you wait," she said immediately. "California isn't going anywhere. You come back and you finish school. You give Stella time to adjust to the idea. I think you owe her that, don't you?" she said, and I nodded even though she couldn't see me. "And then you leave when it makes sense. When your decision isn't based around a baby or a boy or being caught up in the rush of being in a new place, a big city."

I heard Ryan and Cassie's door open, and the sound of someone's bare feet on the wood floor, heading toward the bathroom.

"I love you, Lemon," Emmy was saying, "but you have to be certain. A road trip is different from a move to the other side of the country. One doesn't just become the other," she said. "Not like this. What's the rush?" she asked.

"I just want something more, something bigger than what I had before," I told her, my voice quieter by then. "I feel like I could find that here," I said.

"And that's a good thing," she said. "But just take your time. That's all I'm saying. Come home and take your time making the decision."

I nodded and flipped the conversation back to her applications, her plans to enroll at WVU in the fall even though I could tell she wasn't interested in talking about college.

"I should go," she said eventually. "Keep calling, though. I want to hear what's happening. I want to know what's going on."

I told her that I missed her. And then I thanked her. "For being honest," I said.

"Someone's gotta keep your ass in line," she said. "I miss you too."

After we hung up I imagined her huddled on her front porch finishing her smoke, her mom folding laundry, maybe, or grabbing her purse and heading out to Walter Reed. I imagined what it would be like to be there with her, and I knew it would be different. Different from how it was when I was there last, and different from how it was in California, but being with Emmy would always be a good thing: It would always feel like being home.

CHAPTER TWENTY-TWO

ON TUESDAY, AFTER WORK, I headed to the hotel to see Stella, and when I got there she was sitting cross-legged in the center of the bed, with a red colored pencil in one hand and her cell phone in the other. There were papers everywhere: balled-up sheets torn from her notebook on the floor, shredded scraps from her sketch pad on the nightstand, and pieces of poster board littering the love seat and desk by the window. She smiled at me when I let myself in but held up her pointer finger, needing a minute or two to wrap up the call.

"I know, but—," she said, stopping to look at me and mouth Simon's name.

"Take your time," I whispered. I eyed a sketch of an Asian family outside the post office on Geary, which Aiden had taken me to when he shipped extra demos up north for the band.

Under it was a drawing of a child in a school uniform waiting at a bus stop with headphones in his ears, a black-and-white ink of the Rollerblade stunt skaters in Golden Gate Park, and a pencil drawing of the storefronts on Haight Street. They were good—better than I remembered her being.

"But that doesn't make sense," she said to Simon. "I haven't been working. You can't just give me a paycheck if I haven't clocked any hours."

There were take-out food containers spilling out of the trash can, and she had three pairs of underwear and two bras draped over the TV set, drying. The dresser was littered with empty water bottles, snack packs of crackers, and pens and pieces of paper. Beside the bed she had piled her dirty clothes in a heap, and next to it was a CVS bag. I saw that it was full of shampoo and soap and a pack of disposable razor blades, as well as a small bottle of Woolite detergent for washing clothes in the sink, I guessed. I realized she had probably packed quickly when she left for San Francisco, that obviously she never planned to stay for as long as she had. I remembered she only had one carry-on suitcase when we checked into that hotel, and I realized she'd been in the city for over two weeks.

"It's fine," she said. "I'll haggle a discount from the guy at the front desk, show him my boobs. You know the drill." And then she winked at me and told Simon, "I'm fine, Simon. We're fine."

I moved her coat and a stack of sketches from the chair so I could sit down, but I couldn't figure out where to put them. The room suddenly seemed too small. Miniature. Claustrophobic.

"Just put them on the floor," she said to me, and then, to

Simon, "Listen, I should go, Lemon's here." After a quick pause, she said, "Simon says hi, baby."

"Hey, Simon," I shouted as I sat down. "Miss you," I said.

She told him they'd talk soon. That she loved him. Talk soon.

After she hung up she took one look at me and said, "You look better," and I nodded.

"I feel better." I glanced around the room. "And you probably feel like a pack rat, or a homeless person, like a kid living in a dorm room."

"It's not so bad," she said, but I said, "It kind of is," and then we were quiet.

"I'm sorry," I said finally. "Thank you. For being here, I mean. For letting me stay."

"Watching you leave on the bus like that, knowing that I had to let you go if you wanted to," she said as she traced her fingers over the sketch pad in front of her, "it shook me up, I guess. Plus, it's good that you get some closure before we go back. It's good that you have some time."

She asked how work was going, and I offered to use my discount to get her any art books she wanted, and then she asked about Aiden.

"I know it's superlame, but I'd like to meet him," she said.

I tried to imagine the three of us sitting at a coffee shop or meeting at a café for lunch, and I knew instantly they would like each other. Just because of me.

"That makes sense," I said. "I'll plan something." And then I took her out to dinner at the Italian restaurant around the corner, where we gorged ourselves on garlic bread and lasagna before I headed back to the Mission.

The next afternoon Ryan and I loaded up a day pack with

water and snacks and extra layers of clothes, and he borrowed a truck from a friend so we could drive to Marin County to take that hike. We left the city, headed over the Golden Gate Bridge, and drove north, traveling past joggers and bikers who were making their way along the path on the side of Highway 101. The bridge was an orange-red color, just like in all the travel books, but I hadn't imagined the cables so large and looming as they stretched above us while the traffic moved under the steel beams. I would have liked a picture of me and Ryan standing over the water, posed on the path with the arches of wire above us. The shot of him and Cassie in that same spot was by far my favorite photo in their house, but he was too excited to get out of the city for me to bother to ask him to pull over to take a picture. It was the beginning of February, and the fog had burned off in the morning, but even though it was cold out, the sun was warm beating down through the front window of his buddy's Chevy. We moved out of San Francisco into the brown slopes of Marin, the mountains getting larger the farther out we went. Ryan navigated through the hills and I played with the radio, our conversation casual and unimportant as he drove. Eventually he exited the highway, and turned onto a small road while I watched the buildings of the city growing smaller in the side-view mirror. I rolled down the window and felt the heavy dampness of the air—the winter breeze was wetter and cooler on the other side of the bridge. We parked at a trailhead, and the lot was empty.

"It's a pretty mellow hike," he said when we were outside looking up the hill. He grabbed the pack from the truck bed and locked the doors. "If you get tired, just say so. We'll stop, no big deal."

The incline was gradual as we began the walk up the dirt path, and the switchbacks were slow and measured as they lifted us away from the truck. There was a rhythm to the back and forth, and I walked behind Ryan and followed his tempo through the trees, staring at his footprints in the dirt. The wind picked up, and we stopped on the side of the path to pull on sweatshirts we had brought in the backpack.

"Look," he said, and for the first time since we'd started, I glanced behind us and realized that we were high enough to see San Francisco on the other side of the bay.

The water was bluer than I remembered, the white waves spitting foam throughout the surface of the Pacific, and the city was a map of building-covered hills, a chart of colors and angles. The roads looked like ribbons weaving through the peninsula, linking the neighborhoods like lines in a child's connect-the-dots book.

"Want to go farther?" Ryan asked, and I nodded.

We kept moving up, and the light-headedness came in small waves, but I pushed through until we reached a flat landing littered with cigarette butts, a dirt lot enclosed by trees on three sides but overlooking San Francisco on the fourth. There was a bench with empty beer cans underneath and graffiti spray painted on the seat, and I sat down and tried to catch my breath.

"It's amazing," I said, and stripped off the sweatshirt. My skin was a filmy mixture of sweat and dampness from the air, and I imagined my face was red, because Ryan asked if I was all right.

He sat down on the bench too and pulled a bottle of water from the pack, opened it, and handed it to me.

"It feels good to get some exercise," I said. "How far did we go?" I asked, realizing the trail continued up from where we were, and that we hadn't even made it to the top.

He shrugged. "Far enough," he said, taking the water back and swigging it down. I watched his Adam's apple bobbing in his throat. He looked at me and then looked down the hill. Looked back at me again. "You're pretty sturdy, considering all the shit you've been through lately." He smiled.

The wind was ripping through the trees by then, and the air cooled me down while we rested. In front of us the city looked like a web of wires, a map of ebbs and flows, the streets running into one another like music.

"I hate the thought of leaving," I said, and I felt Ryan shift on the bench as he crossed and then uncrossed his ankles.

"You're leaving?" he asked. "When?"

"I can't stay here forever," I said, thinking of Stella back at the hotel, stalling her life with Simon because she didn't want to leave me, thinking of our three-week deal. I could tell Stella had changed just as much as I had since I left West Virginia, maybe because of Simon or maybe because of her painting, and it wasn't fair that I had asked her to put all those good things on hold while I hung around the city. She'd given up a lot by staying there with me, and I figured it was time I began planning what I was going to do with myself. I knew that whatever it was, it would start by going back home.

"Look how amazing it is," I said. "All that energy in motion." I took the camera out from the backpack and snapped a shot of the view. City buildings on top with a vast ocean of blue and white waves below. I turned the wheel on the disposable and watched the number shift from twenty-two to twenty-three.

"I fell in love with that city so long ago I can hardly remember anything from before it," Ryan said. And then he paused before he said something about wishing we had more time together. "I know I've kind of sucked at this father thing, but I promise it'll only get better from here. And you can always come back," he said. An empty can of Budweiser rolled out from under the bench, and he kicked it away.

"I'd like that."

"I should have done more sooner," he said. "It's like when you're a kid and you're taught that if you work hard enough, you'll eventually get what you want. That work and success are undeniably entwined. But then you find that one thing you won't ever be good at no matter how hard you work. Math or football. Writing or art class. It doesn't really matter what, because everyone has at least one thing. No one can be good at everything, regardless of how hard you try," he said.

I thought of how Molly-Warner was never good in gym class, and how Emmy never passed Advanced Chemistry. How I was still terrible at Spanish conjugations even though Simon had explained them to me a hundred times.

"I was worried being a parent would be one of those things for me, something I'd never be good at, so I never tried, because I was scared." Ryan looked out at the view, the waves growing violent under all that wind, and the white crests getting sharper as the clouds blocked the sun. "I didn't want to risk it, because I didn't believe I could do it," he said.

And when I thought about it that way, it made me realize Stella was brave for being scared and doing it anyway, for having faith in the fact that if she worked hard enough at being a good mother, eventually she'd succeed. Because each time she failed at making things good for us, we moved and tried again.

"I get it now," Ryan said. "That failure is better than copping out. But Stella's obviously taught you that."

I realized that's what Stella had given me, the recognition that even if I failed to find all the answers, just being in San Francisco, going there with the openness to look, made me brave too.

Ryan's fingers were tracing the names carved into the wood bench when he said, "I'm sorry, Lemon. For . . ."

But I stopped him before he could finish and told him, "We get to be new now," and I guess he understood what I meant, because he nodded and didn't say anything else after that. We stayed there awhile and watched the fog spread away from the hills and over the bridge.

On the way down it started to drizzle, as the smell of the ocean mixed with the smell of trees and dirt, and it was tricky working our way back to the truck. The trail was steeper on the trip down, with gravity pulling at my body and testing the muscles in my legs. I lost my footing once or twice, stumbled midswitchback, and had to stop to catch my balance, but Ryan offered me his hand and let me steady my weight on his before we started down again.

Later that week I set up a time for Stella to meet Aiden since she'd asked me to introduce them. I waited until she had somewhere to be, an art gallery she promised Simon she'd stop by to get the name of a contact he could submit his photos to, and then I told her we could all meet at Stella's hotel and go to the gallery together. Short and sweet: It would be easier that way.

Stella was wearing skinny jeans, ankle boots, and a snug black turtleneck when she came out of the hotel to meet us. The perm had mostly grown out by then, and her blond hair was twisted into a low, knotted bun. She was wide-eyed and shiny lipped, with just the right amount of makeup. She looked amazing.

Next to me Aiden fidgeted, so I hurried through the introductions and pointed in the direction we'd be walking. The art gallery was about eight blocks away.

Aiden asked about Stella's trip out and then asked about Simon's photos, and he even remembered she was an artist too.

"Will you be pitching your work to the gallery also?" he asked, but she shook her head.

"God, no, I'm not ready for that yet. I'm just starting to take some classes," she told him when we got caught at a crosswalk and had to wait for the light to change. "Being a student again feels like a big enough commitment as it is."

My mother never went to college and didn't push it on me like a lot of kids' parents did, though I knew that after Denny ripped us off, she'd started another savings account in case I ever decided to go. She bought a bottle of champagne when I nailed my PSAT but didn't harp on it when my SAT scores weren't as high as I wanted. I figured she knew she had to pick her battles.

We crossed to the other side of the street and moved past a bus stop where a group of retro mod-kids huddled, looking at a map.

I'd missed over a month of school by then, and even though Stella hadn't asked, I knew she was wondering what

I was planning to do about it. I figured I'd have to repeat my senior year and start researching colleges that summer. I was thinking of a lit major and writing classes, of a small liberal-arts college with a strong art and music scene.

"Lemon says you're a writer. And a musician?" Stella asked.

Aiden told her about the band he managed, about their tour up north and the gigs he was trying to land them back in San Francisco. He talked about writing music reviews, his love of finding new bands, and discovering new styles and up-and-coming talent.

"It feels good to write a positive review for a band that's still struggling to make a name for itself. If the band's sound turns me on, I try to do everything I can to get the word out."

By the time we got to the art gallery I was pretty sure he'd won Stella over 100 percent. Inside, Aiden and I wandered through the small room, eyeing the artwork: black-and-white photographs of mountain ridges, desolate campgrounds, and stark landscape shots of fire damage in the hills of Southern California. Stella worked her magic and flirted with the lanky young guy sitting behind a mahogany desk in the back corner, an art student manning the gallery part-time, I guessed. Eventually she landed a contact name, and a business card for the owner, who also worked as the curator for most of the shows.

Back outside we lingered on the sidewalk by the door. Stella had planned to visit the San Francisco Botanical Garden, but Aiden and I decided not to go.

"Thanks for keeping me company," Stella said when we realized we were heading in opposite directions from there. "And thanks for being so good to Lemon since she's been here," she said to Aiden, which was kind of embarrassing but also kind of

nice. "I would've felt a lot better about her being out here if I'd
known she had you keeping an eye on her," she said.

Afterward, Aiden and I hopped on a bus and headed to a
coffee shop on Fillmore Street near the venue where Ryan
worked. Ryan had scheduled a meeting there that afternoon
to introduce Aiden to the events manager. Aiden was hoping that if all went well, he'd be able to line up a gig for his
friends' band in the spring.

We sat on a window bench facing the street, and Aiden
bought us green tea and blueberry muffins even though I said
I wasn't hungry.

"I've kind of got bad news," he said, and then he told me
the band would be back by the end of the week. "You're officially unemployed."

"I figured I'd have to give up my shifts soon anyway," I
said. I didn't tell him I'd already used my discount to buy
the rest of the books I wanted and that I'd said good-bye to
Miller after my shift the day before, had thanked him for the
job, and told him I was leaving town soon. My three weeks
were up.

Aiden and I talked about the music review he'd been
working on, and then we talked about Emmy, how she'd been
spending most of her weekends in D.C. visiting her dad in
the hospital.

"Emmy says he's quieter now, that it's like he's lost his stories and he can't remember any of his jokes," I said, thinking of the rotten knock-knocks. "It must be terrible," I told
him. "It's good I'm going back soon. I figure it'll be easier for
Emmy if I'm around."

Outside, the sun was shining, and I could feel the window warming up against my back. A woman walked by with a

blue-eyed husky. A tall, lanky kid sped through the sidewalk crowd on a skateboard.

"I wish you never had to leave. I wish you could take me with you," he said.

"No you don't," I said, but it didn't sound right when it came out that way. "I just mean that you have a good life here. That you shouldn't walk away from the band and the writing gig, all the things you've worked for. You belong here," I said, wondering if I'd be able to get the words right and then knowing I wouldn't. "We can make it be okay, though," I told him, wanting to believe it. And I knew that Aiden would always be a part of me but that our relationship would most likely never be as big as we would have liked it, though I also believed it would never fully fade away. Because of him, I would never give myself to people like Johnny Drinko again.

"We're, like, train-wreck tragic, you know that?" he said, and pushed the mugs of tea out of the way so he could reach my hands across the table. He brought them to his face and rubbed his nose across my knuckles, serious then.

"Say you'll be back to visit," he said.

"I'll be back to visit."

"Say you won't forget this."

I looked straight into those green eyes. "I could never, never forget," I told him.

That weekend, I went to the Palace of Fine Arts before Stella and I left for West Virginia. I didn't take her with me, though. I went alone, but it seemed better that way, to be on neutral ground. The monument was set in a park with a small lagoon near the giant rotunda with colonnades and statues scattered about. The grounds were decorated by Roman-style sculptures and flower beds planted around the edge of the lawn. It was the middle of the day and it was quiet, the sun cutting into the water in strips of white light. The pond smelled fresh like mud, like nature, unfiltered and hopeful. It was one of those days when the sun was shining strong but the wind blew steadily. It was warm and cool at exactly the same time. Inside and out.

Aiden told me the Palace of Fine Arts was originally built for the 1915 Panama Pacific International Expo, or the World's Fair, and the Roman-style constructions, the renditions of ruins from another era, were created to represent the mortality of material beauty and the vanity of human desire. Like all the other structures at the fair, it was supposed to have been torn down at the end of the exhibition.

"The city saved it from demolition because it became a symbol of hope to people in San Francisco. It represented the gathering that welcomed the city back to the world after the 1906 earthquake," he explained one night while we paged through a historical book about the Bay Area. "Hosting the World's Fair was a public acknowledgment the city had survived."

"So they saved it," I said, eyeing the photos in the book.

He nodded. "To remind themselves and the rest of the world that as bad as the disaster was, they'd recover. They couldn't be ruined."

I wandered from the lawn into the rotunda, and the structure looked just like the pictures, though the columns were layered with traces of moss and the walls were cold and shadowed with age. Kids had tagged parts of the building with spray-painted names and quotes, and I ran my fingers over the splits in the walls, thinking of all the other people who had been there before me. I knew from the book that it was a popular place for brides and grooms to go for postwedding photos and that art students often visited to study the architecture and to photograph the winged statues and gargoyles, the columns and arches. The towers were originally made from plaster and wood, but in the sixties San Francisco raised the money to cast them in concrete and make the structure permanent. I pressed my body into the coolness of a shadow and looked up to watch the birds above me dodging in and out of view.

I'd said good-bye to Ryan and Cassie that morning and had left Aiden the night before. The leaving part was terrible, and I'd searched for the right words to let them know how important my time there had been, but in the end the words weren't all that significant. We knew what had passed between us.

I'd left Stella at the hotel and gone to the purple house to say good-bye, and while Cassie went to the bedroom for a gift she said she had for me, Ryan nudged me into the living room and showed me a plane ticket he'd bought for that fall.

"I talked to Stella, and we decided I should come in September. For your birthday," he said. "Eighteen years old. I know now." He smiled and handed me the ticket. He'd booked a five-day trip and said he wanted to come alone the first time, but that next time around he'd like to bring Cassie.

"We're getting married in May," he told me after he took the ticket back. "Figured it's time I make an honest woman out of her," he joked. "One more year and it'd be common law, but I want to do it the right way," he said, which sounded good to me.

I imagined Cassie in a white dress, something simple and elegant, and my father in a suit with that goofy smile slung across his lips. It was easy to picture it, the two of them making a promise I figured they'd have no problem keeping.

"It'll be small. Just us out near the water somewhere, but I think it's important," he said. "It's good we make it official."

And then Cassie came into the room and handed me two small packages wrapped in newspaper.

"Nothing fancy," she said, "but you know, something to take with you, a little reminder."

The first was a framed copy of the picture of them in front of the Golden Gate Bridge, their heads tucked together and their lips open and laughing. The second was an unlabeled CD.

"It's the New Year's show," she said. "I downloaded it. I figured you'd like a copy."

I thanked her.

"Your friend's band is good," Ryan said. "I hope my boss gives them a shot."

And I hadn't told them yet, but Aiden and I had agreed to split the cost of a plane ticket if he landed the band a gig at the Fillmore. I'd fly back for the show so I could finally see where Ryan worked.

But I wasn't really thinking about plans for the months ahead that afternoon in the ruins; I was thinking how Aiden had been right: I didn't notice when it happened, but as I got ready to leave California, I realized I'd let go of all that blame and fault I'd been carrying around like a suitcase. I'd gone to San Francisco looking for someone to hand it to, thinking once I had somewhere to put it, all the sadness and anger wouldn't be mine anymore. The funny thing was that I never did pass it off to either of them, to my mother or my father. Instead it got lost somewhere between them, really.

Somewhere between West Virginia and the grounds of the Palace of Fine Arts the suitcase had emptied itself out. The loneliness had faded, and the anger had finally disappeared. Maybe on the bus with Emmy, on that wide-open road that led me from one place to another. Or maybe in the Mission, in that purple house, or out on Haight Street. I'd been dropping pieces of all that weight in the rooms I'd moved through during those past weeks, and later, when the fog lifted and I looked for it, it was gone.

Acknowledgments

I'm extremely thankful to have had the opportunity to work with an incredible team at Simon & Schuster, who amazed me by the attention and care they devoted to *Fingerprints of You*. From copyediting to design to publicity, I couldn't have imagined a more compassionate group of people to turn my manuscript over to: Krista Vossen, Jenica Nasworthy, Michelle Kratz, and Lara Stelmaszyk. I am especially grateful for the generosity and guidance of my brilliant editor, David Gale, and his assistant, Navah Wolfe—while I know it certainly was not true, they made me feel as though this book was their only project in process during their time working with me. And, of course, to my feisty friend Gail Hochman—your energy and passion are an inspiration, and no writer could ask for a better agent than you.

This novel would never have come to be without the invaluable gift of time and space from the following organizations: Vermont Studio Center, Virginia Center for Creative Arts, Hedgebrook Writers' Retreat, Millay Colony for the Arts, the Studios of Key West, and the Key West Literary Seminar. In truth, this book belongs to you. I am also grateful for the wisdom and encouragement of my mentors and colleagues who supported the writing of this novel in more ways than I can count: Stephen Cooper and the California State University, Long Beach MFA faculty; James Blaylock of Chapman University; Josh Weil; Jill McCorkle; and Hope Mills. But above all I would like to thank Judy Blume, the most generous and insightful mentor a young writer could ever hope for.

I can't imagine having embarked on this journey without the continuous inspiration of my families, the Madonias, the Lomases, and the Gordons, but particularly my sister, Lisa, whom I admire and appreciate equally for the ways that we are different and the ways we are the same. This book could not have existed without the love, support, and patience of my husband, Christopher Gordon, who has always provided me with the invaluable gift of both roots and wings. And finally, I've dedicated the novel to my mother and father, who consistently said I could when I worried that I couldn't, then helped me find a way to prove them right.

ABOUT THE AUTHOR

Kristen-Paige Madonia is the 2012 D. H. Lawrence Fellow and the recipient of the Tennessee Williams/New Orleans Literary Festival Fiction Prize. Her short fiction has appeared in various anthologies and journals including *Upstreet, New Orleans Review,* and *American Fiction: The Best Previously Unpublished Short Stories by Emerging Authors.* She has received awards or residencies from the Sewanee Writers' Conference, The Hambidge Center, The Vermont Studio Center, Juniper Summer Writing Institute, Virginia Center for Creative Arts, Hedgebrook, The Millay Colony for the Arts, the Key West Literary Seminar, and The Studios of Key West. She holds an MFA in Creative Writing from California State University, Long Beach, and currently lives in Charlottesville, Virginia, where she teaches fiction. Visit her at kristenpaigemadonia.com.